When an injured Irish greyhound named Degsey arrives at Oyster Gables Animal Shelter in the village of Swiftly, the lives of everyone who works there are dramatically affected. The dog seems to possess a mystical sixth sense which can influence people's actions and drastically alter the course of events. Horses are being stolen from various locations in England, and Sky Patakin, female manager of Oyster Gables, plus trainee Shack Skinner and new assistant Daniel Rusk, find themselves thrown into a fast-moving plot which involves a great deal of danger as they attempt to discover the horse rustlers.

A whirlwind of adventures follow—and Degsey is at the forefront of the chase as the net closes around the thieves. It takes all of the greyhound's special powers to protect the people she loves, and in a dramatic twist-ending things are never quite what they seem . . .

Swiftly

Michael Maguire

authorHOUSE®

AuthorHouse™
1663 Liberty Drive
Bloomington, IN 47403
www.authorhouse.com
Phone: 1-800-839-8640

First published in Great Britain, 1998.
Updated and published by Authorhouse 2011.

ISBN: 978-1-4678-7769-5 (sc)
ISBN: 978-1-4678-7770-1 (hc)
ISBN: 978-1-4678-7771-8 (ebk)

Printed in the United States of America

Any people depicted in stock imagery provided by Thinkstock are models, and such images are being used for illustrative purposes only.
Certain stock imagery © Thinkstock.

This book is printed on acid-free paper.

Action and adventure fiction
By Michael Maguire

Shot Silk
Slaughter Horse
Scratchproof
Scorcher
Mylor: The Most Powerful Horse in the World
Mylor: The Kidnap
Superkids
Swiftly 2

CHAPTER ONE

M arshwood Stables. Two a.m. on a cold, grey damp Saturday in July. Martin Griggs reluctantly opened the cab door of Ryker's travelling horsebox and shivered as the fresh south-westerly wind tore hungrily at his leather jacket.

'I hate the early mornings,' Griggs muttered, accepting a head collar, halter and a pair of bolt-cutters from Tony Ryker's outstretched hand. 'They always give me nosebleeds.'

'Stop moaning.' Ryker sucked and chewed on a matchstick. 'Just go for the nags in the first four boxes. They're the livery horses. The rest are racehorses and we don't want them . . . too much trouble. There are no stable security lights and no alarms. It'll be like taking candy from a baby.'

Griggs didn't reply. He knew what he had to do and his cheekbones looked sharp and projected as he adjusted the face-hugging material of his ski-mask. He was 26 years old, small and scarecrow thin with pale olive skin, curly fair hair and regular almost feminine features. He made his way cautiously forward, his long bony fingers unclipping a flashlight from his belt.

Marshwood Stables were set back from a narrow lane and screened by trees and thick evergreen shrubbery behind a high

1

stone wall. Large ornately carved stone gateposts supported heavy wrought iron gates.

Ryker waited for Griggs to reach the gates before pulling on his own ski-mask. He glanced quickly in each of the side mirrors, checking for light or movement before slipping the catch on the driving door and dropping to the ground. He made his way to the rear of the vehicle.

All quiet. Perfect.

Tony Ryker had done this operation many times before. Between them, he and Griggs were responsible for the theft of more than five hundred horses from the South West of England. It was a profitable trade. Steal up to ten horses a week and keep them out of sight in a deserted Devon warehouse. Then, when the trail had gone cold, sell the younger ones at horse markets in other parts of the country. The unfortunate old stagers which nobody wanted to buy were shipped via Harwich to continental abattoirs for horse meat.

It was a sleazy business, but it had made Ryker a very wealthy man. Not that his current lifestyle reflected it. For six months of the year he lived in Martin Griggs's rented mobile home in the Devon hamlet of Hele, near Ilfracombe. It was a ramshackle dwelling, far away from the tourist trail and mostly ignored by local people. The mobile home sat in six acres of straggly undergrowth which doubled as a paddock and backed on to a derelict fertiliser warehouse.

Very handy. Total isolation.

The ideal hideaway for horse rustling and shady business dealings—a far cry from Ryker's respectable, alternative lifestyle as a law-abiding husband and father who owned an elegant Tudor house in Berkshire.

'Gotcha,' Griggs murmured, as the bolt-cutters sliced effortlessly through a thick padlocked chain which shackled the main gates. They opened smoothly, and Griggs wasted no time in streaking across the stable compound to the first of the loose boxes.

'Well done, Griggsy,' Ryker mouthed the words, allowing himself a satisfied smile as he watched Griggs's flashlight wink twice. Ryker reached up and slid the metal pegs from their keepers, then took the strain with both arms outstretched as he slowly lowered the vehicle's ramp.

Rolls of fat bulged through his shirt at his stomach, but he was still in reasonable shape for his 42 years. There was a great amount of power in his neck muscles, in his broad shoulders and thick wrists.

Ryker was the one with the aggressive character, the backbone, whilst Griggs was the born follower. They'd met three years ago at Exeter racecourse. Ryker was there winning money; Griggs was there losing it. The partnership had been formed the moment Griggs had foolishly tried to steal Tony Ryker's wallet. The big man knew all the tricks of the pickpocket trade and he had immediately caught Griggs's thieving fingers in a vice-like grip. Griggs pleaded for his freedom and Ryker (subject to conditions) had duly granted it.

The conditions were met and the alliance was formed. Ryker needed a sidekick, a gopher who would do the dirty jobs; and Griggs needed this big, businessman's know-how. They also both shared one common interest . . . Easy money.

Some of that was about to be earned now as Griggs took the bolt-cutters to each flimsy padlock securing the first four loose boxes.

A shrill whinny speared the early morning air.

'Easy, easy,' Griggs whispered through clenched teeth as the padlock fell away and he entered the first box.

A large bay mare flared her nostrils and backed up as Griggs carefully fastened the head collar he had with him to the horse. 'That's my beauty,' he breathed, running a soothing hand over the mare's muzzle as he wrapped the halter round his arm. 'No noise. Be a good girl for Griggsy.'

Ryker waited well out of sight by the ramp. Muscles rippled in the mare's hindquarters as Griggs whispered comforting words to coax the horse towards the travelling box. A well-practised routine now followed:

Ryker took the halter from Griggs's hands and led the mare up the ramp and into the first of a dozen wooden stalls. Griggs grabbed another head collar and halter from a row of hooks and quickly retraced his steps back to the loose boxes.

This time he emerged with a black colt and the system continued. Horse to Ryker . . . collect head collar and halter . . . back to loose boxes. He worked like clockwork. The last two horses quickly followed, a washy dun gelding and a piebald mare. Speed was the key to success and in total the whole operation had taken less than eight minutes.

Ryker glanced at Griggs as he fastened the ramp. Through the ski-mask he could see Griggs's mouth sucking in air as he puffed with exertion. 'You look done in, my little ferret,' he sniggered. 'You need building up. For lunch *you* can cook us both some nice steak and chips.'

Griggs was an excellent cook, and Ryker being wifeless on his Devon trips used this expertise to the full.

'Make it horse meat and chips if you like,' Ryker said with sour amusement as they both climbed back into the cab. 'Lots of protein if you cook it rare. Tastes best if you have your chips floating in half gravy, half blood.'

'You're disgusting.' Griggs pulled off his ski-mask.

Ryker did likewise, giving a throaty laugh as he selected reverse gear. The travelling horse-box eased its way out Marshwood Lane and onto a narrow country road.

'We'll stick to the back doubles,' Ryker stated, 'Less chance of meeting the cops.'

Griggs gave a grunt.

Ryker scratched at the scorpion tattoo on his right forearm. 'I'm well pleased with tonight's work, Griggsy. I reckon we'll get a thousand a piece for the bay, the black, and the dun and maybe up to eighteen hundred for the piebald.'

'S'pose.'

'Come daylight and the owners are going to be weeping buckets. Bet some of them belong to a load of posh kids. Heart-breaking, isn't it? Their loss is our gain, eh?'

'Yeah.'

Martin Griggs's eyes were closing. Ryker flicked the match he'd been chewing towards Griggs's face.

Griggs jumped. 'Pack it up and watch the road!'

'Now don't go all sulky on me just 'cause you're tired. Worse than a moody old woman you are.'

Griggs controlled his irritation with visible effort.

'I love horses,' Ryker continued. 'I can't get enough of 'em, my little ferret. I'm greedy, Griggsy. I'm a greedy man who likes to be satisfied.'

Griggs said nothing. He'd heard it all before. Many, many, times before. Ryker loved babbling on after a successful job. He couldn't help voicing his pleasure, mainly at Griggs's expense. Any minute now he'd make his usual crack about DVD machines, Griggs thought.

As if on cue, Ryker gave another throaty laugh and said with relish, 'Sure beats stealing DVD players, eh Griggsy?'

Griggs offered a bored grunt.

Tony Ryker's big hands swung the wheel this way and that as he went through the gears with practised ease. The travelling horse-box cruised through the tiny villages of Sherwood Green, Huntshaw Cross and Brownscombe. Griggs was hunched down in his seat, dozing.

Time passed. Ryker kept to his plan of avoiding the main roads and the vehicle bypassed the A39 and skirted the picturesque hamlet of Westleigh.

Suddenly Ryker's forehead creased.

The piercing beam of the headlights had illuminated a movement in a nearby piece of moorland. Ryker applied the brakes a touch too fiercely sending Griggs catapulting against the dashboard.

'What the hell's going on?' Griggs flared.

The travelling horse-box coasted to a halt in a lay-by.

'There's a shaft-horse tethered over there.' Ryker indicated a piece of moorland. 'It's just begging to be taken, Griggsy.'

Griggs cursed under his breath and pulled himself up to look. His sleepy eyes focussed on a wooden caravan and a heavy-shouldered chestnut cob of about fourteen hands standing peacefully under a clump of trees. Its back was slightly bowed and its leg joints appeared stiff and swollen with age.

'What d'you want that for? Looks twenty years old at least.'

'I told you, I'm greedy.'

'Crazy more like.' He sniffed and pulled out a handkerchief. 'Just let me rest. I can feel a nosebleed corning on.'

'You're always getting nosebleeds.'

'I'm a born sufferer . . . always have been. Let's get off home. We can do without another broken-down old hack.'

'That hack's worth six hundred pounds on the continent. We've got five back at the mobile, so we need one more to make up the batch. They go over from Harwich in sixes, right?'

Griggs thought for a moment. He didn't like the old horses. They were kept in the paddock at Hele, and they caused problems. Unlike the weekly markets for the warehoused young horses, the Harwich shipments for the old crocks were monthly and that meant extra work. Water troughs to be filled, the odd bit of hay to top-up the outdoor grazing, and, because of their age, the very real risk of illness.

'I hate the old nags,' he whined to Ryker. 'If they get sick it's always me who has to sort out the problem.'

Ryker played with his diamond-studded ring, twisting it round and round his finger. 'Stop complaining. What do you expect me to do, run up a bill with a vet? You've only got to keep them fed and watered until they've left for the knackers yard.'

Griggs shifted uncomfortably and looked at the old cob again. 'What about that wooden caravan?'

'What about it?' Ryker consulted his watch. 'It's ten past three in the morning. They're not going to worry about us, they'll be sleeping.'

Griggs considered carefully. Doubt, apprehension, confusion flashed across his eyes. He sensed something. He wasn't sure what at first, but as the tiredness cleared, he knew exactly why he was feeling uneasy.

He sensed trouble.

* * *

The greyhound stirred. The snap of a twig underfoot sent tiny electrical impulses racing to the nerve-ends of Degsey's ears. The ears lifted, and then pricked as she listened. There was an uneasy thumping inside her rib-cage as she heard a shuffle of feet outside the caravan. No human would have picked up the noise, but to Degsey's excellent hearing it sounded loud and threatening.

She didn't want to leave the three greyhound puppies snuggled warmly against her breast, but the outside noise had caused her instincts to race ahead of her rational thoughts. She stood up carefully, easing her long, long legs from under the soft little six-week-old bodies and stretched her muscles, shaking the drowsiness from her body.

Seamus Horrigan was sleeping. A huge patchwork quilt covered most of his face leaving only his pink scalp showing between the thinning strands of grey hair.

Degsey's liquid-brown eyes turned towards her master. She knew Seamus was fast asleep, and recognised the signals. She watched as the quilt rippled with his breathing; saw his chest rise and fall; heard the deep nasal sound of his snoring. She thought about waking the old Irishman with a quick nudge of her muzzle, but brushed off the idea as the voice of Griggs demanded her urgent attention.

'Stupid rope,' he was muttering to himself. 'Tied with a load of granny knots.'

The chestnut cob named Mister Rafferty looked at Griggs with guarded curiosity as his thin fingers worked at the knotted fibres. Slowly they began to loosen and the rope worked free, rattling the brass ring attached to the tethering stake.

The noise fired Degsey's muscles into action. Her powerful haunches flexed and she sprang through the hinged flap in the caravan's front door, built by Seamus exactly for an emergency such as this.

It was like a bullet leaving a gun. Degsey powered her way through the flap and sailed over the caravan's front wooden steps. Her sleek body speared the early morning air and she landed softly, now treading purposefully through the lush grass.

Degsey's colour was predominately white, with three small splashes of dark brindle on her body. Her head was a combination of white and brindle, as was her tail.

Griggs heard her exit. The flap had banged against its housing and he went rigid, his fingers stiffening around the rope halter. He turned towards the noise, expecting to see the barrels of a shotgun being pointed at him. But the only movement came from the scurrying clouds in the almost black sky.

Degsey had dropped low, eyes fixed unblinkingly on Griggs. It was a proven fact that a greyhound had the best eyesight of any dog, and Degsey would now use this gift to the full.

Tony Ryker was getting impatient. He'd lowered the ramp and was gesturing to Griggs to hurry up. A matchstick flicked from side to side in his mouth.

'C'mon! C'mon!' Griggs urged, clicking his tongue at Mister Rafferty.

Degsey looked from Griggs to Ryker to the travelling box. She glimpsed the other four horses. Three were weaving their heads in obvious distress whilst the fourth blew a fine mist of moisture from nostrils that flared red as it whinnied uncertainly.

Degsey was aware that the whinny was a cry for help and the same awful fate that had befallen the other horses would soon befall Mister Rafferty unless she acted quickly. She instinctively knew that Griggs and Ryker were evil.

'Greyhound!' Ryker yelled, as Degsey broke cover. She veered towards Griggs, every nerve screaming with urgency.

Griggs began to run. He still had a firm grip on the rope halter and this forced Mister Rafferty to follow at a rather lumpy trot.

Degsey's supple body slashed into Griggs's legs causing him to stumble awkwardly. He staggered, slithered and swayed, but he didn't release the halter. The action caught him just below the knees, but the impact had left Degsey temporarily winded. She fought for breath, spinning round on her front paws, sending damp little clods of grass flying into the air.

'It's coming at me again!' Griggs choked out the words as he appealed to Ryker.

Ryker had disappeared into the travelling box, then reappeared holding a pitchfork.

'Leave the dog to me,' he instructed, his eyes flashing. 'Just get that horse up the ramp!'

Degsey's lean, muscular body shot towards Griggs. She didn't intend to bite him—it wasn't in a greyhound's nature to be savage—but she would try to use her speed to make him drop the halter.

She homed in with long, purposeful strides.

Ten metres . . .

Five . . .

Ryker was suddenly there, standing between Griggs and the greyhound, holding the pitchfork like a javelin and ready to hurl the twin spikes at Degsey's fast-closing body.

She saw him and swerved. The muscles in her forelegs and thighs caused a braking action and the pads of her feet stretched in an attempt to stop. She very nearly somersaulted, but somehow her thick toenails managed to get enough of a grip in the soft turf to keep her upright.

The pitchfork left Ryker's hands . . .

It was a powerful throw. He had been aiming for the shadowy outline of the greyhound's neck, but her sudden actions had changed things drastically.

Degsey felt a little rush of air on her cheek as the deadly prongs whooshed past her face . . . then a thick clotted cry bubbled in her throat as she felt pain.

Both prongs had briefly speared her left shoulder, tearing through skin and muscle and causing blood to streak down her leg and puddle in the clefts of her paw. She stood still, dazed slightly, as the pitchfork continued its flight before thudding into the ground.

'Got the dog!' Ryker seemed jubilant. 'Shoulder, I think. Switch on your torch.'

Griggs was still fastening Mister Rafferty into a free stall in the travelling box. He wiped a sheen of sweat from his face, then bounced back down the ramp. 'Did you kill it?'

'Not sure . . . Can't see properly.'

As Ryker raised the ramp, Griggs unclipped the flashlight from his belt.

Degsey had tucked herself behind an upturned tree. She'd flattened her body against it, moulding herself into the tangled wooden roots. She gathered both her strength and her wits as she licked away blood from her shoulder wound.

Griggs snapped on the flashlight letting the beam ripple over the grassland around him. It illuminated a patch of turf where Degsey's blood still glistened wetly. The fringe of the beam swept briefly across the shaft of the pitchfork.

'Can you see the greyhound?' Ryker asked, looking over his shoulder as he fastened the ramp with the little metal pegs.

Griggs had already dashed forward to retrieve the pitchfork. 'No, but I'll find it . . . and then I'll stick it properly!'

'We haven't got time for games,' Ryker made an impatient gesture. 'Get in the cab before we wake the caravan people. If the greyhound's gone, it's gone.'

Griggs ignored him. The yellow beam from the flashlight rippled over the bark of the upturned tree. Suddenly Degsey was framed in its blinding glare.

'Gotcha!' Griggs's tongue circled his lips.

'Leave it!' Ryker motioned towards the cab. 'You told me earlier not to push my luck, so don't push yours.'

No words were going to stop Griggs. He moved forward smelling blood-lust, the pitchfork wavering menacingly in the greyhound's direction.

Degsey watched him come. She didn't move. Her muzzle was drawn back in a quivering vicious snarl, her lips shimmering pinkly as a warning growl began to build in her throat.

Griggs suddenly stopped . . . rooted to the spot.

Something in Degsey's lower jaw was glinting in the beam of the flashlight. It held Griggs in a trance. Was it a tooth? A sharp canine tooth? His thoughts spun wildly. Gold? Was it a gold tooth?

It was so bright he had to screw up his eyes. He felt a sudden tightness in his chest. His palms were sweaty, his throat dry.

Degsey held Griggs's mystified gaze. Her growl deepened.

Griggs stood locked to the spot, unable to look away. It was as if the gold glint had a life-force of its own. The pitchfork fell from his fingers as he shielded his eyes with a quivering hand. The tooth, the gold, or whatever, was blinding him, sucking the strength from his body. The glint seemed to bounce into the glare of the flashlight, willing him to blot out the beam.

He fumbled for the 'off' switch. 'H-help me,' he stammered.

His fingers clawed at the flashlight and the piercing glare flickered and went out. Degsey was plunged into shadowy darkness.

Griggs backed away. Sweat was trickling down his backbone and his legs felt like lead. He paused for a moment, sucking air in his lungs.

Gradually . . . very gradually, things began to get back to normal. As he stumbled back to the road his head cleared and he felt his strength begin to recover. He tried desperately to compose his thoughts as he made his way round the back of the travelling horse-box to the cab.

Ryker was behind the wheel. He chewed on a match. 'Well?' he asked, 'Did you get it?'

'No . . . I didn't.' Griggs slumped into the passenger seat. 'Just drive. I don't want to talk about it.'

'Frightened you, eh?'

'Not in the way you think. It was weird, Tony, very weird.'

Ryker laughed. 'You're the only weird thing around here, my little ferret.'

Griggs gave a stubborn stare. 'I'm telling you! That's some sort of devil dog. It's got supernational powers.'

'Supernatural,' Ryker corrected.

'Yeah, that as well. It was spooky. It stopped when I switched off the flashlight.'

'You're crazy.'

'I think it's got a gold tooth . . . I think that's what gives it the power.'

'Gold tooth? What gold tooth?'

'Sharp bottom canine. Left one I think'

Ryker's face now showed a mixture of amusement and irritation. 'I suppose the greyhound's now got its slippers on and is reading a paper in front of the fire!'

Griggs's jaw bunched. 'Take the pee if you wanna, I don't care, but I know what I saw. And I never want to see that damn dog again!'

Ryker's brow creased as he glanced in his off-side door mirror. The reflection showed Degsey running at full stretch, keeping pace with the travelling box.

'Looks like you will see it again, Griggsy,' he let the words out gently. 'I don't believe it, but it's following us. Must be after that flamin' horse!'

Griggs gave a grunt. 'Yeah, very funny, Tony. Ha, ha!'

'Look for yourself.'

'I'm not stupid. Stop trying to be clever.'

'I said *look!*' Ryker's left hand grabbed Griggs's leather jacket and he heaved him across his own body, pushing his face towards the off-side door mirror.

Degsey was still there, muscles rippling, legs just a blur of speed as she kept close to the vehicle's rear end.

Griggs's lips were bloodless as he glanced from Degsey to the dashboard instruments. 'L . . . Look at the speedometer,' he stammered. 'That dog's injured but we're still clocking 38 miles an hour!'

This fact hadn't escaped Ryker's attention. His mind was working overtime on how he could put Degsey's speed and stamina to personal use.

'Flapping tracks.' Ryker scratched at the growth of bristles on his chin. His jaw had been broken sometime in the past and was lumpy and out of line with the rest of his face. 'A dog with that sort of speed could beat any other greyhound and make us a pile of cash.'

'Count me out,' Griggs replied, hunching back in his seat. 'That dog's jinxed.'

Flapping tracks were not registered under the National Greyhound Racing Club and therefore rules and regulations counted for very little. Meetings were held up and down the country, and unlike licensed greyhound tracks you didn't have to prove that you were the legal owner. It was done in the name of sport, but large amounts of money changed hands if you had a successful greyhound.

Ryker was driving with fingers steepled, tapping a spoke of the steering wheel with his thumbs. 'I'll be coming back for that dog,' he said. 'I've got plans, Griggsy.'

'Coming back! When?'

'Tomorrow, maybe. We know it belongs to the caravan, and that won't be moving far without a horse.'

Griggs shifted his bony shoulders angrily but remained silent.

'That dog's going to make me rich,' Ryker added with a satisfied smile. 'Oh yes, my little ferret. That little beauty is going to make me a fortune.'

As the travelling horse-box negotiated a long bend in the road, Degsey decided on a woodland short cut. She left the tarmac and veered right, slicing through a tangle of bracken, and spanning the width of a hawthorn hedge. An elderly badger crossed her path as she picked up the smells of the forest—the pheasant, the fox, the hedgehog, the rabbit and the hare. She identified each one by its own special scent, remembering all the secret places where they would be hiding. But this was no time for giving chase or playing games. A voice was pumping in her ears, prompting the same message, over and over again . . . Save Mister Rafferty . . . Save Mister Rafferty . . . Run . . . Run . . . Run . . .

She scooted over wild honeysuckle, heather and prickly gorse, dipped through tractor ruts and across open farmland. She ignored the needle-sharp pains in her left shoulder and tried to ignore the sticky blood that was drying on her leg. Her thoughts now turned briefly to the love for her three puppies. She tried to reassure her motherly instincts that all the activity at the caravan would have woken her master. Seamus would be comforting them, she convinced herself. They would be safe. Safe, snug, and warm.

'Dog's burned itself out,' Ryker said to a disinterested Griggs. 'No sign of it'

The travelling horse-box had covered the two miles from Westleigh to the small Swiftly turnoff which led to the beach. Ryker increased acceleration, sticking to the main road which would take him through Barnstaple and on to the hideaway at Hele.

Suddenly, without warning, Degsey launched herself over a five-barred gate and into the path of the travelling horsebox. She was panting, staring at the faces behind the cab windshield. She was illuminated by the headlight beams and she was unmoving.

'Hellfire!' Griggs covered his eyes.

Ryker jammed on the brakes, and the vehicle's springs groaned noisily as the tyres screamed for grip. He swung the wheel left in a frenzied slide, mounted a grass verge and uprooted some newly planted saplings.

Griggs felt the vehicle right itself and once again pick up speed as it trundled back onto the road. He also heard Ryker exhale in a sigh of relief. Slowly he opened his eyes.

'W-where's the dog?' Griggs peered into the near-side door mirror, blinking constantly. He saw that Degsey had given up the chase and was now padding across the road to the grass verge. 'You shouldn't have swerved,' he stated irritably. 'You should have run it over while you had the chance.'

Ryker increased acceleration. 'What, and kill the goose that might lay the golden egg?'

'I told you it's a devil dog.' Griggs replied. 'What's the use, you don't understand.'

'I *understand* you're talking rubbish.'

'Did you see the gold tooth? It must have showed up in the headlights. Did it glint? Is that why you swerved?'

'I told you, I swerved to miss the dog.'

'The tooth *made* you swerve.' Griggs mulled this over as things began to snap clear. 'Think, Tony. Did you see anything glint?'

Ryker shrugged and looked uncomfortable. He had seen something shining in the dog's mouth but he wasn't going to admit the fact to his partner.

'The disc on the collar, maybe,' Ryker said, thinking quickly. 'I don't know. I can't remember.'

Griggs shook his head in a slow, exaggerated movement.

'What?' Ryker asked, looking defiantly at him. 'What's up with you now?'

'The greyhound wasn't wearing a collar.'

'Then I don't know.' Ryker's patience was wearing thin. 'I suppose I didn't see anything . . . Alright!'

The big man concentrated on the road ahead. He threw a glance that told Griggs that if he was thinking about continuing the subject then he was in very real danger of being thrown from the cab.

Griggs tilted his head back as he blotted the beginnings of a nosebleed with a handkerchief. 'Damn devil dog,' he muttered.

Degsey watched the fast-fading rear-lights of the travelling horse-box. It cruised smoothly past Horseshoe Coppice and negotiated the brow of a hill. Then it was gone.

She was weak through the loss of blood; far too weak to make the journey back to the caravan. With her head hanging limply, almost touching her muscled shoulders she took the beach road that led to Swiftly village. She padded very slowly, taking one carefully placed step at a time. Her thoughts centred on Mister Rafferty. She couldn't remember a time without the old cob horse—he had been there when she was a puppy, and there again when she had puppies of her own. He had pulled the caravan mile after mile, strapped proudly between the shafts wearing a harness and huge collar that glittered with silver mountings. He was a true friend to her and her master Seamus. Loyal and faithful. Solid as a rock. Now this friend had gone out of her life and she felt a terrible sadness. She also blamed herself for letting it happen.

She walked. Minutes dribbled away.

To the right of her were sprawling sand dunes studded with tufts of grass which rippled when caught by the wind, and beyond these was the sea and a few flickering lights of human habitation.

The early morning air smelled salty fresh as she paused at the Swiftly quayside. She passed one cottage, then another, feeling herself drawn to a large creeper-covered house where a red chimney protruded boldly on either side, promising warm, cosy fireplaces in winter. It stood in three acres of land which sloped gently down to the beach and lay well back from the road, with a pair of enormous conifer trees flanking a driveway to the front door.

Degsey stood at the entrance, lifting her neck painfully so that her eyes could focus on the white-shuttered windows and their gable-shaped canopies. They were overlaid with oyster shells, pearl side up, and shimmered with a brilliance in the moonlight.

This was the place to rest.

She sensed it, smelt it, felt it.

Each step was becoming more and more painful as she made her way past the trees and shrubbery to the porch. She walked under a hanging sign which announced: *'Oyster Gables Animal Shelter.'*

Little pools of orange light seeped from beneath the front door, making her welcome. She lapped gratefully at water from a bowl placed nearby . . . then exhaustion took over.

She folded her legs under her and sank down onto the porch mat. The blood on her shoulder had streaked and caked to a brittle crust, but the pain began to run beyond the wound, surging hotly, then icily, then hotly and icily again . . . making the heat and the cold feel the same.

She tried to ignore it, telling herself that in a few hours her strength would recover and then she would walk back to her master. Seamus would make things right . . . he always did.

She closed her eyes.

Slowly, blissfully, sleep finally washed over her and she drifted off into a pain free world.

CHAPTER TWO

'Don't they make alarm clocks with bells in them any more?' Sky Patakin asked, her eyes dark and direct.

'Sorry.' Jonathan yawned an apology and took his place at the well-scrubbed pine breakfast table. 'It's only eight o'clock.'

'Spring was down at seven,' Sky continued, looking briefly towards her younger sister. 'We have rules at Oyster Gables, and the animals come first.'

Jonathan was twelve, tall and slender, with short springy fair hair and mischievous blue eyes. 'It's no wonder you haven't got a boyfriend,' he said. 'You're always complaining.'

'There's more to life than boyfriends. They just complicate things. Besides, I'm very lucky to have a job which provides me with a home. Running an animal shelter takes up all of my time.'

'It's not natural. You're nineteen.'

'And that's old is it?'

'Old enough. I've already noticed a few wrinkles.'

Sky made a disapproving face. 'When I want your opinion, Jonathan Patakin, I'll ask for it.'

The sweatshirt she was wearing matched her tawny hair. There was a wiry strength in her build, a warm suppleness as she moved to the old coal cooking range. She broke two eggs into a frying pan alongside the sizzling bacon, tomatoes and slices of frying bread.

Scooter, the shelter's pet boxer dog was having problems ignoring the delicious aroma. He lazily uncurled himself from his basket, padded across the stone-flagged floor and rubbed his face against Sky's legs. He was a fawny red with a flashy white chest, and he had the habit of drooling whenever cooking smells alerted his taste buds.

'Stop slobbering, Scooter . . . *No!*' Sky said firmly.

Spring had finished her bowl of muesli. 'Have we any releases today?' she asked Sky, helping herself to orange juice. 'If Beethoven's fit to go, I'd like to help.'

'We could release him today.' Sky flipped over the bacon with a spatula. 'His neck wound's healed nicely, but the badger has the most powerful bite of any wild british mammal . . . so I'd rather wait for help. A job like that needs two adults and the new assistant manager should be here shortly.'

'His name's Daniel.' Jonathan pursed his lips to avoid grinning. 'I wonder how big sister will fancy a man about the house?'

Jonathan had seen an official-looking letter pinned to the notice-board in the outside office. The shelter was run by a charitable trust, and the letter notified Sky that they had appointed Daniel Rusk to fill the temporary live-in vacancy. Not that Sky was too pleased with the decision. She'd hoped for another female to replace her usual assistant, who was away on maternity leave.

'How old is he?' Spring asked, helping herself to toast.

'Eighteen,' Jonathan piped up before Sky could answer. 'He's taken a gap-year between school and university to gain work experience. He sounds really cool. He's already spent six months at a safari park'

'Anything else you'd like to tell us?' Sky flicked back a strand of hair from her forehead and fixed Jonathan with a sharp gaze. She wore her hair coiled on top of her head in a loose disorderly mass that threatened to come undone at any second.

'He's got tons and tons of A-levels in zoological and biological stuff . . . and he's coming from Brighton.'

'Bristol,' Sky corrected, dodging round an ever-hopeful Scooter and handing Jonathan a plate of eggs and bacon. ' . . . and in answer to your original question, I've no worries about having a man about the house. It'll make a change . . . It'll be different . . . A new face, and all that.'

Jonathan said nothing, just picked up a fork and took a healthy mouthful of his breakfast. Spring, who was vegetarian, clicked her tongue. 'You're turning your stomach into a graveyard.'

'It's my stomach.'

'It's unhealthy.'

'If we were meant to be carrot crunchers we'd have been born with long floppy ears and we'd be hopping everywhere.'

'One in five people in this country don't eat meat,' Spring stated.

'Well I'm one of the four who does.'

The opening of the back door ended further argument as Shack Skinner entered the kitchen. He wasn't very tall but he was stocky and muscular. He was clad in jeans which were beginning to wear thin and fray at the knees, blue trainers, and a tattered denim jacket emblazoned with animal rights badges. He had very direct hazel eyes and curly brown hair and carried himself with a careless ease, his face full of confidence.

This was Shack's third week of a six-month Job Skills training scheme at Oyster Gables. He was sixteen, currently out of work, and had been sent to the shelter by the Employment Centre at Barnstaple. Sky found him slightly self-confident, a bit of a hotshot, but he was hardworking and anxious to learn. He hoped eventually to join one of the national animal welfare groups, but until then he was glad to be getting valuable hands-on training.

'I've mucked out the stables and the donkey pen,' he told Sky. 'And I've checked the aviaries and the animal recovery cages—all okay.'

'Thanks, Shack.' Sky filled the old cooking range with some more coal. 'Like a coffee?'

'I'd better not. It's my morning to attend the animal husbandry class at Bideford College, so I best be off.' He collected his crash helmet from a wall peg and motioned towards the front door. 'See you after lunch.'

He tucked his thumbs into the waistband of his jeans and grinned as he passed Spring and Jonathan. 'Bet you two guys are glad to be away from your mum and dad?'

Spring smiled, crimping her eyes. Jonathan lifted a knife in a sort of wonky salute.

Sky busied herself at the sink. 'When you've finished breakfast,' she began, 'I'd like you to feed the small mammals first, then . . .' She broke off on hearing Shack talking to somebody, or something, at the front door.

'Is everything alright?' she called out.

'You've got a visitor.' Shack's voice came and went, as if he was moving about.

Sky pinched her lips tight before murmuring, 'Oh good grief, not Daniel Rusk . . . it can't be . . . not this early.'

'A dog,' Shack called back, easing her fears about Daniel. 'A greyhound bitch. I think she's been injured.'

There was a clatter of cutlery as Spring and Jonathan hurriedly left the breakfast table. Sky unhooked Scooter's collar and lead from a hook on the wall, and all three headed along the hall to the front door. Scooter lumbered behind.

Degsey swayed uncertainly, looking dazed and confused as she sniffed gently at Shack's hand. Her body movements were sluggish as she raised cheerless eyes towards Sky.

'Out of the way, kids,' Sky ordered, and took over.

Scooter's collar was immediately buckled around Degsey's neck and the lead handed to Shack. Sky ran an experienced eye over the greyhound, her gaze settling on Degsey's injured shoulder. She took a pinch of neck skin between thumb and forefinger and watched as it stayed peaked instead of springing quickly back. A brief examination of the dog's gums revealed a sickly paleness rather than the normal deep pink colour. Her tongue was dry, her eyes sunken and her pulse weak—all signs of fluid loss.

'Has she been hit by a car?' Spring posed the question.

'No, she's been pierced by something sharp . . . probably last night. Two small puncture wounds.' Sky indicated without touching. 'She's very weak through loss of blood.'

'Bet she's been dumped,' Jonathan stated. 'Where's the owner?'

'Goodness knows, but we can't worry about that now. She needs warmth and fluid replacement.'

'An intravenous drip?' Shack suggested. 'Dextrose and saline?'

Sky nodded and tapped her forehead with the heel of her hand. 'Can she walk, Shack, or will she need carrying to the treatment room?'

The question didn't need an answer. Shack had already cradled one beefy forearm under Degsey's bottom, and the other around her chest. 'She's a big girl,' he said, getting his balance before making his way back down the hall. 'She's incredibly muscular. Must weigh around thirty kilos.'

Sky walked quickly ahead, her thoughts concerned only with giving Degsey correct and speedy treatment.

Oyster Gables Animal Shelter had been set up solely as a haven for sick or injured wild mammals and birds, and Sky was far more familiar dealing with creatures of the forest than treating domestic animals. As a general rule callers with injured dogs or cats were always referred to the vet's surgery or the animal welfare clinic. This was an Oyster Gables regulation.

Two livery horses and two donkeys were the only exception to the 'wild-life-only' rule. The horses brought in additional income to the shelter in the form of rent; and the donkeys, both now unwanted and formerly used for seaside rides, brought in small sums when hired out for local fund raising events.

Sky wasn't used to stray dogs spending the night on the shelter's doorstep. Badgers, foxes, squirrels or barn owls she could handle . . . a sick greyhound posed more of a problem.

* * *

Daniel Rusk had made good time. He'd left Bristol at eight a.m., journeyed via Bideford, and was now turning east onto a minor road which would take him to the Swiftly turn-off. The wheel was smooth under his hands and the tarmac hummed as the tyres cruised over it. He glanced at his wristwatch. It had taken just under two hours to cover the one hundred miles.

Rich, rolling farmland flanked the narrow country road as Daniel's old grey Volvo estate car negotiated a roundabout and skirted the hamlet of Westleigh. The sky was blue and cloudless, tinged in the east with a soft pastel tone. The sun shimmered against the windshield lighting Daniel's face with a study of contrasts—high tanned forehead, broad cheekbones, and intelligent brown eyes. His dark hair was combed straight back off his forehead and ran to small black curls which trailed over the line of his collar.

He was looking forward to the challenge of Oyster Gables. From working with the largest form of wildlife, he'd now be working with some of the smallest.

'Please report to Shelter Manager Sky Patakin' his job sheet had said. He'd never worked for a female before. He grinned at the prospect. Sky Patakin. He repeated the name twice, saying it out loud. It sounded nice, unusual.

He didn't mind that the vacancy was only temporary. It suited his plans. In another six months he would be going to study at Exeter University where he hoped to graduate with a degree in zoology.

The road ahead curved into a bend. Daniel was only half concentrating as a pheasant darted out of the undergrowth, and streaked in front of the Volvo. He took swift action, swerving slightly, clicking his tongue as he watched the bird dive into the cover of a hedgerow . . . then something else flickered at the corner of his eye.

Through some brown-fringed gaps in the hedgerow he could just make out the colourful outline of a wooden caravan parked in the middle of moorland, and an old man sitting on one of the shafts, his head buried in his hands.

Daniel cruised the Volvo into a lay-by and applied the handbrake. He guessed the old man was in need of some sort of help so he made his way towards the caravan.

Seamus Horrigan looked as if his world had just crumbled around him. The shock registered in his pale features, in his obvious distress and the equally obvious effort he was making to control his emotions.

He looked up at Daniel, fluttered his hands in a gesture of helplessness, and asked simply, 'Have you seen them?'

Daniel caught the hint of an Irish accent. 'Seen who? What's happened?'

'Me family. Missin' so they are.'

'Can I help?'

'It's too late, boy. I've been lookin' since daybreak.' He sighed and fingered a large gold earring which pierced his right ear. 'Mister Rafferty and Degsey be gone . . .It's an awful, awful day in me life.'

Daniel studied the old man's features. It was a pleasant, country face with the winds of the Irish glens etched upon it in a hundred separate wrinkles which mapped the surface of his skin. His grey hair was tied back in a pony-tail and his eyes were flinty blue, quick and all-knowing.

'Degsey would never leave me wagon,' he went on. 'Not without reason. Y'see she has the babbies to look after.'

'Babies?'

'Ay.' Seamus climbed up the wooden steps to the caravan's footboard and opened the top half of the porch doors. He beckoned a puzzled looking Daniel to join him. 'See, there they be. Little lost souls.'

Daniel followed him onto the footboard and gazed into the caravan. The Venetian-style shutters to the side and rear windows were closed against the morning brightness causing the floor to be lined with alternate slats of sun and shadow.

'The wee ones.' Seamus indicated. 'Right next to the policeman in the comer.'

'Policeman . . . ?' Daniel's mind was reeling.

Seamus rasped the bristles on his unshaven chin and managed the briefest of smiles. 'The old brass Colchester stove there. Sorry, boy, I see so few folk that I be forgettin' you're not used to travelin' talk.'

Daniel craned his neck towards the stove. There was a locker seat just beyond it and this was covered with a sheepskin rug. Three pairs of inquisitive eyes turned to face him.

'Jeez, puppies!' Daniel grinned broadly; showing very white, even teeth.

'Degsey's babbies so they are.'

'And I thought . . .' Daniel sheepishly rubbed his nose with the back of his hand. 'So Degsey is a dog?'

'She be a very special sort o' dog. The most beautifullest greyhound bitch to ever walk God's green earth.'

'And Mister Rafferty?'

'Ahh, me old cob horse. Pulls the wagon so he does.'

There was a glint of amusement in Daniel's eyes. He looked at the pups and they looked back at him making tiny squeaky noises. An all-white one licked an all-brindle one's ear, whilst another which was mostly white with three brindle patches screwed up its face, curled its tongue and yawned, before giving a wheezy little bark.

'I can help,' Daniel said. 'I'm on my way to Oyster Gables at a village called Swiftly. It's an animal shelter. We could take the puppies there, and then make enquiries about Degsey and the cob horse.'

'I'll not be leavin' me wagon.' Uncertainty seemed to flicker in Seamus's eyes. 'Could be weeks before me animals be found.'

'But you can't stay here . . . you're stranded without a horse. Supposing Mister Rafferty doesn't come back?'

He let his breath out slowly. He said nothing.

'Leave the caravan here, locked up,' Daniel suggested. 'Stay at Oyster Gables until the horse is found. They're bound to have a spare room. They're won't be a problem.'

'But I be the problem,' he said. 'I couldn't do it me boy. Ah sure no, not sleepin' in a proper bed, and washin' wi' new-fangled plumbin' an' tings. Ay, I remember 'em before me travellin' days . . . brass taps wi' hot and cold wrote on those little twisty tings.' He paused, adding, 'I'll be too old now to be doin' with change. I have me habits y'see, so I'd be fair twizzled stayin' in a proper house wi' me own room an tings.'

Daniel told him he understood. He thought for a long moment before the answer hit him.

'Of course!' He looked triumphant. 'We'll take the caravan to Oyster Gables and park it in the grounds.'

'And how will we be movin' it boy?'

'I'll figure that out once we're at the shelter. Perhaps we can tow it . . . I'm not sure yet.'

'It's me home. I'll not live anywhere else.'

'Trust me. I won't let you down.'

The worry had gone from his face; his hands were no longer trembling; his eyes were direct and steady. 'Ay, I trust you me boy. Take us to this shelter of yourn.'

Daniel nodded, pleased with the solution. Seamus collected an old corduroy jacket and his pipe from a locker then scooped up the three puppies and handed two to Daniel. His face was immediately licked by pink tongues which felt like sandpaper as the pups smothered him with fluttering kisses. For such small creatures they seemed to have legs that went up to their ears. Long, lanky, and dangling.

Seamus secured the porch doors and both men made their way across open moorland to the parked Volvo estate car. Daniel shifted his two pieces of luggage, fixed the dog-guard, and set the puppies down on a car rug.

Seamus was having trouble with his front seat-belt. He explained that he'd never worn one before, adding, 'The most mechanicallest ting I've ever driven is a tractor . . . and that be more than sixty year ago.'

The Volvo's exhaust burbled sweetly as they headed towards the Swiftly beach road. The fair weather; high, scattered clouds and warm temperatures had brought the tourists out in force. They paraded at leisure, cameras hanging from their necks, guidebooks in their hands.

Daniel and Seamus talked during the brief drive. They discussed odd, unrelated things about themselves which all came together to help build a mutual respect. The welfare of all kinds of animals was the special link—an ongoing scrapbook of stories filled by both their lives.

'Oyster Gables,' Daniel announced, indicating right before swinging the estate car across the road and between the pair of large conifer trees. He parked beside a motorbike and a white Escort van which displayed the name of the shelter in gold lettering.

'Tis the most whimsicallest place I've ever seen,' Seamus admitted, his eyes wide with curiosity as he gazed at the glittering pearl-oyster roof shells. 'It's fine, very fine.'

Daniel was seeing the shelter for the first time. He looked beyond the house to the smooth, golden beach, breathing in the salty, slightly fishy air as he listened to the lapping waves.

'Hello!' Spring's voice brought him back to the moment. Her hair was the golden colour of ripened wheat, long and thick and with a sheen that fell to the lower edges of her shoulder blades. She looked slightly older than her eleven years. Her whole face was alight with energy as she asked, 'Are you Daniel Rusk, Sky's new assistant manager?'

'Yes, I am.' Daniel exited the Volvo, prompting Seamus to do likewise. 'And you must be . . . ?'

'Spring Patakin. Sky's sister.'

'Then it's great to meet you.' He snapped open the estate car's rear door and reached in for the puppies. 'Can you help me with these little devils . . . they belong to my friend Seamus.'

'Hello, Seamus.' Spring shot the old man a winning smile and gathered two of the puppies into her arms. 'Oh, they're bigger than you think. Are they greyhound pups?'

'To be sure they are, missie,' Seamus said, lifting the third pup from the car rug. 'Do you like greyhounds?'

'I like all dogs. We have Scooter, he's a boxer, and then we have . . . well I don't know what her name is, but she's a greyhound. She was badly hurt. We found her this morning.'

Her words made Seamus feel a sudden fear of asking the most obvious question.

Daniel had no such fears. 'What colour is this greyhound, Spring?'

'The same colour as the pup that Seamus is holding.'

Seamus was cradling the white pup with the three splashes of brindle. He breathed out long and hard, experiencing a great wave of thanks. Dry-mouthed, he said, 'It's Degsey. You've found me darlin' Degsey. Praise be to God and Mary, Peter, Paul and Patrick!'

A frown came and went. Daniel was confused but happy. 'This is great news. What amazing luck.'

'Ach no!' Seamus said, hugging the pup tightly. 'This be no luck, boyo. I tink this be Degsey's doing.'

'I don't understand?' Spring glanced questioningly at Daniel. He leaned against the Volvo, his brown, bare forearms folded against the whiteness of his shirt.

'How can it be Degsey's doing?' he asked Seamus.

'Did I not tell you she was a very special dog? Special enough to arrange for you and me t'meet. Special enough to bring us both to Oyster Gables . . .'

'But I was coming here anyway. The fact that I met you on the road was just chance.'

'You didn't have to stop, boy.'

'No, but a pheasant shot out in front of the car . . . and then I saw you . . .'

'Twas Degsey's doing. She can influence tings like, with her special powers. She's had them since she was a wee babby.'

Daniel looked sceptical. He fingered a tiny scar on his forehead which was all that remained of a school rugby tackle.

'We were meant to find her,' Seamus went on. 'Oh ay, Degsey leads an enchanted life.'

'Wow!' Spring's eyes sparkled with curiosity.

Seamus said nothing, just lifted his bushy eyebrows.

Daniel felt a smile coming to his lips. 'I think,' he said slowly, giving a sideways glance to Spring, 'that we've just been listening to some good old-fashioned Irish exaggeration.'

The front door opened and Sky stepped out into the sunlight. She was wearing a white surgical coat and holding a mug of coffee. Her skin was shining where the sun had caught it the previous day, highlighting the smattering of freckles across her cheeks and the bridge of her nose.

'I'm Sky Patakin,' she announced, looking Daniel over from top to toe as she crossed the forecourt. Her smile seemed stiff and formal.

Daniel gave Sky a strong, brisk and no-nonsense hand-shake. 'Daniel Rusk, I'm very glad to be joining you.'

She saw the greyhound puppies and tilted her head back. 'This seems to be my day for greyhounds. I've just left one in the recovery room. She's supposed to be woozy from a pain-killing drug, but she's pining and snuffling at the door . . . It's most peculiar.'

'It's Degsey.' Seamus's voice sounded relaxed and amused. 'Twas I not just sayin' that the wee darlin' dog knows I'm here.'

'Are you the owner?' Sky queried.

'Horrigan, ma'am. Seamus Horrigan. And Degsey's owner so I be.'

'Well, she can't possibly know you're here, Mr Horrigan,' Sky continued bluntly. 'The recovery room is at the back of Oyster Gables. It's soundproofed and has no windows.'

Seamus looked at Spring and winked as he tapped the side of his nose with a forefinger.

'She has special powers', Spring murmured.

Daniel slowly shook his head in confused disbelief.

'The wound', Sky asked, 'do you know how it happened?'

'I be tinkin' it must be poachers', Seamus said. 'Me wee girl must've disturbed 'em.'

'And do the three pups belong to Degsey?'

'Ay', Seamus nodded. 'They be her little ones.'

'Then perhaps you'd like to reunite Degsey with her puppies and Mr Horrigan.' Sky turned to Spring. 'Maybe that will calm her down.'

Spring cradled the two pups in one arm and took hold of Seamus's roughened hand. She led him, holding the other puppy, towards the front door. Relief showed in the old man's grizzled features and there was a definite bounce in his step as he tilted his face towards the heavens and muttered a faint prayer.

'Is Mr Horrigan a friend of yours?' Sky asked Daniel, brushing a trailing hair back from her forehead.

'No, we met by chance. He'd lost his horse and his dog and I just happened to be in the right place at the right time . . .' He paused, swallowed. 'At least that's what I think happened.'

'Only think?'

'It's all a bit strange . . . Seamus would have us believe that his greyhound has mystical powers.' He laughed weakly, adding, 'Forget it, I'm beginning to sound like an idiot.'

'Well, it appears to have ended happily enough.' Sky spoke gently a false sound which made Daniel feel uneasy. He was fairly certain that although she was putting on a polite front, she didn't really want to make the effort of liking him.

'We don't make a habit of taking in domestic pets.' Sky sipped her coffee and continued, 'But the greyhound was found on our doorstep, and she did have nasty puncture wounds in her left shoulder.'

Daniel shuddered. 'How the heck could that happen?'

'I'm not sure, but if I had to guess I'd say she'd been stabbed with a pitchfork. The holes were about eighteen centimetres apart, quite deep, and needed four stitches. Her shoulder muscle will be bruised for a week or two.'

As they talked Shack Skinner came round from the back of the house. Sky made the introductions and Shack helped Daniel lift his luggage from the Volvo.

Daniel wanted to be friendly with his new manager, but she seemed determined to make things difficult for him. It was almost as if she resented his arrival at the shelter. He felt a flatness in her voice, and she avoided all but the most essential eye contact. Her full lips told him she had a great smile—but he didn't hold out much hope of seeing it.

'I'll have to call the vet.' Sky walked towards the house with long, purposeful strides. 'Dogs aren't really my territory so it's best if he checks her over. He's bound to give Degsey a shot of antibiotics.'

'Oh, right . . .' Daniel called out, fishing around for something kind to say. 'Thanks for fixing up the greyhound. I'm sure Seamus is very thankful.'

Shack watched her disappear through the front door, and then grinned as he turned to Daniel. 'Don't let her manner put you off, dude. She's a bit anti-man at the moment. Her last assistant manager was female so I expect you'll take a bit of getting used to.'

Shack and Daniel each carried a suitcase through to the kitchen. The large room gave Daniel a pleasant feeling of cosiness. The old coal range and a huge pine dresser sparkling with crockery brought back magical memories. It made him think of his grandmother's kitchen during his childhood.

'Shack's an unusual name,' Daniel said, helping himself to coffee and giving Scooter a friendly pat.

'It's a nickname.' Shack lowered his voice to a whisper and added, 'When I was a kid I helped my dad run a hire business on Swiftly beach. It was called the Surf Shack . . . and I guess the name sort of stuck. I was christened Cedric, but don't you dare tell anyone . . . especially Jonathan . . . or you'll ruin my street cred.'

'Who's Jonathan?'

'Sky's twelve-year-old brother. They're from Sussex. He and Spring are down for two weeks of the school holidays.'

'Do you live in?'

'No, I live at Yelland with my dad. My parents split up a couple of years ago. Mum re-married and lives in Yorkshire, but everything's cool. I usually see her and my new stepfather at least once a year. They've got a camper van and spend holidays touring the West Country.'

'Are you permanent staff?'

'No, part-time work experience . . . which reminds me . . .' He glanced at the kitchen clock. 'I should have phoned Bideford College about three hours ago. A course I'm doing. I'll have to catch up next week. I lost track of time watching Sky stitch up the greyhound.'

'I'm glad for Seamus's sake she's alright,' Daniel admitted, warming to Shack's easy-going manner. 'He loves that greyhound.'

'Seamus being the old guy?'

'Yep. His caravan's back at Westleigh . . . He's lost Mister Rafferty, his horse, so I promised I'd think of a way of getting the caravan back here. He won't live anywhere else.'

Shack's jaw tensed. 'Are you sure the horse wasn't stolen? We've had a load of stealing in the West Country lately.'

'That's possible. It makes a lot of sense.' Daniel tugged at a longish lock of hair as things began to make sense. 'Perhaps Degsey disturbed the horse thieves . . . You know, tried to stop them and—'

'Got wounded for her efforts,' Shack put in angrily, grinding the words.

Daniel's face darkened at the thought of it and he moved his head in a series of slow, deliberating nods. It certainly fitted the facts as he knew them. Seamus had described the animals as his 'family' so Degsey would be protecting her pups and probably Mister Rafferty as well.

'Any ideas on how we can shift the wooden caravan?' Daniel posed the question. 'My Volvo's fitted with a tow-bar.'

'Parts of Westleigh moorland can be boggy. I wouldn't like to chance it.'

'The caravan's cumbersome too. It'll be awkward to move.'

'We'll use Napoleon and Josephine.' Shack snapped his fingers. 'They're knocking on a bit—fourteen I think Sky said—but she's used them to raise funds for the shelter in the past. She had a load of special harness made up so they could pull carnival trailers and stuff.'

'Horses?'

'No, donkeys! They got dumped on us when they got a bit too doddery for beach-rides.'

Daniel grinned, relieved. 'Sounds perfect. Can I see them?'

Shack led Daniel through the back door, and across a small yard which passed the office. It was a purpose-built structure, with red bricks to match the house and large roof windows. Pots of flowers stood neatly around the base and one side was covered in trellis-work where creeping plants were encouraged to grow.

Daniel looked past the office to a variety of animal pens, some open-air, some not. There was a large concrete yard, several open-sided sheds with their own strip of pasture, a wooden feed outbuilding, storehouse, and numerous fully enclosed breeze-block buildings. Finally, another concrete yard led to some stables and a large paddock. Beyond this you could glimpse the beach and the far-off foamy sparkle of the sea.

A large external telephone bell shrilled loudly just as Shack turned the handle on the office door. Jonathan was sitting at a computer work-station playing a car chase adventure game. Shack ushered Daniel inside, and reached for the telephone. Jonathan beat him to it, snatching up the receiver.

'Good morning, Oyster Gables,' he announced chirpily.

'You shouldn't be playing games on the works' computer . . .' Shack glared at Jonathan and made a throat slitting gesture.

'Yes, Shacky's here. Who's calling? Hold on.' Jonathan covered the mouthpiece with his hand. 'And you shouldn't be getting calls at work from girlfriends.'

'Who is it?'

'Somebody called Claire.'

Shack flushed angrily and took the receiver from Jonathan's now outstretched hand. He pressed himself into a corner and began a whispered conversation.

Daniel introduced himself to Jonathan, glancing round at the office furnishings. There was a roll top desk with maps of the area above it, three filing cabinets, a workbench and a small stove with a kettle and two electric rings. A ceiling fan whirred overhead and one wall was totally dominated by a huge bookcase. A quick scan of the titles revealed veterinary and care-problem books dealing with every wild animal.

'Would you like an Oyster Gables window sticker?' Jonathan was asking, opening a drawer and pulling out various coloured strips of printed vinyl. 'I can fix it to your car's rear window.'

Daniel nodded agreement, pointing to a blue one.

'Sky did a terrific job on the greyhound,' Jonathan went on, his lips parting in a toothy grin. 'If you ever want a button sewn on your shirt she's an expert with a needle.'

'Cheers, Jonathan.' Daniel returned the smile, thinking that he seemed very young, very confident.

'Strange about the tooth, though,' Jonathan added.

'What tooth?'

'Haven't you seen the greyhound?'

'Not yet.'

'W-e-l-l . . .' he dragged out the word, playing Managing Director, swivelling back and forth in a squeaky chair behind the desk and fiddling with the numbers on a cube desk calendar. 'I was assisting with stuff, pushing a tube in the dog's mouth . . . and there it was . . . a lower canine tooth . . .'

'Jonathan,' Daniel said, a trifle harsher than he'd meant, 'I don't know what on earth you're talking about.'

'A solid gold fang.' He did an impression of a werewolf. It wasn't a very good impression. It reminded Daniel of a tame sea-lion wanting to be thrown a fish.

A puzzled look flickered in Daniel's eyes. He was about to ask Jonathan to explain more fully when Shack slammed down the phone.

'Evil goons!' Shack exhaled deeply, to ease his emotions. 'Four livery horses were stolen from Marshwood last night. That was Claire Morgan, a stable girl who works there . . . an old girlfriend. She says they just busted the padlocks and helped themselves.'

Daniel's face darkened as he considered various aspects of the situation. 'So Mister Rafferty . . .'

'Was probably stolen by the same damn bunch of crooks,' Shack put in, opening the office door. 'Better not say anything to Seamus—not yet. Old horses can sometimes end up as dog meat.'

They talked over this fresh development as Shack steered Daniel towards the donkey pen. Most of the outbuildings had heat—the small mammal casualties having the comfort of a heated pad under their bedding, the larger mammals an infra-red lamp above the holding cages. In one building Daniel was shown mice, voles and shrews who were housed in small plastic fish tanks with top opening lids and in another he saw squirrels, weasels, rabbits and hares who were kept either in wooden cages or hutches with small mesh aviaries.

'All casualties,' Shack informed him as they walked. 'Either attacks from other animals or victims of road traffic accidents. As soon as they're well enough they'll be released back into the wild.'

They passed deer that had fresh hay as bedding and were kept in a small outside paddock, then entered a breeze-block building housing badgers, foxes and stoats. Here, the cages were built with far more strength. Daniel noted the thick vertical bars as Shack explained that the construction was designed to securely hold even the most dangerous animal.

Next, Daniel was shown the isolation shed. It was a small structure, but you couldn't enter unless you'd washed your rubber boots in a tray of antiseptic fluid. New admissions were quarantined for hours, Shack explained, so as to prevent the possibility of cross-infection.

Daniel was suitably impressed. At the safari park he'd been used to large compounds with far fewer animals which, apart from the occasional zoo-swap were never released. Here at Oyster Gables, animals came and animals went. With such a large turnover of different types kept in close proximity, space was short so cleanliness and hygiene was obviously of great importance. Every concrete floor and walkway, Daniel noticed, had been hosed clean and there was the sharp smell of disinfectant in the air.

'Napoleon and Josephine,' Shack announced, as they crossed to the donkey pen. He leaned on the securing rail. 'This old pair will shift the caravan—no problem.'

Daniel fondled the donkeys' huge ears, feeling little puffs of vapour pump from their nostrils as they sniffed his hand, their velvet lips touching his palm and curling up. He grinned as their tongues rasped against his fingers. They were bright-eyed, alert, and looked in excellent condition for their fourteen years.

'Leave it to me,' Shack continued. 'I'll harness them up, and then walk them to Westleigh. Should be a good laugh driving the caravan back to Oyster Gables.'

'Will you need help?'

'Nope, all cool. I've finished for the day . . . you haven't. And as this isn't strictly shelter business then the boss-lady can't moan.'

'Cheers.'

'It's nothing. You go and unpack'

Daniel lifted a hand in thanks and made to move off. He paused as a question nibbled at the corner of his mind.

'Jonathan mentioned something odd.' He turned back to Shack. 'Something about Degsey having a gold tooth . . . ?'

'Oh, that.' Shack shrugged. 'Yeah, I noticed it during surgery.'

'So what did you reckon?'

'Sky thought it was probably some sort of dental thing. Old Irish guys like Seamus can have funny ways . . . they use gold and stuff because of superstitions. Do you think it's important?'

'Not really. Just curious, I suppose.'

Shack gave a lopsided grin. 'Sky said it was a damn nuisance because it was glinting in her eyes under the surgery lights!'

*   *   *

'Degsey's not havin' any antibiological injections, so there's an end to it! The dog was raised with the fruits of the forest; herbs, plants and roots all provided by the good lord. Chemicals be no good for her. I'll make the wee dog better meself. You'll not be lettin' no veterinary touch her with no hypo-thingamy needles. Ah sure no, no, never. Never!'

Seamus was raising his voice as Sky listened to him in white-lipped silence. Daniel also remained quiet, not wishing to voice an opinion and probably put his foot in it on his very first day. He stroked Degsey's silky ears as her nose nuzzled his legs, seeing for the first time the greyhound bitch which had captured everyone's imagination. Her mouth was closed, so he couldn't see the tooth, but she had a very beautiful face, he decided, admiring her markings and the solid thickness of her muscular body. She had a deep chest with plenty of lung-room, strong neck, powerful hindquarters and she stood high on her feet. All excellent qualities, Daniel thought, remembering a lecture he'd attended at college on animals that were purpose built for speed. She had a surgical dressing on her left shoulder and walked with a slight limp, but this didn't appear to be causing distress.

Scooter was lying on the kitchen floor, flicking the odd glance at his basket and wrinkling his forehead even more than usual to show his most wounded expression. Spring had put Degsey's three pups in his personal wicker retreat, and his big brown eyes were expressing disapproval.

'Mr Horrigan,' Sky spoke coldly, defensively. 'Earlier I cleaned Degsey's wounds and stitched them. Now I'm advising, most strongly, that she has an antibiotic injection to fight any remaining infection. I could do it myself, but I'm not too familiar with greyhounds. Therefore, the amount of drug to body-weight should be given by a qualified vet.'

'Have you ever seen creatures find wellness by seeking out a cure for themselves?' Seamus asked the question.

'Of course.' Sky shifted her weight from one foot to the other, looking slightly angry as she absently inspected the palm of her hand.

'Then you'll be knowin' that when a dog eats grass it's most certain it has a stomach ache.'

'I've seen that.' Spring's blue eyes, bright as a squirrel, swerved to Sky. 'Scooter sometimes eats grass.'

'It's nature's way.' Seamus pulled a pipe from the pocket of his old corduroy jacket and sucked on the stem. 'Oh ay, animals know about these tings.'

'No smoking, Mr Horrigan, please!' Sky tut-tutted disapprovingly.

'It's not lit.' Daniel came to Seamus's defence, then wished he hadn't as Sky glared at him, her eyebrows moving in annoyance.

'You may only smoke outside,' she said to Seamus.

Seamus nodded, put the pipe away and moved to the back door. He fingered his earring thoughtfully, and then turned. 'Degsey has mystical powers and wi' me help she could have healed her own wounds, but . . .' He raised his hands before Sky could jump in. 'I'll not let you be tinkin' I'm an ungrateful old man, because full of gratitude I am. You did a fine job . . . very fine. But me wish now is that you leave poor Degsey to me own healin' ways.'

'She's your dog, Mr Horrigan,' Sky's words came out reluctantly. 'I've given you the facts, but the decision in the end is your own.'

Seamus looked comfortable with the arrangement. He exited the back door and Degsey limped outside with her master.

Daniel watched Sky's every feature as he explained about Shack, the donkeys, and the caravan. She smiled at him, but it wasn't very reassuring.

'So Shack's bringing the caravan back here?'

'If that's okay with you?'

'Of course. It can stay on the forecourt till Mr Horrigan's ready to leave us.'

Daniel looked pleased and slightly confused. Sky's tone seemed pleasant enough and she was actually agreeing with something he hadn't asked permission to do.

'Sorry to plunge you in the deep end, Daniel,' she went on, not sounding sorry at all. 'But we have a badger that's due for release today. Do you feel confident enough to handle it?'

'His name's Beethoven,' Spring said amiably. 'He's always getting into scrapes and he seems to spend more time at Oyster Gables than he does in the wild.'

'Yes . . . I'll take him . . . You're the shelter's manager,' Daniel agreed, nodding to Sky. 'I'm here to learn.'

'Good,' she replied curtly. 'Remember that fact and we'll get along famously.'

'What were your favourite animals at the safari park?' Spring asked.

'I liked the monkeys, chimps and gorillas. I worked a lot with the orang-utans . . . so they'd have to be pretty high on my list of favourites.'

'No exotic animals from far-away lands at Oyster Gables,' Sky put in quickly, pressing her lips together. 'I'm afraid we're far more basic . . . much more down to earth.'

'I'm looking forward to the challenge.'

'We're all very pleased you're here.' Spring smiled, glancing quickly at Sky from under long lashes.

'Yes . . . yes, of course we are.' Sky didn't sound particularly convincing. She turned the conversation back to business. 'So use the Escort van and take Beethoven to Scamperbuck Ring at Fremington. You'll find it clearly marked on the map in the office. That's where he was rescued—he was in a nasty fight and came off worst. We always try to release badgers exactly where they're found, and there's an established sett in that part of the woodland.'

'Shouldn't I wait until dusk?' Daniel queried.

'Normally, yes . . . but Beethoven knows the release routine backwards. Daylight won't worry him. He's a regular casualty at

Oyster Gables . . . an easy going old boar who won't give you any problems.'

'I'll take you to the sett.' Spring crinkled her nose at Daniel.

'I'm afraid not,' Sky tried to sound reasonable. 'I'll need you and Jonathan to help me with the midday feeds.'

'What about Hannah and Megan, can't they help you?'

'You know they're only volunteers who assist during the school holidays. Besides, they're not due in until later.'

'Will you be going to Scamperbuck Ring?'

'No, just Daniel.'

'Oh, poo! You said earlier . . .' Spring frowned at her sister and fidgeted awkwardly. 'You said that Beethoven had a powerful bite and it needed two adults to—'

'I know what I said, but I've reconsidered. I'm sure that someone who has safari park experience won't have any kind of problems with a plain, old badger.'

CHAPTER THREE

Beethoven decided to make life difficult for Daniel. The lid of the transporting cage had been unlocked and was now hinged down flatly on a piece of mossy turf awaiting the badger to make an easy exit.

A dash for freedom, Daniel assumed.

No such luck.

Daniel had positioned himself in a clearing, well inside Scamperbuck Ring. He'd carefully studied the office map and knew that his location was within a 100 metre radius of the badger sett where Beethoven had been found. Spring had made him a few written notes and he double-checked these as he stood at the rear of the cage. All okay, he was in the right spot . . . brook to the left, broken stile to the right, a far-off fringe of silver birch straight ahead. He began stamping his feet and making shooing noises in an effort to encourage the badger to exit the steel-barred container.

Sky had equipped him with a short wooden rod, and this was meant to be used as a prodding tool in times of difficulty. Daniel crouched and tried rasping it across the top of the cage, then when this had no effect he resorted to a metallic banging which was loud enough to wake the dead.

The dead maybe, but not Beethoven.

The badger looked inquisitively out of the escape door, but seemed in no hurry to go anywhere. He weaved his long snout back and forth, twitching his whiskers at the warm smell of sun-kissed leaves and forest grasses. His dark, tiny eyes were barely visible, blending in with the facial black stripes which ran sleekly up from his nose to the bristles of his ears,

Daniel peered through the top bars of the cage and eyed the badger cautiously. Beethoven looked back at him with an 'I'll-leave-in-my-own-good-time' expression . . . but time wasn't on Daniel's side. This was the first real duty he'd been given at Oyster Gables, and he wanted to make a good impression on Sky. Arriving back late at the shelter would only give her cause to complain and prompt her to ask awkward questions.

Beethoven's rump was now towards the rear of the transporting cage, so Daniel took the stick and gave a hefty prod into the badger's fleshy fur. He didn't expect such a violent reaction, and wasn't really aware that he'd let his fingers stray briefly between the bars. The badger's coat immediately bushed out and he turned with lightning speed, the great power in his jaws making a clacking sound as his teeth snapped high up on the stick, catching the tip of Daniel's thumb.

'Holy Moley!' Daniel cursed as pain lanced up his arm to his elbow. He felt the sudden stickiness of blood. It was seeping into the right thumb-piece of the protective trapper's mitts loaned him by Spring.

He instinctively jumped back, pulling off the damaged glove, and temporarily easing the blood flow as best he could with the tail-piece of his shirt. The crimson redness leaked out on the white cotton material . . . making it look far worse than it was. A brief examination of the injured thumb showed a small piece of flesh missing from under the nail. No more than a bad nick, Daniel told himself, deciding to make things easier by tearing a strip of cloth from his shirt-tail and winding it round his thumb.

Beethoven still remained obstinately in the cage. Daniel watched as, with a flick of the animal's neck, the stick was tossed out of the escape hatch.

What now? Daniel was turning a few options over in his mind when, much to his amazement, the answer presented itself in the form of a big sow with three members of her family. The female badger and her four-month-old youngsters emerged from a large burrow and stood cautiously in front of the fringe of birch trees.

Daniel stood stock still. Badgers were nocturnal creatures and seldom, if ever, did they venture out in daylight hours. Daniel watched as the group were lit briefly by a shaft of sunlight which coiled down through the branches and glistened in shimmering tints off their sleek, stripy faces.

Beethoven spotted his family immediately. The sow called to him with a soft whickering sound and he stretched out his thick neck to respond in kind. He carefully edged his way out of the escape opening, shook himself, and gouged wavy little lines of earth in the mossy grass as he lazily extended his powerful front claws. Daniel felt a glow of excitement course through his body as he watched the badgers' greeting ritual. He momentarily forgot the throbbing in his thumb, just grinned and breathed a sigh of relief as Beethoven finally lolloped away to join his family group. He saw them exchange playful nudges, scooting round in circles before disappearing into the shadowy depths of Scamperbuck Ring.

Daniel lifted the empty cage and closed it. The torn shirt was hanging raggedly out of his jeans. He looked and felt a total mess as he tucked the shirt in the best way he could before tying the ripped piece of material more firmly around his thumb. He pulled the glove back on and made his way to the Escort van, trying to ignore thoughts of Sky's reaction when she saw his messy state.

It was Shack Skinner who spotted Daniel first. Seamus's wooden caravan dominated the forecourt of Oyster Gables, and Shack was leading Napoleon and Josephine across to the shelter's large double gates. He waited as Daniel parked the Escort van. He held a donkey by a halter in each hand, and had numerous pieces of harness and leather tack slung across his chest and over his broad shoulders.

'I got a load of dodgy looks from motorists, but the donkeys were well up to the job,' he called out as Daniel crossed to meet him. 'Seamus, Degsey, and the pups are inside the caravan. You wanted to see the old guy's face when we rolled up. He could hardly believe it.'

'Great stuff. Well done.' Daniel pulled off his right glove and displayed his bloody thumb.

'Beethoven?'

'Beethoven,' Daniel nodded and explained briefly what had happened at Scamperbuck Ring.

'You look in a right state, dude.' Shack eyed his tangled shirt.

'I need a shower.'

'Have you had a tetanus shot?'

'I had a booster before I left the safari park.'

51

'The boss-lady will clean up the bite. You know, antiseptic and stuff. She's in the office.'

Daniel gave a brief nod.

'Unless you're into herbal medicine.' Shack displayed a wicked grin. 'Seamus has got all these potions in the caravan. He's mixing some up for Degsey. I bet he'd love to play doctors with your thumb.'

Daniel grinned back. 'I'll take my chances with Sky,' he said.

They went their separate ways. On his walk to the bathroom Daniel stopped at his bedroom to pick up a clean denim shirt. It was a large, low-ceilinged room, neat and clean, with a fresh smell to it. There were three china geese flying across the pale blue emulsion paint of one wall and covering the floor was a faded carpet patterned with huge swirls. An over-stuffed armchair filled one corner of the room and a big old fashioned wardrobe rested against a wall which creaked as he trod on a loose board beneath the carpet. A single bed sat under the window and, lying there at night, you could hear the sea hissing and thundering in.

Daniel had a hot shower and changed into his fresh denim shirt before grabbing a cola from the kitchen fridge. He made his way to the office, and on pushing open the door, wondered faintly who or what would be colder, Sky or the fizzy drink.

On this occasion it was the drink.

'Hi, Daniel.' Sky smiled, deciding to be nice. 'Everything go alright?'

'Beethoven's back with his family,' Daniel said.

Sky gave a relaxed nod, stretching her legs against the work-station's footrest. She was transferring handwritten information from a box of record cards onto the computer database. Each mammal or bird casualty was initially issued with a card stating where and when it had been found, what injuries it had suffered, the treatment it had received, plus notes on drugs and diet. Finally, it was given a pet name and a release date.

'So Beethoven was released at Scamperbuck Ring on . . .' She checked the desk cube calendar and tapped in the date using the computer keys. 'Oh, heavens!' She glimpsed the makeshift dressing on Daniel's thumb. 'You've hurt yourself.'

Daniel wasn't sure whether she was genuinely concerned or just putting on a caring voice. She had this strange way of saying one thing, whilst her eyes expressed either nothing, or faint amusement.

She crossed to the first-aid box hanging on the wall by the bookshelf and picked out some items. 'Sit,' she ordered, pointing to the work-station chair.

Daniel sat.

He could smell a faint trace of perfume as she leaned over him, expertly working with scissors to cut free the shirt bandage from his thumb. In no time at all she'd cleaned the bite, swabbed it with iodine, applied some antiseptic cream and dressed it.

'You'll live,' she said brightly, her long fingers plucking at the collar of his shirt, straightening it . . . then she looked quickly away, almost embarrassed by her actions.

'There are two portions of shepherd's pie in the oven,' she announced, now using her flat professional voice. 'Plenty for you and Seamus. Jonathan and Spring have both eaten and I've fed Degsey and the pups.'

Daniel murmured a thank you and stood up. He was certainly getting used to her mood swings and wasn't going to say anything to ruin his lunch. Sky smoothed a wandering lock of hair back behind her ear, trying to appear unruffled.

'See you for a ride later,' she said as he reached the door. 'We usually exercise the livery horses on the beach at weekends.'

'Fine.'

'You *can* ride?' The question was asked with a hint of scorn.

Daniel was an excellent horseman, but he said, 'I expect I'll get the hang of it.'

He left Sky staring at the computer monitor, her fingers busily rat-tatting at the keyboard.

* * *

Seamus Horrigan's caravan was carved and gilded both inside and out. It sat on the forecourt of Oyster Gables with all the beauty of an ancient galleon in harbour.

The oak spokes of its huge wheels were painted in the brightest of bright yellow—twelve spokes on the front wheel, fourteen on the rear. These supported thick iron tyres and were secured to the fore-carriage and hind-carriage by hubs with gleaming brass ends.

Its roof was white lead which dazzled when caught by the sun; its body a dark red colour decorated with gold and green. Two brass lamps, a candle in each, were fixed either side of the door.

There was a mass of exterior carving, set with tiny cut-glass mirrors; and the shafts, once carried proudly by Mister Rafferty, were glowing with lines of colour.

The caravan's porch-brackets were carved in a design of flowers, leaves and twisted stems. The shutters were bright yellow with sunflower decorations, and the door panel showed a St George-killing-the-Dragon pattern against a background of spade-shaped leaves.

For Jonathan and Spring it was a magical, breath-taking world.

They sat on a locker seat beside a chest of drawers opposite the stove. Both listened wide-eyed as the old Irishman told them travelling stories. He talked of the old times as he ground up herbs and tree bark into a thick paste. Degsey and her pups were curled asleep on a skin rug at his feet.

'Ah to be sure, Mister Rafferty could pull me wagon for eighteen mile a day,' Seamus told them, 'and I've crossed and re-crossed the Irish Sea many times.'

'Will you ever find Mister Rafferty?' Jonathan asked.

'Who can say, Jonathan boy.' He lifted his shoulders in a despairing gesture. 'It's for sure I miss the old devil. To grip the reins in yer hands and hear the rumble of the wagon beneath you, listening to the clink and rattle of the bit and harness links . . . It's the most beautifullest of feelings.'

'You have a lovely home.' Spring began talking in rapid little bursts. 'Can I live here? Can I travel the country with you and Degsey? Oh, please say yes.'

'And can she drive your caravan?' Jonathan asked.

'Wagon, boy, wagon!'

'How big is the wagon?' Jonathan corrected himself. 'You know, size and weight and stuff?'

'It's called a Reading and she be about twelve feet includin' the front porch, and about thirteen-and-a-half feet includin' the back porch.'

'What's that in metres?'

'Don't know metres.' He lifted grey wisps of eyebrows. 'It's seventy year since I went to school.'

'How about weight?' Jonathan pressed on.

'Lordy, lordy, boy, you ask enough questions to annoy a saint! She be thirty hundredweight . . . and before y'be askin' her age, she be older than yer dad and his dad before him. Built in the early nineteen-hundreds so she was.'

Seamus had finished his grinding and mixing. He replaced pieces of twig, bark, herbs, and oil into different drawers of a tiny tabletop cabinet, then turned his attention to Degsey.

'Up, me wee darlin.' He smiled easily, coaxing Degsey to her feet. The greyhound yawned, showing a glint of gold, looking up at her master with trusting eyes.

'When will you tell us how she got her tooth?' Jonathan asked anxiously.

Seamus stroked the edge of his jaw. 'You be curious to know of Degsey's mystical powers?'

'Bursting,' Spring admitted.

'Well, we don't want you to burst, wee Spring,' he said, after a moment's reflection. 'It's a long story. It's the most magicallest story you'll ever hear . . .'

'So you will tell us?' Jonathan pressed.

'Ay, tonight, after dark. 'Bout ten o'clock. Ask permission to stay up and we'll drink tea round the wagon. Bring Sky, the donkey man and Danny boy.'

Spring and Jonathan exchanged grins of delight.

'I'll ask Sky to make some Cornish pasties,' Jonathan said.

'I be likin' the pasties.' Seamus nodded approval. 'Will y'sister be mindin' the task?'

'Of course not,' Jonathan told him. 'She makes the best pastry in Swiftly.'

'Jus' so long as she pricks it to let the wee spirits out.'

'She always pricks it,' Spring put in, 'but I'll remind her if you like.'

'Good, good, then pasties it be. I'll be cleanin' Mister Rafferty's harness tonight. It's a weekly chore, but must be done . . . even though the ole horse not be wi' us.'

'Can we help?' Jonathan asked.

'To be sure you can. It will be hard work, mind.'

Both nodded eagerly.

Seamus got on with the task in hand asking them to hold Degsey still. He carefully peeled Sky's dressing from the greyhound's shoulder, noting that the wound was weeping slightly under the stitches. Degsey didn't flinch as he replaced it with a fresh dressing smeared with the sticky mixture he'd been preparing. He spoke of the healing effects of the blend, telling Spring and Jonathan that the dog's limp would be cured within 24 hours.

'Hi, all!' Daniel stuck his head through the top half of the front porch door. He held up some slices of bread and two steaming plates of shepherd's pie. 'Grub up, Seamus.'

'By Jaminee it's me pal, Danny.' The old Irishman sniffed the air. 'I can smell me favourite . . . Meat and taters.'

Seamus waved him in, clearing the table to make room for the food. He produced two sets of knives and forks from a drawer and stuffed a napkin into the front of his shirt.

'Place 'em down, Danny me boy.' He smiled gleefully, rubbing his hands. 'And let's be tuckin' in.'

Daniel sat on the locker seat beside the stove, opposite Spring and Jonathan.

'Any news of Mr Rafferty?' Seamus asked.

Daniel gave his head a mournful shake. 'Not as yet'

The puppies were still fast asleep but Degsey stretched her neck forward and sniffed at Daniel's shoes. Her tail slashed at the air like a whip as she moved her firm-muscled body under his hands, craving love.

'So what have you been doing to her?' Daniel asked, noticing the fresh dressing as he stretched a hand to stroke Degsey's ears. 'What magic potions have you been brewing?'

'Bashing bits of old leaves and trees and stuff,' Jonathan put in, 'with a club-shaped thing in a bowl.'

'Fruits of the forest,' Seamus said, taking a forkful of shepherd's pie.

'Which are?' Daniel showed genuine interest.

Seamus spoke between heaped mouthfuls of pie, explaining how he'd used the herb comfrey to promote healing of the skin wound, creosote bush to help Degsey's body fight infection, calendula oil to reduce fever and relieve pain, and the bark of an elderberry tree for its mystic powers.

'It's good to plant an elderberry near your house,' Seamus added, his eyes flickering with amusement as he glanced at Spring. 'It'll bring you good luck and protect against disease.'

'Sounds total tosh to me,' Jonathan said positively. 'When I'm ill I go to the doctor.'

'Ay, very wise, Jonathan,' Seamus agreed. 'But don't you be forgetin' that plant medicines have been used since the beginnin' of time.'

As if to agree with Seamus, Degsey crossed to her water bowl and began lapping gently at the contents.

'And does the wee dog not agree with me words?' Seamus's flinty eyes beamed as he nudged Daniel to look. 'The water has white willow bark in it, so it does. A cure to help bring fever down and ease pain.'

Daniel couldn't resist smiling as he finished his meal. He wiped his plate clean with a slice of bread . . . then wished he hadn't. Seamus glimpsed the bandage on his thumb.

'Hurt y'self, boy?'

'A nick. It's nothing.'

'Will you not be lettin' old Seamus treat it? It should have been bathed in garlic . . .It's the bestest ting for a wound.'

'Sky sorted me out.'

'Antibiologicals?'

'No, iodine, and antiseptic cream. It's healing nicely.'

'And you be sure you wouldn't like me to take a wee look at the wound?'

'Very sure . . . thanks.'

Seamus nodded slowly, accepting the decision. Daniel watched the old Irishman eat the last few forkfuls of his pie, then let his gaze wander over the fittings of the caravan's interior. He hadn't noticed much on the last visit due to the panic over Degsey's disappearance.

The cabinet work was of dark-red polished mahogany with the glazed cupboard shelves trimmed with bobble-fringe and held in place by brass-headed studs. To the right side of him was the old Colchester stove with its mirror polished brass front, curved mantel shelf, and floor rail guard which held a brass shovel, tongs and poker. Both front corners of the caravan had a small cupboard displaying china, and immediately opposite him was a chest of drawers. His eyes were drawn to a splendid brass lamp, fixed to one side of the window, and Seamus followed his gaze calling it, 'Me Angel lamp.'

At the back of the caravan were the two-berth sleeping quarters. These comprised bunk beds; the top bunk just below the rear window.

Daniel was impressed by the quality of the fine linen sheets and fringed pillow cases. The upper bed, for guests, had a satin-covered eiderdown; the lower, which Daniel presumed was Seamus's bed, a patchwork quilt. The curtains were lace-edged velvet, looped as drapes, and tied back to the bedposts with gold-tasselled cord.

Daniel was impressed. Everything sparkled with long hours of cleaning, and the rich colours of the woods could only have been acquired with years of polishing. The furnishings, Daniel thought, would certainly have done a large country house proud.

'Me belly be full.' Seamus broke into Daniel's thoughts, rubbing his chin with his napkin and reaching for his pipe. 'God bless the kitchen and all belongin' to it.'

'Sky cooked your pie,' Spring told him. 'I had cabbage and mushroom hotpot.'

'Do you not be likin' the pie of the shepherds?'

'She's a veggie freak.' Jonathan sniffed.

Seamus tapped out his pipe. He frowned at Daniel, not understanding the words.

'Spring only eats vegetables,' he explained. 'No meat.'

'What do you do when you're on the road?' asked Jonathan. 'Do you hunt and trap things? Have you got a gun?'

'No gun,' Seamus said, noticing that Spring was glancing uneasily at him. He paused before saying, 'It's vegetables I eat, given to me by farmers in trade for a few hours work.'

Spring smiled, giving a nod of approval.

He exchanged a sideways glance with Daniel and began filling his pipe. He could have told Jonathan how he relied on Degsey to catch him a rabbit or hare or even the odd pheasant or grouse, but he decided not to upset Spring.

'You must eat meat . . . sometimes.' Jonathan pressed Seamus for an answer.

'Oh, ay, I have a bit sometimes . . . like today. I be admittin' I'm not a true veggie freak like y'sister.'

'Thought not.' Jonathan gave a grunt of satisfaction.

All heads turned towards the front porch as steps rattled on the footboard. Seamus stood up, looking relieved at having escaped any further quizzing on his eating habits.

'Mr Rusk?' A girl's head peered over the top half of the porch doors. 'Mr Daniel Rusk?'

Her face was delicately shaped and framed with short, fair hair. Daniel guessed her to be around fifteen.

He stood to greet her and she introduced herself as Megan Fairchild, one of Oyster Gables volunteer helpers.

'Sky says to tell you the horses are tacked up and ready for your ride,' Megan said.

Daniel had virtually forgotten about exercising the livery horses. As he said his goodbyes to Seamus, Jonathan and Spring, he wondered whether Sky's mood would be friendly, or whether he would be given the cold-shoulder treatment.

They picked their way across the concrete yard and past the storehouse. Megan spoke about the various cases of injured animals and birds at Oyster Gables then guided Daniel towards the breeze-block outbuilding which housed the small mammals. There, he briefly exchanged smiles with Hannah Fullerton, another of the shelter's young volunteers. She had springy, red-gold hair, a freckled complexion, and wore a waxed jacket and green rubber boots about four sizes too large. He left them hosing down a flagstone path and pressed on to the stables.

Sky was sitting astride a grey mare which pranced around the curve of the building, tail up, neck arched, the nerves in its flanks twitching as it halted to face him.

'You're not dressed!' She looked down at his jeans and trainers and made a tutting sound. 'I expected as much. You'll find a pair of riding boots and a hard hat in Sir Galahad's box . . . I had to guess at the size.'

Daniel glanced at her pale cream jodhpurs, having presumed she'd be wearing them, and admiring the way they suited her. He also liked the wild way her tawny hair spilled from under her hat. She looked scrubbed and shining and wore only a hint of make-up.

'The mare's called Excalibur.' Sky made some effort at politeness, assuming Daniel was admiring the horse rather than her. She slipped her feet from the stirrup irons, stretching her legs. 'Whenever you're ready, Daniel.' She smiled tolerantly. 'Take your time.'

Daniel made his way to Sir Galahad's box. The horse was a showy chestnut gelding with a lot of Arab in him. He sported a white blaze and three white socks and stood around sixteen hands. His ribs were well sprung, giving way to broad, muscular hindquarters. Daniel found himself being nuzzled playfully as he pulled on the boots and fastened the hard hat.

Compared to the rest of the animal units, the stable area appeared run down and ancient looking; comprising three loose boxes which had seen far better days. They weren't really needed, Daniel thought, knowing that the shelter didn't deal with horses apart from the extra funds collected in livery money. He gazed round at the cracked mangers, the lopsided doors badly in need of re-hanging, and the powdery moss-covered brickwork which had probably been standing for hundreds of years. There was new hay in the hay-nets, and fresh straw on the floors. Everywhere was clean and tidy—he couldn't fault it—but unless the Oyster Gables' Trust were prepared to spend money upgrading the structure, then the weather, over time, would force the stables into total disrepair.

Sky was waiting for him by the paddock. She leaned forward in the saddle, her fingers working loose the metal keeper that held the five-barred gate. Daniel coaxed Sir Galahad to move at a collected trot just as the gate swung inwards. He held the reins almost loose, his manner secure and confident.

'See you on the beach!' Daniel took a deep breath and grinned wryly. Suddenly he was enjoying himself.

A mountain of chestnut haunch swung past Sky's face as Sir Galahad responded immediately to the pressure of Daniel's heels, springing straight into a gallop. The big horse was literally flying, crossing the paddock at full stretch with Daniel coaxing him towards a gate on the far side. Through the wisps of streaming mane Daniel could see the beach and the sea beyond. Terns, herring gulls and guillemots bobbed on the creamy foam of the breakers.

Sky's pulses were racing wildly as she sent Excalibur forward into a faster pace, encouraging the mare with soft words. She began closing on Sir Galahad's rump, preparing to rein in as Daniel pulled up at the gate . . .

Only he didn't.

Daniel's blistering gallop continued.

He was perfectly balanced and his hands were moving with great force and rhythm as he concentrated on Sir Galahad's pacing, correcting the horse's leg action slightly before pushing forward and effortlessly spanning the gate . . .

It was an expert jump, with the chestnut's heels showing the wooden framework plenty of daylight. Sky felt an angry flush run up her cheeks as she reined in, watching the big gelding's hooves dig into the soft sand as Daniel slowed to a halt. Sir Galahad was quivering and steaming as Daniel swung the horse round to face her.

Sky boiled with anger as she unhooked the gate and gently walked Excalibur through to the beach. Her hazel eyes got smaller as she met Daniel's gaze.

'Of all the stupid, irresponsible, hare-brained . . .' She broke off huffily. 'You could easily have injured that horse.'

'Nonsense, he loved it.'

'T—that gate's never been jumped before. You were just showing off.'

'I felt Galahad wanted to do it.' He fingered the damp hair off his brow. 'Is it against the rules?'

'No, of course not.'

'Then no harm done.'

Sky looked away and smoothed imaginary wrinkles from her jodhpurs. 'Peggy would have never behaved like that.'

'Who's Peggy?'

'My previous assistant manager.'

'Well Peggy's not here and I am . . . only temporary, I know. So you'll just have to put up with my funny little ways until Peggy returns.'

She flushed hotly, her chin uptilted. This was the first time she'd seen a touch of annoyance in his expression and she didn't like it. She wanted to reply . . . to perhaps apologise for her anger. Certainly a small voice inside her wanted to tell him it had been a brilliant jump—a well judged piece of riding—and that he was obviously a good horseman . . . but common sense told her to say nothing.

'Chill out, Sky, it's a beautiful day so enjoy it.' Daniel remained cool as he jogged Sir Galahad on.

It wasn't easy to shake off her anger but as her face softened she managed to force a ghost of a smile. For the first time in a long while, she found herself enjoying some male company, so she switched her tracking position and eased Excalibur alongside to join Daniel. They trotted forward in the sheltered bay, reaching the sea and then skirting it, letting the lacy foam of salt water gurgle around the horses' fetlocks. Small waves combed the sleek silvery beach, sucking back and shifting pebbles and tiny marine creatures into nearby rock pools.

'What's this place called?' Daniel was very impressed.

'Delight Cove.'

'Delight Cove.' He repeated the words, squinting into the sun and giving a soft whistle. 'Wow, it certainly lives up to its name.'

Sky indicated a strip of breakwater which ran from the far side of the paddock to the sea. 'Oyster Gables own this section of the beach. We're very lucky. It came with the house.'

The promenade was alive with people. All wore T-shirts, or summer outfits, or swimming costumes. Sun cream soaked into skin as temperatures nudged 30°C. The public beaches were rapidly filling with glistening, oily bodies. Hotels and guest houses along the seafront wavered in the heat haze.

Sky and Daniel went from trot to canter, doing various fun movements with Excalibur and Sir Galahad as they caught the spray from the breakers. They were totally unaware that their every move was being watched by two men from the quayside.

'Two little beauties. One chestnut, one grey.' Tony Ryker lowered his binoculars. 'They're nice lookers. They'll fetch good money at auction.'

Ryker had returned to the area with the aim of capturing Degsey. On finding Seamus and the caravan gone, he'd dragged a reluctant Martin Griggs onto Swiftly for some sun and sea air.

Griggs sucked tomato ketchup off the drooping end of a sausage wrapped tightly in a long, soggy roll. 'You don't know where they're stabled,' he murmured, biting into a third of the bread, his words puffing around the load in his mouth. 'They could've come from anywhere . . . might even have been brought by trailer.'

'Wrong, my little ferret. It's a private beach.'

'So?'

'So the beach belongs to an animal rescue place called Oyster something or other. They keep a couple of livery horses to make a bit of money on the side. I've passed it many times in the car. It's just up the road.'

Griggs said, 'So you plan to steal 'em?'

He nodded. 'Sir Galahad and Excalibur.'

'You know their names . . . ?'

'I have my contacts.' He fiddled with his diamond-studded ring, twisting it. 'I listen and learn, Griggsy. I never turn a deaf ear when there's dishonest money to be made.'

Ryker put the binoculars back to his eyes and indicated the various ways of gaining rear entry to Oyster Gables. His tattooed forearm made a sweep as he pointed out the breakwater and the beach gate which led to the paddock, informing Griggs that the stable area was blocked by the roofs of other buildings.

'Are you barking mad?' Griggs burped loudly and looked uncomfortable. 'I'm not climbing over breakwaters and crossing beaches just to get two horses. The sea can be dangerous. What about tides and stuff?'

'Are you frightened of the water?'

'You know I can't swim.'

'You don't wash much either. Are you allergic to the liquid that comes out of taps?'

Griggs burped again. 'I shower once a week and sometimes I use your deodorant. So don't try and be funny.'

Ryker ignored him, deep in thought as he tapped a fingernail against his teeth. 'The beach method is less dangerous,' he said. 'You're well away from the house. I'll get a local timetable that lists the tides.'

'I'm still not doing it,' Griggs rasped. 'I'm liable to get a nosebleed, so you'll have to think of something else.'

Ryker's eyes roamed over the roof of Oyster Gables. 'Okay, we'll use our normal routine . . . front entry. With two horses on the premises there has to be easy access.'

Griggs rolled the empty hot-dog wrapper between his palms and tossed it into the sea. 'When do you plan to get 'em?'

'Soon. I've had a tip off that three livery horses are being kept temporarily at a farm at Penhill. That's just down the road from Swiftly, so we'll make a night of it.'

Griggs's bony shoulders lifted moodily. 'Thought we were supposed to be looking for the wooden caravan owners?'

Ryker set his jaw. 'Well we couldn't find them, could we? No caravan at Westleigh . . . nothing.'

'I'm glad they're gone—especially that damn devil dog.'

'Luckily we haven't had a wasted journey.' Ryker gave a nasty chuckle. He watched Sir Galahad and Excalibur trot back to the paddock gate, before adding, 'Two more for our collection, my little ferret. And they're ours for the taking.'

CHAPTER FOUR

It was a clear, warm night, and for the past hour Seamus, Spring and Jonathan had been carefully cleaning every section of Mister Rafferty's strap harness.

There was a mountain of it.

They'd used a bucket of water with sponges, some bars of saddle-soap, and a can of silver polish. Spring and Jonathan had sat beside Seamus on the footboard, listening as he explained the purpose of each piece of harness. Spring had cleaned the bridle fitted with blinkers and snaffle bit, while Jonathan had struggled with the huge collar and thick leather traces which connected onto a back-strap in order to hold up the shafts. Seamus finished saddle-soaping the crupper strap, which went around the base of the tail, then all three had got to grips with the mass of leather reins.

They were four-and-a-half metres long, hand-stitched and decorated with silver crests. When the leather had been thoroughly cleaned, three pairs of hands had worked briskly away with the polish, buffing and brightening every little silver crest and motif. It was a complicated job but both Spring and Jonathan had thrown themselves into the cleaning and eventually the reins glittered and twinkled as Seamus lit the candles in the two carriage lamps.

The cleaning now complete, Seamus had packed the gleaming harness in the pan-box at the caravan's rear end, and sent Jonathan and Spring off to wash and change at the house.

Seamus did likewise, putting on a clean white shirt with stiffened collar, beige corduroy trousers and suede waistcoat. The black belt of his trousers was punctuated with silver diamond and heart designs, similar to those on Mister Rafferty's harness. He changed by the light from two candles fixed in brass mounts attached to the bed posts. He carefully combed his long thinning wisps of grey hair, fastening them back in a pony-tail with a bright strip of cloth, then he consulted his pocket watch. Almost ten o'clock . . . time for him to go through his nightly business of lighting the paraffin Angel lamp.

It was an Irish tradition that the quality of the Angel lamp reflected the personal pride taken in owning a caravan. Seamus Horrigan's lamp was particularly splendid—having been cast in solid brass, and displaying a flying cherub holding Pan-pipes to its mouth. The oil container was made from ruby red cut-glass, and the globe had been hand-painted with forest scenes.

Seamus carefully removed the globe and the chimney and put a match to the wick. As the flame licked at the air he replaced the glass pieces and adjusted the burner so that a warm, flickering glow spilled out through the porch doors.

Degsey was curled on the skin rug with her pups, but when her eyes sensed the light from the Angel lamp she stretched, turned her head, and stared unblinkingly into the globe. She'd watched her master do this nightly since the day she'd been born, and this evening was no exception. Seamus looked at the lamp and took a few seconds to thank his blessings.

Two of the pups remained sleeping, but the third, whose markings matched her mother's so closely, stretched her head into the soft hollow of Degsey's throat and followed her to the Angel lamp. This pup, the only bitch in the litter, had been fittingly named 'Little Degsey' by Spring.

Seamus gathered some clean, but old, woollen rugs from inside a locker seat and left the caravan. The light from the Angel lamp flickered out of the nearside window illuminating the grass verge alongside the parking area. Seamus placed rugs down at certain points along the verge so that wherever his guests sat the caravan's footboard would be in full view.

Earlier, Spring and Jonathan had taken the still-limping Degsey for a short walk and gathered driftwood from Delight Cove for the fire. Now, freshly washed and changed they were back and setting up a metal tripod which Seamus called a 'chittie' to support the large copper kettle. It held four and a half litres of water and Jonathan had struggled to fill it.

Seamus built a nest with tightly twisted strips of newspaper and placed some pieces of driftwood in a close-knit pattern around it.

'Plenty of air', he advised Jonathan and Spring as he carefully added more sticks to the arrangement. 'Build it right and the old kettle'll boil faster than usin' any modern gas ring.'

Earlier, Daniel had placed a large piece of aluminium sheeting in front of the caravan to stop any scorch marks spoiling the forecourt's tarmac. It had last been used on Guy Fawkes Night and it was now serving a double purpose as Seamus put a match to the wigwam of driftwood. The fire caught immediately, popping and crackling as it sent up a spiral of sparks which danced like silvery spirits in the warm night air.

The noise of a motorbike announced the arrival of Shack and his girlfriend Sophie. They removed their crash helmets and crossed the forecourt like two dark mystery figures, in shadow against the camp-fire's brightness.

'It's the donkey man and his wee girl,' Seamus announced, extending a leathery hand as Shack introduced Sophie.

She was seventeen, dark and plumpish, with green eyes that held a glow of intelligence and a sparkle of fun. She asked to look inside the caravan and Spring gave her a guided tour, taking the opportunity to load up a tray with seven mugs, a huge teapot, tea caddy, sugar, milk and spoons. Shack's arm muscles bulged beneath the short sleeves of his tightly stretched black shirt as he carried the tray down the wooden steps. He placed it beside Seamus, then he and Sophie sat with knees clasped on a rug on the grass verge.

The fire was blazing nicely and the water in the kettle was already beginning to hiss. The caravan towered behind Spring and Jonathan, its bright colours picked out by the flames as they sat around the chittie, adding pieces of driftwood to the fire.

Shack and Sophie asked countless questions about Seamus's lifestyle, and the old man recounted many interesting stories from his past. He made enough money to feed himself, Degsey and Mister Rafferty, he told them, by stopping here and there and doing odd jobs. If really pushed for some odd pennies, then he would rely on his ancient craft of making baskets from willow and strips of split hazel, and sell them by the roadside. Shack replied jokingly that Seamus had better teach him the art, so that he could save enough cash to rebuild the stables.

'This looks cosy.' Daniel appeared from the blackness and joined the fireside group. He was wearing a short-sleeved cotton shirt, worn outside combat trousers.

'Hello, everyone.' Sky was a few paces behind him with Scooter at her heels. She held a mobile phone in one hand and a carrier bag in the other and smiled easily at Seamus as she stood by the chittie. 'Freshly cooked Cornish pasties,' she told him, taking foil-wrapped little parcels from the bag and handing them to all. 'They're piping hot, so be careful.'

'Oh, more than kind.' Seamus's face creased with delight as he juggled the heated silver wrapper between his fingers. 'I be admittin' I'm a poor cook when it comes to pastry.'

Spring was eyeing Sky with caution. Sky turned to meet her gaze.

'And before you ask,' she said, moving her head in a series of slow, thoughtful nods. 'Yes, your pasty contains soya and vegetables, and yes I did prick them as instructed.'

Spring bobbed her head and looked at Seamus. He nodded back, his lips pursed into a smile.

The lid of the large copper kettle was beginning to rattle under the pressure of steam. Seamus lifted it from the chittie, thoroughly warming the teapot before adding tea from the caddy. It was now Jonathan's turn to fill the pot and following Seamus's instructions he placed it close to the fire.

'Do you need any help?' Sophie called out, wrapping an arm tightly around Shack's waist.

Seamus signalled that all was well, but Sophie's actions prompted a question from Spring to Daniel.

'I expect you have tons and tons of girlfriends,' she said, her eyes mischievous. 'But is there a special one?'

Daniel gave a small grin. 'There was one . . . an assistant at the safari park. She emigrated to New Zealand about three months ago. Her parents were going to live there, so she went too.'

'Don't embarrass, Daniel,' Sky said, quietly pleased with the answer. 'You shouldn't ask personal questions . . . It's very rude.'

A smile lifted the corners of Jonathan's lips. 'You could say girls travel to the other side of the world to avoid Mr Rusk.'

Daniel grinned at that and Sky wanted to smile too, but for the sake of correctness she tut-tutted and gave Jonathan a fierce look, keeping her amusement under control.

She, Daniel and Scooter crossed to a rug on the grass verge, Sky curling her legs under her as she sat. She was wearing fashionable sandals which looped behind her heels, jeans and a white, lace blouse buttoned high on her throat. Her hair had been pulled upwards and secured by a small beaded band.

Seamus checked the fire and then carefully stirred the tea leaves in the pot. He counted five circles with a long-handled spoon one way and then five circles the other way before asking Spring to fill and distribute the mugs. He stood upright, wincing slightly as he stretched his old bones. Cleaning the harness and the general bustle of the day had prompted some aches in his joints and he walked stiffly to the caravan, resting against one of the shafts before making his way up the steps.

Degsey, padded out onto the porch and lay on the footboard beside her master. Seamus sat with her head resting on his thigh, fondling her ears, her outline darkened by the feathery shadows cast by the light from the Angel lamp.

'Any news of the lost horse?' Sophie asked, genuinely concerned as she took a bite of her pasty. Shack gave her a nudge, remembering the call from Marshwood Stables and wishing she hadn't asked the question.

'Ahh! Nothin'.' Seamus's gentle face clouded over as he stared at the empty shafts. 'And miss him so I do. Mister Rafferty be pullin' me wagon for the last seventeen year, and he be hard to forget.'

'Can't you buy a new one?' Jonathan asked, peeling the foil from his pasty. 'A younger horse would pull your cara . . . I mean . . . wagon much faster.'

'True, boy, but it's not youngness I be wantin', it's knowledge,' he said, with a sigh. 'A 'sperienced horse knows how t'get a heavy wagon rollin' by usin' his own weight. Gentle, y'see, young 'un . . . Gentler than a summer breeze in the glens of Antrim. Mister Rafferty would lean slowly forward in his harness 'til he felt the traces tighten . . . then off . . . smooth as moleskin. No jerkin' old Seamus, Mister Rafferty be tinkin' . . . no rattlin' his master's old bones . . .' He paused, toying with his unlit pipe. When he spoke again it was almost if he was talking to himself: 'Oh ay, the old devil was even too clever to let Seamus use the brake . . . might strain the old boy's back, he be tinkin'. So, on a steep hill he'd use his muscles by sittin' back in the shafts, takin' the full weight of the wagon on himself.'

There was a few seconds awkward silence. Glances were exchanged as nobody knew exactly what to say.

Eventually Daniel forced a hopeful note into his voice and said, 'We'll do everything to get him back for you, Seamus. That's a promise.'

'It's faith in you I have, Danny boy. Forgive me for gassin' on . . . Me brain be fair twizzled with the loss.' He crinkled some life into his flinty blue eyes and took a huge mouthful of his pasty.

'Please tell us about Degsey,' Jonathan piped up.

'Me wee dog?' Seamus stroked Degsey's long, athletic neck. 'So what do you want to be knowin'?'

'The tooth! The tooth!' Spring's blue eyes were fixed pleadingly upon Seamus.

'We . . . ll,' he began, 'then I shall have to be startin' at the beginnin'.'

He finished his pasty, took a gulp of his tea and told of the story of Degsey's birth. He explained that Degsey's mother was a retired racing greyhound called Deggoran Odyssey whom he'd adopted when she was just three years old.

'She be a kind, faithful female greyhound,' he went on, 'but she not be wanted by her owners 'cause her racing days be over. So I took her and loved her as me own.'

'What about Degsey's father?' quizzed Shack, leaning forward with interest.

'An Irish Derby winner. One of the finest racing dogs in the land . . . They romanced each other whenever they met; while I be doin' a few odd jobs at the race-track in Dublin. The result of their lovin' be me darlin' Degsey.'

Every time her name was mentioned, Degsey nestled her chin more firmly against Seamus's thigh, watching the sparks burst from the fire and blinking sleepily at her master.

'So how many pups did Deggoran Odyssey have?' Sky asked.

'Only the one.' Seamus's eyes were misty, faraway. 'Me wagon be stopped for the night near Knockgrafton at the foot of the Galtee mountains . . .'tis the beautifullest of places and me wee girl went to sleep outside. As the sun went down she lay on a rich green carpet of four-leaf clovers stretching as far as the eye could see . . . It be a sight to behold. It was magical. Then—' He paused, swallowed hard, tears pricking his eyes as he relived the memory.

'Then . . . me wee girl had trouble givin' birth. It be hard for her . . . Somethin' be wrong. There be more than one pup, but they be still . . . still . . .'

'Stillborn,' Sky said softly.

'Ay, 'twas terrible.' He drew a ragged breath. 'She managed just the one . . . Degsey . . . then, god-love-her she died wi' me fingers strokin' her face . . . In me arms she be when she was taken up to heaven.'

The words held everyone spellbound. Shack and Daniel both swallowed large lumps in their throats, Sophie's small white teeth worked on her lower lip and Jonathan noisily gulped down his tea trying not to show his feelings. Tears came so suddenly to Spring that she couldn't stop them.

'Now, now, me wee Spring.' Seamus said gently 'It's not me wish t'be upsettin' you with me stories.'

There was a momentary silence. Everyone seemed puzzled as to what to do next.

'I think I've worked out how she came to be called Degsey,' Sky eventually said, trying to lighten the moment. 'You took the "DEG" from Deggoran and the "SEY" from Odyssey to make an unusual first name.'

'Ay,' Seamus nodded. 'Me darlin' girl be named after her mother so she is.'

'How did you wean her?' Shack asked.

'By hand usin' a dolly's bottle. She be on solid food after 'bout three week.'

'Have you ever raced her on a track? She looks as if she could run a blinding race.'

'I not be believin' in it. Racin' dogs spend their lives in kennels . . . so 'tis no life at all. As long as old Seamus has his health then Degsey will run free t'chase the wind.'

'And the pups?'

'Ay, them too.'

Jonathan had put on a manly front. He topped up his mug from the teapot and coughed a couple of times to clear the thickness in his throat before saying, 'Please go on. Don't leave the story about the tooth half told.'

Seamus carefully filled his pipe with herbal tobacco from an old leather pouch and tilted his head to Spring. She met his gaze with slightly bloodshot eyes which begged him to continue. His brow creased as he exchanged a quick glance with Sky who nodded.

He struggled on, a little painfully. 'I buried Deggoran Odyssey under some wild daffodils, where the sun peeps over the Galtee mountains . . . but 'twas strange. As I lifted her from the carpet of four-leaf clovers they be pale . . . not dark green . . . and the paleness exactly matched where she lay. 'Twas like a pattern of her body. Says I to meself, she must've drawed all the power from the clovers whilst giving birth to wee Degsey. All the god-given Irish luck had been passed to me new wee babbie girl.'

Everyone looked at everyone else. Spring was wide-eyed, staring at Degsey, Sophie's jaw hung slightly open as she gazed at Shack, Daniel blinked in astonishment at Seamus, and Sky's mouth had gone dry as she fixed Daniel with a puzzled look.

Daniel said, 'So is that why you think Degsey has special powers?'

'Be sure, it's one reason . . .'

'And the other?' Daniel pressed.

Seamus put a match to his pipe and puffed out a cloud of fragrant smoke. Slowly, his hand moved down Degsey's neck to her muzzle. He lifted the pouch of pink flesh to expose her sharp, bottom left canine tooth. All, apart from Daniel and Sophie had seen it before, but now in the shadows thrown up by the firelight, the soft glint of gold made everyone stare.

Seamus said, 'A cluricaun knocked out me wee girl's tooth when me wagon pulled in near Donegal on the banks of Lough Swilly. 'Twas a spiteful, evil little devil . . . screechin' curses. 'Twas jealous of Degsey's good fortune.'

'Who or what is a cluricaun?' Sky asked, intrigued.

'A banished relative of the leprechauns,' he told her, his voice very soft. 'A lazy cousin or twin. Oh ay, I see him clear as I'm seeing you. A slouchin', jeerin' little person in a green jacket and red cap. He saw Degsey be sleepin' so he swung his wee hammer. Crack it went on her tooth . . . breakin' it clean. Planned so it was, 'cause it not be her milk tooth. The devilish cluricaun had waited five month 'til her permanent teeth be fully growed.'

Spring shifted her position, snuggling closer to Degsey so that she was cushioned against the softness of the greyhound's warm body.

'Why would the little man want the tooth?' she asked, gazing up at Seamus.

'To steal some of the luck. To make a charm to hang in his den, maybe . . . It's a fact they be corrupt and sinful little people.'

'So you had an implant tooth made of gold?' Sky asked the question, giving a drooling Scooter the last piece of her pasty.

'Ach no!' Seamus stroked the edge of his jaw and permitted himself a smile as he sucked on his pipe. 'Not that I know what an implant be . . . but the tooth be Fin's doin'.'

'Fin?'

'Fin the leprechaun. He be an elder, and seen the cluricaun's antics so he had. He'd been watchin' over little Degsey since we left Knockgrafton, guessin' that the cluricaun be up t'mischief. He knew about the luck from the clovers and he knew Degsey be special.'

'We've read about leprechauns at school.' Jonathan pressed his lips together thoughtfully. 'They're not real. They're sprites or elves or something. They look a bit like those plastic gnomes you buy for the garden.'

Shack grinned and even Daniel had difficulty hiding a smile. Sky glanced from Scooter to Seamus, lifting a doubting eyebrow.

'So y'not be believin' in leprechauns at all?' Seamus looked at Jonathan, tapping the bridge of his nose with his pipe stem. 'You be tinkin' old Seamus be imaginin' Fin's visits?'

'Well I . . .' Jonathan hesitated, then smiled warily. 'No, I'm not sure . . . I suppose if you say you saw him, then you must have.'

'What was Fin wearing?' Spring broke in, her eyes huge and bright.

'Well, let me tink . . .' Seamus puffed on his pipe as he collected his memories. 'He be all in red . . . Ay, leprechauns always wear red, 'cause that be the colour of wizardry. His coat had seven rows of buttons, with seven buttons in each row, and his hat be three-cornered and sewed with gold lace. Leprechauns be shoemakers so Fin's shoes were grand . . . soft scarlet leather sewn together with huge silver buckles. Twas the splendidest wee fellow you could wish to see.'

'How tall was he?' Sky asked with a polite smile.

'He be about a span and a quarter tall.'

'Span?' Sophie looked inquiringly at Shack, who shrugged.

Seamus spread the fingers of his hand. He explained that a span was the distance between the tip of his thumb and little finger.

'So Fin was a very little man,' Spring said.

'Leprechauns be the littlest people who have fallen from heaven and landed on earth.'

'Have you seen them making shoes?'

'Not seen, little Spring, but often heard 'em. When me and Mister Rafferty be pulled up for the night, I be laid in bed many a time listenin' to leprechauns playing music on pipes, flutes or fiddles . . . and hearin' the tap, tap, tap of the wee hammer as they be busily makin' shoes.'

A grin disturbed Sky's features. She turned to Daniel, asking softly, 'Are we supposed to be taking this seriously?'

Daniel glanced from Spring to Jonathan, then from Shack to Sophie. Nobody appeared to be taking it as a joke, or the lunatic words of an old man . . . and certainly no-one looked bored.

'I think we should just enjoy the story,' Daniel said, pulling his legs tight to his chest and linking fingers around knees. 'Everyone else seems to be.'

'But it is *only* a story?'

'Is it?' Daniel threw the question back her.

'Oh, I don't know what to think.' Sky shifted uneasily, shrugging her narrow shoulders.

'Fin spoke to me,' Seamus continued. 'The wee man promised t'make the tooth as good as new by usin' leprechaun gold.'

'It is very shiny,' Spring remarked.

'Leprechaun gold be the most enchantedest and powerfullest gold in the world. It be mined a tiny speck at a time and the tooth be built up wi' wee pieces, day after day, week after week.'

'Mega! It must have taken ages,' Jonathan beamed.

'Oh ay, two month of work. Fin added the golden specks each evenin' while Degsey be asleep. He would come to me wagon wearin' his little leather apron and carryin' the littlest of hammers and a file. He'd work until the early hours, bangin', filin', and shapin' so he would.'

'Where did the gold come from?' Sophie asked, intrigued.

'Secret wee mines, missie . . . well hidden from us folk. It's not meant for us to be findin' 'em. Fin and his family would work all day collectin' the gold. To be sure they are very hard working little people.'

'And when the tooth was complete,' Spring added glowingly, 'Degsey became a greyhound with mystical powers.'

'Ay, she got her luck from the clovers and her special strengths from the leprechaun gold.'

Seamus banged the remains out from his pipe by tapping it against the footboard. Grey layers of fragrant, herbal smoke hung in the firelight.

Sophie, was unsure whether Seamus was about to continue. Shyly, she found herself asking, 'How exactly do Degsey's powers work?'

Both Spring and Jonathan seemed to grow a few extra centimetres as they held their breaths, gazing up at the old man's weather-beaten face, waiting for him to answer.

'It's an energy or force . . . but I not be rightly knowin' how it works,' Seamus admitted mildly. 'I do know that Degsey uses her powers to take care of her old master, and it's got me out of a scrape many a time. It's a strange ting . . . but it happens sure enough it does. Ay, there have been some odd happenings . . . and most times she has to be smilin' so the sunshine or a bright light can glint off her tooth.'

'But dogs don't smile,' Jonathan put in.

Seamus's pouched eyes looked at him with amusement from under the shaggy eyebrows. 'To be sure they do, young 'un. Have you never seen wee Scooter smile?'

'I've seen him pant when he's hot, or curl up his lip in a growl.'

'And when he pants can you see his tongue?'

'Yes.'

'His bottom teeth?'

'Of course.'

'Then 'tis most likely you be confusin' some of his pants with some of his smiles.'

'Hmph.' He frowned and thought it over. 'I—I suppose he might have smiled . . . sometimes.'

'O'course he has. Does me darlin' Degsey not be givin' old Seamus lots of smiles?'

'So when she was injured,' Spring gulped as a thought flashed in her mind, 'she used her special powers to bring you to Oyster Gables. I remember that her tooth was glinting under the surgery lights . . . Sky was stitching her shoulder and she complained that it was making her blink. That must have been the energy working.'

Sky exchanged a knowing glance with Shack. Both remembered the incident well.

Spring raised herself on an elbow and gave the greyhound an affectionate hug. The dog turned to gaze at her, her lower jaw dropping and quivering with excited curiosity as the scent of a rabbit wafted in on the night air. 'She's doing it now,' Spring announced glowingly. 'Look everyone, she's smiling!'

Sky's mobile phone was resting on the rug next to Scooter. Its musical ring-tone filled the air.

'Oyster Gables Animal Shelter,' Sky said putting the phone to her ear, listening, then adding, 'Yes, alright. We can be there in ten minutes.'

'Problems?' Daniel asked.

'That was Roy, a petrol attendant from the garage we use at Muddlebridge.' She stood up and stretched. 'A fox has been hit by a vehicle and taken refuge in a gap alongside the forecourt.'

'So we're needed?'

'Absolutely.' Sky turned to Seamus and made apologies for leaving early, and then she asked Sophie to take care of Spring, Jonathan and Scooter until she returned. 'Shouldn't be much more than half-an-hour,' she added.

Shack was already on his feet. 'Do you need my help?' he asked cheerfully.

'Daniel and I can cope . . . besides you're not supposed to be working this time of night. You'll get me in trouble with the Job Centre people.'

He ran ahead, pulling keys from his pocket as he reached the shelter's padlocked front entrance gates that led to the yard. 'As it's a fox then you'll need a holding cage, the Grasper and the protection of some trapper's mitts,' he called back. 'I'll get them.'

As used by dog-catchers, but equally effective for wild animals, the Grasper was a simple device consisting of a flexible loop which poked out from the end of a hollow pole. Slid around the neck of a possible biter it enabled the user to bring the animal under control from a safe distance and therefore reduced the risk of injury.

Sky and Daniel ran past the Escort van to the side door of the house. They kicked off their shoes and quickly changed into rubber boots. Sky collected her first-aid case from the hall table and within seconds they were both back outside.

Shack had loaded the holding cage and the Grasper and was closing the van's rear doors. 'You're ready to go,' he said, giving a couple of taps on the roof as he handed two pairs of protective trapper's mitts to Daniel.

Sky was already at the wheel as Daniel slipped into the passenger seat. She signalled her thanks to Shack as the van's engine coughed noisily into life.

Seamus, Sophie, Jonathan and Spring all waved as the Escort's headlights flashed past the caravan. Daniel turned to see Little Degsey put in her first visit of the evening. The pup was caught in the light from the porch carriage lamps as she squeezed between Seamus and Spring, stretching out her long forelegs and dipping her back as she yawned before edging down cosily beside her mother. Daniel had to admit that seeing the pair side-by-side, in the half light, that the likeness was remarkable. Both sets of brindle splashes on white were identical—three irregular patches at exactly the same point on each body, with the brindle and white mix on the head and tail. Give Little Degsey another nine months, Daniel thought, and the pair would be impossible to separate.

The van had left Swiftly village and was now heading north-east to Muddlebridge. Sky's slim fingers made swift turns of the wheel as, barely within the speed-limit, she covered the three-mile journey with ease. She swung right into the garage forecourt, and halted the van by an attendant who was leaning against one of the petrol pumps. He was early twenties, swarthy and thick-set. He looked fit and hard.

'Hello, Roy.' Sky removed a flashlight from the glove box and was out of the door before Daniel had even released his seat-belt. 'Is the fox badly injured?'

'Reckon it's busted a rear leg,' Roy said, turning to indicate a gap between the workshop and toilets where the creature had hidden. 'It seemed to be dragging it after it got hit. Whacked by a council truck, I think.'

Sky nodded, looking towards the hiding place. 'Is there an exit the other end?'

'No, it's blocked off. It can't get out at the rear.'

'Did you notice which direction it came from . . . before it got hit?'

'Horseshoe Coppice, I think.'

Daniel lifted the holding cage and Grasper from the back of the van and pulled on the thick gloves, known as trapper's mitts. Sky did likewise as a couple of cars pulled in for petrol.

'Must get on, Ms Patakin,' Roy said keenly, lifting a hand to a waiting motorist. 'I'll leave you both to it.'

Sky switched on the flashlight and followed Daniel to the space between the two buildings. The gap was about a metre wide; certainly room enough for a person to move quickly if the need arose.

'You or me?' Sky asked.

'You or me what?'

'To use the Grasper.' Sky's face couldn't conceal a hint of impatience. 'Have you handled one before?'

The early easy manner around the campfire had gone and her voice had switched back to its superior tone. Daniel had hoped that the general cosiness of the evening would have helped ease her snippy manner, but she stood before him with an uppity look, lips pressed firmly together.

Daniel showed her what he hoped was a cheerful smile and confirmed that he had used a Grasper, many times. He added with deliberate cheekiness that he'd noosed the young of most safari park big cats with a similar, though more sturdy type of instrument.

'Then you shouldn't have a problem,' Sky said briskly. She let her flashlight beam into the gap, lighting up dead leaves, an old tyre and various pieces of litter.

'I see the fox.' Daniel edged forward, holding the Grasper with two hands, the noose dangling at the ready.

'Vixen,' Sky corrected, unable to resist a smile which Daniel couldn't see. 'I can see swollen teats on her belly. She must have cubs somewhere.'

'Alright; *vixen* then.' Daniel briefly raised his eyes, and then concentrated on the job in hand.

There was a flurry of movement as the vixen spun crazily round in circles when she realised that there was no rear escape. She eventually settled, crouching to face Daniel, a small growl forming in her throat as she showed him her tiny, but very white needle-sharp teeth.

Daniel gently teased the noose around the animal's neck.

She was stock still. Unmoving.

In one quick wrist movement, he gave a sharp tug on the loop below the Grasper's handle and the noose closed. The vixen was trapped. A high-pitched squealing made Daniel shudder as the vixen twisted, turned, fought and scratched at the pole with her paws. He breathed out gratefully, backing out of the gap, keeping the pole fully extended as he dragged (rather than cause further damage by lifting) the vixen's supple body towards Sky.

'Well done.' She nodded agreeably and bent to apply a mittened hand to the animal's scruff of neck.

Daniel was pleased with the ease of the capture and although his nerves screamed he looked cool and professional as he opened the sprung door of the holding cage.

'Okay to release the Grasper?' he asked.

Sky nodded.

There was plenty of squealing, but the vixen stilled as Sky took a tighter grip. The noose was now loosened and Sky ran an experienced eye over the long, dangling body looking for signs of head and jaw damage and any other injuries. As Daniel removed his mitts she held the vixen at arms length, mouth towards her, and asked him to do a quick, on-the-spot examination.

'Now?' A frown appeared just above the bridge of his nose. He knew she was testing him.

'Have you a problem with that?' Sky spoke patiently, as to a tiresome child. 'If you think there's a broken bone then I have a temporary splint in my case.'

Daniel ran quick, experienced fingers over the vixen's body, pinching the toes for a reflex action, and carefully folding each joint to check for movement.

'I can't tell positively without an X-ray,' he informed her, 'but I don't think there's a break anywhere.'

Sky was quietly impressed, but her voice was still a little stiff as she asked, 'Any further thoughts?'

At this point the vixen decided to pee over Daniel's shirt. It was warm and slightly sticky but he deliberately didn't make a fuss, knowing this was the natural reaction of a frightened animal.

Daniel fought down a smile as he glanced at Sky. Her eyes were large and held a look of faint amusement. He cleared his throat, considered, then said, 'In my opinion she has muscle or nerve damage in her right rear leg. There's no external bleeding and she seems reasonably healthy.' He looked closely at some bald patches of fur. 'There's a touch of ringworm, but that can be easily sorted out.'

'Good.' Sky sounded somewhat irritated at Daniel's thorough review. She placed the vixen without difficulty in the holding cage and shut the sprung door. 'I suggest we keep her at Oyster Gables overnight, and if she's mobile and fit in the morning then we release her back into Horseshoe Coppice. If we hang onto her for too long then her cubs will be at risk.'

Daniel nodded agreement and bent to collect the Grasper. He ignored the strong smell of pee caused by the wetness on his shirt which was now clinging uncomfortably, to his body.

'Are you alright?' Sky asked.

'I expect I'll pong a bit in the Escort.'

'You can clean up back at the shelter.'

'I'm actually quite pleased. I feel as if I've been through some sort of Oyster Gables welcoming ceremony.'

'It could have been avoided.'

'Avoided?'

'Mm, we needn't have used the Grasper at all.'

Daniel looked at her blankly. His forehead creased as he raked his dark hair back with a hand. 'No Grasper. I don't follow?'

A grin tensed at the corners of Sky's mouth as they walked to the van. 'All you had to do was borrow Degsey from Seamus Horrigan,' she said, unable to resist a final poke of fun at the old man's story. 'I'm sure she would have given you one of her golden smiles and charmed the vixen into the cage.'

There was no answer to that, and Daniel didn't even try to invent one.

CHAPTER FIVE

M artin Griggs was 24 hours overdue, and Tony Ryker was not best pleased.

Ryker was a creature of habit. A man who liked routine. A man who always worked to a well-tried system, where delays didn't happen and excuses wouldn't be accepted. The trip to sell ten horses at the Southall horse auction had been planned to take three days—it always took Griggs three days—one day to cover the journey to Greater London, one day to attend the auction, and one day to return to Hele. But this time it had taken four. Griggs had phoned to explain the situation, but excuses would not pacify Ryker. As far as he was concerned time was money. Griggs should have been back, and what was left of the week used for stealing new stock.

He paced, snatching a look at his watch every now and then. Two p.m. and no sign. He ambled past his gleaming red BMW car, polishing a mud mark from its wing with his tattooed forearm. As he walked he cast a critical eye over the six old horses that would journey from Harwich to a continental slaughter house. He chewed on a matchstick as one by one the animals crossed to a rusted gate to greet him.

If they were hoping for a sugar lump or a mint sweet or even a kind word—then they were to be sadly disappointed. To Ryker they were just cash on legs, perishable livestock which were costing him money the longer they stayed.

At least, during the time Griggs had been away, Ryker had tossed down some hay and given them a small daily portion of oats.

Not that Ryker was playing stableman out of the kindness of his heart—far from it. He didn't expect prime meat, but it made good business sense for the horses to look reasonably fit by keeping on a bit of bodyweight. Dull coats, tangled manes, body sores, and ribs which showed through flesh would not be welcomed by Ryker's foreign buyers.

One horse looked okay, he told himself—the chestnut cob from the caravan. He watched it prance arrogantly past him, tossing its neck, bright-eyed and still full of spirit. He actually allowed himself the hint of a smile as he watched the old cob's antics. There was a few years work left in the horse and the thought crossed his mind that he could possibly sell it on for a bit extra . . . but he brushed away the idea as being more trouble than it was worth. Mister Rafferty would join Saturday's slaughter house shipment, and that was an end to it.

With Griggs away, Ryker had been occupied in his usual illegal activity of searching the Devon countryside for yet more horses to fill the now empty Hele warehouse. He'd spotted three at an Okehampton smallholding and two at a Tiverton riding school. These, coupled with the three short-stay livery horses being kept at Penhill, and Sir Galahad and Excalibur at Oyster Gables, rounded up nicely to his magic figure of ten. The sooner

Griggs returned, he thought, the sooner they could continue their rustling activity.

An ever-deepening throb of a noisy engine announced the arrival of the travelling horse-box. Ryker strode from the paddock to meet it. He watched it exit a fork in the track by the warehouse and rattle over a couple of acres of lumpy ground. He avoided the clouds of dust as Griggs stamped on the brakes, narrowly missing the BMW. Griggs reversed the vehicle into a shabby iron structure concealing it from prying eyes, and jumped from the cab.

'About flamin' time.' Ryker gave him a level, unsmiling look. 'I thought you'd decided to take a London vacation.'

'Don't start moaning, Tony.' Griggs's brown eyes flared. 'I've had a lousy time of it . . . delays all round. The Southall guest house kicked me out 'cause you only booked two days. I had a terrible nosebleed and spent last night sleeping in the cab.'

'Good. I'm all for saving money. You're pampered too much as it is.'

Griggs reached inside his leather jacket and pulled out a zipped-up money pouch. He slapped it into Ryker's outstretched open hand. 'Nine thousand, seven hundred pounds,' he said, lifting and sniffing at his underarm. 'I'm smelly and I need a shower. Shall I wait while you count the money,' he added moodily, 'or have I your permission to use the bathroom?'

'I'd reckoned on £10,000.' Ryker strode ahead of him, making a line for the mobile home. 'How come the money's short?'

'I told you on the phone that the market was heaving with horses. I think I did well, considering.'

'So give me the auction figures?'

'Seven went for nine-hundred each, two fetched a thousand each, and the piebald made fourteen-hundred.'

Ryker swung on him as he reached the home's glass-panelled kitchen door. His eyes were probing. 'Haven't stuffed a few hundred pounds in your back pocket, have you?'

'There's an official receipt in the pouch.' Griggs rubbed a grimy palm over his face and met his gaze angrily. 'I don't know why I bother. I work my fingers to the bone, go without sleep, drive the two-hundred miles back without even stopping for the loo, then get accused of stealing.'

'You were a thief when I first met you, Griggsy, and you'll always be a thief. Leopards don't change their spots.'

Griggs pushed past Ryker and headed moodily for the bathroom, grabbing a can of beer from the fridge. 'Pity we're not dealing in leopards,' he grunted. 'I would have got a heck of a lot more cash for 'em.'

He stamped off along the corridor, irritation in every line of his body. Ryker suppressed a chuckle as the bathroom door slammed . . . hard.

'And don't forget to flush the loo,' he called out, unable to resist another stab of ridicule. 'You keep blocking up the U-bend with toilet paper!'

Ryker sat at the kitchen table, his stubby fingers drawing back the zip on the money pouch. There were nine banded packs of a £1,000 each, plus £700 in loose notes.

Griggs received 20% of the auction money, less expenses. Ryker left one pack of a £1,000 on the table plus the odd £700. He struggled to hold back a smirk as he replaced the bulk of the money in the pouch.

'Your wages are on the table,' he called out, looking towards the bathroom door. 'Your share comes to one thousand nine-hundred and forty-pounds, but I've deducted expenses plus the cost of the hot dog I bought you at Swiftly.'

'You're *soooo* flamin' good to me.' Griggs's thick, muffled voice was barely audible above the flush of the toilet. 'Pretty soon my expenses are going to be more than my earnings!'

'You've been skimping on food for the old nags,' Ryker retorted loudly. 'I allow you two pounds a day for each horse, but I'm not blind. It's obvious you haven't been giving them any extra feed. I reckon you've been spending the money on beer. Some of the horses are downright skinny. I've seen more fat on a butcher's pencil!'

Minutes ran by. Griggs was taking a shower as Ryker crossed to a wall safe in the lounge. He clicked it open and placed the pouch inside.

Griggs enjoyed the occasional put-down, he convinced himself, closing the door and spinning the combination. That's what made their partnership work. The mocking kept Griggs in line, kept him from straying, and stopped him getting fancy ideas. Sneering comments came naturally to Ryker. He'd been a bully at school and never lost the habit.

He thought of that, and he liked the nasty memories.

'What you cooking for lunch?' Ryker collided with Griggs as he re-entered the kitchen. He was jamming the money into the back pockets of his black jeans with one hand and pulling a clean T-shirt awkwardly over his head with the other.

'I thought *you* might offer to do the cooking for a change.' Griggs gave him a moody look and added stiffly, 'I've just spent five hours on the road and I'm dead beat.'

'Now don't start doing your whining old woman act on me. Have I not just paid your wages? Am I not just about to start plotting our route for tonight's haul?'

Ryker pulled a map from a kitchen drawer and made a big, over the top effort of unfolding it. He then reached up to a cupboard for a pen and paper before sitting at the table and jotting down some road directions.

'I've been busy, my little ferret . . . no let up at all. I've found two horses which are kept in a paddock at Tiverton, and three which are boxed at Okehampton.'

'Tiverton's a fair journey,' Griggs said.

'I'll be driving,' Ryker murmured soothingly, laying on some fake charm, 'but the actual stealing should be like taking candy from a baby for someone with your experience.'

'Oh, yeah . . . right.' Griggs liked the sudden compliments. He snatched a glance over Ryker's shoulder as he began jotting down places and journey times.

'Five tonight,' Ryker said, twisting his diamond-studded ring. 'And five tomorrow night. How does that suit?'

'Alright.' Griggs heaved a sigh. 'So can't we do the short run tonight? The three at Penhill and the two at that Oyster place?'

'Of course, Griggsy. However you want to play it.' He displayed a smile that curled up like a frosted leaf. It wasn't very convincing but it had the right effect on his partner.

Griggs was once again fooled by Ryker's manner. 'Chicken and chips for lunch?' he asked.

* * *

Sky, Shack and Daniel were busily engaged on a rescue mission.

A dog walker had alerted Oyster Gables that a deer had been caught in a snare at Knightacott Woods, so the hunt was on to find it, free it, and check out any injuries.

It was a short journey, less than five miles from Swiftly, and Sky had taken the van as far as she dare along a narrow track leading past an old paper mill with its now tumble-down water-wheel. The track ended abruptly at a series of marshy pools with spear-grass growing around the edges.

The sun was gaining in strength and the sky a wash of flat blue as all three climbed out of the vehicle and collected their pieces of equipment from the rear of the van. Sky clutched her first-aid case, Shack jammed a rolled canvas stretcher under his arm and an empty bran sack into his belt, and Daniel carefully slipped a rifle out of its soft leather case.

Daniel had loaded the rifle with a tranquilliser dart, known more simply as a knock-out dart. He'd checked that the safety-catch was on, and slung the rifle over his shoulder. He'd received training and been granted a firearms certificate whilst working at the safari park, so he was no stranger to handling weapons. He'd earned the reputation of being a crack shot and the last animal he'd knocked out with a dart had been a leopard which had contracted feline flu.

Since the setting up of Oyster Gables the rifle had only been used twice. Peggy, the previous assistant manager, was the only one licensed for the weapon, and on each occasion it had been fired at deer who were injured and who would have been impossible to catch without firing a dart.

Today was slightly different. If the deer had been snared then it wouldn't be in a position to run anywhere, and Sky hoped to be able to knock-out the animal without the use of the weapon.

'We've brought the rifle along as a safeguard.' Sky was showing her efficient side, which was becoming her usual habit whenever she was in Daniel's company. 'If we're smart we won't need it.'

Daniel nodded, perfectly aware of the situation.

A pair of jays screeched their displeasure at human company as the three followed a winding path through the heather and bracken. They passed an earthen bank riddled with rabbit holes and followed a stream that led to a small waterfall. Ahead of them, in the soft dewy brightness, lay a clump of pewter-coloured willow trees. They had been uprooted by a long-ago storm, and their lifeless branches now criss-crossed the stream.

'I see it.' Shack raised a halting hand. 'It's a male—I can see its antlers. It's lying by the broken willows.'

Sky and Daniel both looked, their eyes spotting the buff brown head and dappled neck of a large fallow buck hanging over the bank, moving restlessly to keep its face clear of the stream.

'The trappers must know deer drink here,' Daniel remarked, 'so it makes them an easy target.'

'It's lying down through tiredness,' Sky said, gesturing everyone forward. 'I can't see the snare but be careful of the hind legs. If they lash about then you'll get badly kicked.'

'Can you quieten it without a knock-out dart?' Shack asked softly.

'I intend to try.' Sky removed a syringe from her first aid case and withdrew a measured amount of fluid from a small bottle. 'Right, I'm relying on you two to hold it as still as possible. Its antlers might be flat rather than branched, but they're powerful. Be very careful.'

Daniel placed his rifle against a tree stump and looked at Shack who nodded his readiness.

The deer was now fully aware of their presence and was flicking its brown ears from side to side as it made an awkward attempt to climb to its feet. The snare was now visible, glinting nastily from a bloodied hind leg. The sight wasn't pretty, but at least it was keeping the very tired animal's movements in check as it tried desperately to stand up.

Shack thrashed forward and was on the buck in seconds. He'd approached it via the stream, slopping through knee-high water to reach it. Daniel followed, and as Shack got to grips with the antlers, pinning them to the bank, Daniel let most of his upper bodyweight slide across the buck's spotted shoulders, clamping his hands around the front hooves.

The team effort worked well. Apart from one hind leg the buck was pinned. Shack's teeth were gritted, and his breath was coming in hot little pants as he held onto the antlers, pressing them into the turf. The muscles in his forearms bulged and his hands were shaking with effort from the strength in the deer's neck, but his expression was one of fearlessness.

Sky skidded to the ground on her knees beside the fallow buck, leaning safely against Daniel's extended arms as she judged the distance in order to avoid being hit by the kicking hind hoof. She found the large muscle mass on the animal's white-spotted rump and punctured the skin with the needle. She pushed on the plunger, watching the plastic syringe empty as the fluid entered the deer.

She was sweating slightly and this strengthened the effect of her perfume as she briefly glanced in Daniel's direction. He'd caught the fragrance and was holding her hot, good looks unblinkingly. Sky was also drawn to his gaze. She found the darkness behind Daniel's eyes to be romantic and tender. She felt a blush rising to the surface so she forced herself to break his gaze, clearing her mind, concentrating her thoughts on the fallow deer and the job in hand.

The buck's beautiful but frightened eyes showed huge circles of white, staring up at her as she removed the needle. Slowly they began to flicker, wanting to close.

'Good boy,' she comforted, letting out a relieved breath. 'You're going to be fine.'

The buck's strength was weakening and the pulling power began to ease on Shack's arms. He released one hand, grinning at the milky blueness of his palm and the tiny marks left by the antlers. He shook life back into his fingers, showing Sky a fake pained expression.

Daniel could also feel the animal's muscles relaxing under the weight of his body. He watched the kicking motion in the hind leg gradually slacken to a gentle movement as the drug found its way round the buck's body.

'He's sedated,' Sky announced, relaxing slightly. She turned to Shack. 'He must weigh around a hundred kilos. Can you cover his head?'

Shack pulled the bran sack from his belt. He lifted the head of the now calm fallow buck with one hand, and slid the sacking over the antlers.

Sky unclipped a pair of strong fencing cutters from inside the lid of her first-aid case. She ran a gentle hand down the deer's trapped hind leg and examined the harsh metal loop which had cut the flesh to the bone. 'It's a locking snare,' Sky's face was taut with concentration. 'Once I've snipped it off I'll cut it into pieces and leave them on the bank. At least that way the trappers will know we're aware of their illegal actions.'

'Blood-thirsty jerks!' Shack's breath hissed as he flexed his jaw. He began to empty the water from his rubber boots.

Daniel watched as the cutters bit into the loop and the snare lashed away. That was the third trapped animal this week, he thought, as Sky snipped the wire into harmless little bits. A rabbit, a fox, and a now a deer. The rabbit and fox had both been caught with legal free-running snares, but the locking snare was illegal and had to be reported to the police.

'I'll treat the wounds back at Oyster Gables.' Sky unrolled the stretcher and laid it flat on the bank alongside the buck 'Okay, let's get the patient on board.'

Everyone pulled, heaved and lifted. There were a lot of sweaty foreheads and a fair bit of cursing, but eventually the fallow buck was eased onto the canvas. Daniel gripped the two metal poles by the animal's sack-covered head, while Shack gripped the two at the rump. The hooves dangled over the stretcher as they lifted; but apart from the odd twitch, movement from the animal had ceased.

'Let's go.' Sky closed her first-aid case and retrieved the rifle from the tree stump. She gave a slight, breathy laugh as she added, 'It's only a few hundred metres back to the Escort.'

Shack and Daniel took the strain as Sky led the way, retracing her footsteps. There were a couple of pauses for extra air to be sucked into lungs, then weak with relief they arrived at the van. Sky opened the rear doors and the stretcher was pushed carefully inside.

Shack jumped into the back, sitting on the floor as he supported the buck's head. He looked a scruffy mess. His jeans were soaked up to his thighs and his face and arms were splattered with mud.

He wiped his forehead with the back of his hand as sweat stung his eyes.

Sky and Daniel looked the worse for wear too. Both knees of Sky's jeans were grass-stained; one was torn, and she was picking little pieces of moss and forest scraps from her hair.

Daniel's jeans were soaked up to the back pockets, his sweatshirt was streaked with leaf-mould and he had picked up a grazed elbow. All three were in need of an urgent shower, plus a hot cup of tea or coffee.

'Well done everyone.' Sky started the van, and reversed back down the narrow track. 'The buck will have to be kept calm and housed in a separate pen. I'll immediately put him on a drip and treat the bruises we can see, but some will take a few days before they fully show up.'

'How long will we keep him at the shelter?' Shack asked.

'Minimum of a week...' Sky paused, and a trace of amusement looked out from her eyes. 'You won't be getting much sleep tonight, Daniel.'

'Post-capture myopathy,' he murmured, surprising her slightly.

'Post . . . what?' Shack wiped a limp strand of hair from his forehead.

'You've dealt with deer before?' Sky shot Daniel a glance.

'We had a kiddies corner at the safari park . . . various tame animals which children could get close to . . . so I do know that an injured deer is the world's worst creature for dying on you.' He looked at Shack. 'In the early stages the slightest stress will kill them.'

'So you'll see the buck through the night?' Sky squared her shoulders, turning the van towards Swiftly.

'Definitely the assistant manager's job,' Daniel agreed. 'I wouldn't expect the boss-lady to lose her beauty sleep.'

Sky said nothing, just gave a small cough and concentrated on the road ahead. Shack grinned cheekily.

'Not that she needs her beauty sleep.' Daniel risked the stroke of a forefinger down the back of Sky's hand. He expected her to shift her position on the wheel, or at the very least to fix him with a cold stare.

She didn't do either. 'Check on the buck about two a.m., and then again about five,' she said smiling cheerfully.

'I can do that job,' Shack put in quickly. 'I was going to ask if I could spend the night at Oyster Gables. My mum and stepfather have driven down to Lynmouth for a short break. They're bound to pop over to Yelland to see me.'

'Perhaps you should make the effort to see them,' Sky said.

'I will . . . sometime. At the moment I'm alright with dad . . . It's cool.'

'Okay.'

'Okay, you'll let me stay and look after the buck?'

'No.' Her voice took on a teasing note. 'If you stay then you go to bed. Daniel's the one who will be losing sleep.'

Daniel found himself smiling. He really didn't mind. A fallow deer for company during the night? No problem. Suddenly everything was okay between him and Sky . . . and for the moment that was all that mattered.

*　　*　　*

'Stop worrying,' Tony Ryker told Griggs, chewing on a matchstick. 'I have it on good authority that this place is run by a bunch of nerdy kids.'

It was 1:50 a.m. and they were both sitting in the cab of the travelling horsebox. Ryker had reversed the vehicle clear of the road and parked just short of the two huge conifer trees which stood either side of the driveway to Oyster Gables.

'I just feel uneasy, that's all,' Griggs said, dipping into a large holdall and handing Ryker a ski-mask. 'I can't help it if I get these strange feelings.'

'We've got three horses in the back from Penhill,' Ryker reminded him in a light, casual tone. 'Did they cause us a problem? No. So now we're collecting two more. Trust Tony, it'll be easy.'

Griggs pulled on his black ski-mask and gloves then rummaged around in the holdall checking the contents. Flashlight, bolt-cutters, head-collar with halter and two sets of four bootees. They were stretch nylon, with soft leather soles, which fitted snugly around the hooves of a horse to the fetlocks. When attached they completely dampened the clacking sound of horseshoes, and with the house being so close to the shelter's front entrance gates Ryker had decided to use them.

'Such easy, easy, money,' Ryker grunted positively to himself, pulling on a pair of gloves and the black ski-mask. He slid from the cab and made his way round to the ramp.

He watched Griggs scoot off into the darkness carrying the holdall, then paused briefly looking up at the house windows for any light, listening for any noise.

Nothing. All asleep.

He leaned back against the ramp, waiting for the signal from Griggs's flashlight. It should only be a matter of seconds, he told himself. It was commonsense that a wild animal shelter wouldn't bother with heavy-duty padlocks.

Time passed.

He looked at the luminous hands of his wristwatch and began to fidget. There was a hint of unease in his eyes as he realised that something must be wrong. No sign of a signal. Griggs was taking too long . . . far too long.

He cursed and decided to investigate. He hadn't taken more than a couple of steps before he saw the wavering shape of Griggs's gangly, light-framed body running towards him.

'Tony . . . Tony . . ' Griggs panted as he swayed to a halt, almost bumping into Ryker. 'I've just seen . . . hellfire . . . It's here . . . the thing's here . . '

'Speak properly!' Ryker grabbed his shoulders with a touch of impatience. 'What have you seen? Make sense!'

'The wooden caravan.' Griggs worked hard at letting his voice out evenly. 'It's parked up by the gates. Y—You can't see it from here 'cause it's lying back on the forecourt.'

Ryker looked at Griggs, his top lip drawn up nervously.

'The red caravan,' Griggs said again. 'The one you've been trying to track down.'

'Did you see the dog?'

'No . . . and I don't want to.'

Griggs went to walk back to the cab, but Ryker's thick fingers grabbed his arm. 'Where the hell are you going?'

'Home. I'm getting stressed-out and I can feel a nosebleed coming on. I'm not stealing horses from here.'

'Forget the horses. I want that greyhound.'

'Then you find it . . . but don't count on me.' Griggs paused to suck in a deep breath. 'We haven't got the gear for dog-napping. Let's get out while we can.'

'Not before I've got the full picture,' he muttered, his jaw muscles fluttering. 'So maybe we can't get it tonight, but I need to take a close look. Are you wearing a belt?'

'Do what?'

Ryker repeated the question, adding, 'I'm wearing braces. Take it off.'

Griggs grumbled under his breath, surly and unwilling as he fumbled to free the belt from the waist of his black jeans.

Ryker coiled it through the buckle and slipped his free hand through the loop. 'Collar and lead in one,' he said, demonstrating—jerking the end hard, so it snapped tight across his forearm.

'You're barking mad.' Griggs's voice cracked. 'You'll never outsmart that greyhound . . . *never!*'

'Just being prepared, my little ferret. The dog might fancy an early morning stroll. So who better than you and me to take it for one?'

Ryker nudged Griggs towards the house. The big man moved forward with deliberate dead-silent slowness. Griggs followed, still muttering curses, one hand gripping the waistband of his jeans to stop them from slipping. Ryker was ignoring Griggs's complaints. An opportunity had presented itself—and now, more than anything, he was hooked on the idea of stealing Degsey.

Daniel didn't see the shadowy outlines as they carefully passed the kitchen window. He hadn't bothered to switch on the light, preferring to make coffee by the cosy glow from the old coal cooking range. He yawned and knuckled tiredness from his eyes, stirring hot water into a mug.

Scooter had left the confines of his basket and was generally being a nuisance. He had heard movement outside and was padding up and down the hall to the side door—an action he repeated several times.

'Scooter, behave!' Daniel added milk and sugar to his coffee. 'I'll let you out in a minute . . . when I check on the deer.'

The dog suddenly stopped pacing, his eyes looking upwards and beyond Daniel. The coffee mug hovered half way to Daniel's mouth as a flicker of movement caught his eye.

He turned to face Shack Skinner as he stumbled into the kitchen. His face was still misty with sleep and his long curly hair looked a mess. He was pulling a Scottish rugby shirt over his head with one hand and hooking moccasins over the back of bare heels with the other. Daniel could hear the rasp of his breath as Shack looked at him with panicky eyes, placing a finger to his lips.

'Intruders.' Shack's voice was barely more than a whisper. 'They're outside on the forecourt.'

Daniel gulped. 'How many?'

'Two, I think. I was coming to give you a hand with the buck, when I spotted them from the bedroom window.' Shack unhooked Scooter's collar and lead from the wall peg and found the boxer immediately at his heels. 'Get the rifle,' he said, fastening the collar. 'They look as if they mean business, so we'd better go prepared.'

'Shouldn't we ring the cops?'

'No time . . . Hurry.'

Daniel dug the key to the gun cabinet from his pocket. He crossed quickly to the cupboard under the stairs and released the padlock on the heavy-gauge upright metal box. The knock-out darts were in sealed containers on a shelf above. He left them, slung the rifle over his shoulder, and made his way back to the kitchen.

Shack was waiting by the side door. He held Scooter in one hand and a heavy rubber torch in the other.

'I haven't loaded the rifle,' Daniel told him.

'Didn't think you would.' Shack's mouth quirked grimly. 'Just so long as they don't know it. Are you ready?'

'Ready.'

A finger of fear crept down Daniel's back as Shack gently turned the door handle.

Tony Ryker had made an inspection by circling the caravan and was now standing on the grass verge deciding on his next move. Griggs was deliberately hanging back, not wishing to play any major part in any plan that Ryker had in mind.

Suddenly both men froze.

The hinged flap in the caravan's front door creaked and slowly lifted. Degsey left the wagon, one carefully placed paw at a time. She moved silently and there was no sign of the pitchfork injury. She looked from Ryker to Griggs, crouching on her haunches as she lay guard across the footboard. A tangle of smells sharpened by the warm night air pricked at her nose, tugged at her memory. Horses . . . the scent of horses was overpowering, bringing back memories of Mister Rafferty. Faintly, she knew she could smell the old cob, and she was also fully aware that she was now face-to-face with the evil men who had stolen him. Her muzzle lifted as a growl began to build.

'Flashlight,' Ryker whispered the word, stabbing an impatient finger towards Griggs.

'N-no.' He shook his head violently. His mind was numb and his actions stiff as he backed away.

Ryker took some hurried steps towards him and wrenched the lamp from his fingers. 'What the hell's wrong with you?' he said.

'D-don't turn on the flashlight,' Griggs managed to choke out. 'I-I'm warning you, Tony. Don't let it glint off the dog's tooth.'

Ryker gave a grunt of irritation and was about to thumb the switch when Daniel stepped out of the shadows. Griggs felt his stomach tighten as the rifle was pointed at his body.

'Stand still!' Daniel said, deliberately throwing a harsh note into his voice. He swept the barrel of the rifle towards Ryker. 'Move closer together!'

Ryker didn't flinch. He said, with relish, 'Grow up, kid. You haven't got the guts to use that.'

Shack appeared at Daniel's shoulder. He held a now-growling Scooter who was straining at his leash. He clicked on the heavy rubber torch, illuminating both men in the brightness of the beam.

'Take off those masks,' he said. 'Let's get a good look at you.'

Griggs, shielding his eyes, had shuffled nearer to Ryker. He hooked his thumbs under the ski-mask, preparing to peel it over his face.

Ryker knocked his hands away. 'No smartass kid gives me orders.' He spoke to Daniel in a dangerously tight voice. 'We're going to walk out of here . . . and there's not a thing you can do about it.'

Scooter looked at them and gave three half-hearted barks.

'And as for that overweight lapdog,' Ryker continued, 'he looks about as dangerous as a ping-pong ball against a tank.'

Daniel exchanged a quick glance with Shack. The words rang true because Scooter was a pet, not a guard dog. Like the majority of his breed he was all bluster and very little action.

Ryker's gaze shifted to the upstairs windows of the house. A light had come on in Sky's bedroom. She'd been woken by Scooter's barking and the curtains were moving.

Several things happened next but they were just blurred movement.

Ryker suddenly pitched himself at Daniel and, with a crazy burst of strength, brought both hands down in a clubbing action against the rifle. It sent the gun spinning away, and the sheer weight and force of the move brought Daniel to his knees.

Griggs reacted instantly by aiming a kick at the now free Scooter. It was not karate or kung-fu, just crude—vicious. His toecap struck the dog's ribcage with a jarring thud sending a painful squeal to Scooter's throat. He rolled over a couple of times, and then limped under the caravan, whimpering slightly, seeking a place to hide.

Shack held the heavy torch at arm's length, swinging it in front of him and threatening to use it as a weapon unless Ryker backed off. The big man laughed and dodged sideways, sending Shack off balance as he tried to catch Ryker with a badly timed lunge. The action carried him towards the caravan's hind-carriage and his legs tangled as he reached it. He fell awkwardly, tumbling head first into the nearside wheel, his mouth bouncing painfully against the hard edge of the heavy iron tyre. There was a hollow click from his teeth as his jaw snapped shut and a stain of blood dribbled from between his lips. He scrabbled for balance and righted himself by gripping the wheel's thick, brightly coloured spokes.

Ryker was on him instantly, allowing no time for his senses to be recovered.

Shack felt the torch being prised from his fingers as the big man used his weight to pin him against the wheel. A scorpion tattoo floated in front of his eyes and he held onto the image, knowing it was desperately important to store it in his memory.

One by one his fingers were being peeled forcibly back from the rubber grips of the torch as Ryker wrestled it from his hand. The big man gave a sickly laugh as he grabbed it and tossed it up and away.

It went high, spinning almost in slow motion, lighting up the greenery, spilling its glow over the forecourt before it tumbled to earth.

Griggs looked stricken as the heavy rubber torch struck the caravan's white lead roof, then rolled slowly past the chimney stack before bouncing down and settling on the footboard.

A yellow hoop of light settled itself across Degsey's face. She was still lying with her muzzle drawn back as she turned her head to look at Daniel.

'No!' Griggs saw the bright glint of gold and let out a shrill scream.

Daniel crawled towards the rifle and grabbed it.

Griggs began to run.

Ryker now had his solid bulk on top of Shack. He was gripped in a head hold and he felt the big man's thumbs forcing their way towards his eyes. He struggled and squirmed but he was hopelessly outmatched in both weight and strength.

Daniel was now on his feet. He knew he had to stop Ryker and help Shack, but he couldn't hold onto that thought.

Get the other one . . . the other one . . . a small voice in his head kept saying.

He looked at the rifle balanced in his hands, stock pressed firmly against his shoulder. It was no good to him, he thought. He hadn't loaded it. So why was he holding it in a firing position?

Degsey held Daniel with her gaze and he blinked rapidly, trying to blot out the shimmer of gold that was blurring his eyesight. No use. His thoughts began to swirl and his actions became numb. The skin between his shoulder blades was sweaty and prickled as he was gripped by the radar-like strength of Degsey's stare.

His tongue seemed to be held fast against the roof of his mouth as he lifted the rifle's telescopic sight to his eye, framing Griggs in the centre spot. He heard a metallic click as, without his touching it, the safety-catch flipped off. Moisture began to puddle in his eyebrows as he had no control over his trigger finger . . . It was pulling back, taking up the slack.

Griggs was fleeing, snatching a glance over his shoulder, running in a weaving path to make him a harder target. Without a belt around his waist he was losing control of his black jeans and his pace now slowed to an awkward stumble as they dropped to his thighs and then to his ankles. He was wearing bright pink underpants with little yellow duck motifs.

As if giving a signal, Degsey blinked.

Daniel fired.

Griggs screamed.

Instead of an empty *'phutt,'* there was a harder sound as Daniel felt the pressure of a knock-out dart leaving the barrel. He saw Griggs grip the left cheek of his backside then stagger forward in a clumsy jumble of limbs as he hit the ground.

Ryker had heard the noise of the rifle and he released his grip on Shack. He got unsteadily to his feet, raising hands to Daniel, looking towards the limp body of Griggs.

'Y-you crazy kid. I-I never thought . . .'

'Go help your friend,' Daniel said bluntly.

As Ryker fled, Shack looked up at Daniel and smiled, stretching his bruised mouth. 'I thought you said you hadn't loaded that thing,' he murmured.

'I must have forgotten to *unload* it.' Sky's voice came from behind them. She was wrapped in a white towelling robe, her hair untidy, her face pink and showing sleepy puzzlement. 'I picked up the weapon at Knightacott Woods, and I locked it in the gun cupboard. I didn't check it, so it's my fault. Daniel's not to blame.'

Suddenly all eyes were on Degsey. She stood up and shook herself, stretching her long legs. A paw caught the heavy rubber torch that had settled on the footboard and it rolled forward, falling between the caravan's shafts and hitting the tarmac. There was a tinkling sound as the lens smashed, killing the light, and sending glass in all directions. It was as if she had completed her task and was no longer needed. She looked from Daniel to Shack to Sky before nosing open the caravan's hinged flap and disappearing back inside.

'That's one hell of a weird dog.' Shack got to his feet, eyeing Daniel. He coughed and spat, leaving slimy streamers of blood down his chin. 'Did she do anything to help us—apart from just lying there?'

Daniel cleared his throat, his Adam's apple jerking, 'She more than lived up to Seamus's story telling,' he said.

'I don't follow . . . ?' Shack frowned.

'Tell you later.'

Ryker had reached Griggs. He helped him to his feet then decided to carry him in a fireman's lift past the two huge conifer trees. He opened the cab's passenger door and threw him face first onto the seat.

'W-where did he get me? Is there much blood?' Griggs burbled.

From the glow of the cab's interior light Ryker could see the knock-out dart sticking into Griggs's left buttock. He gripped the plastic shaft and yanked out the needle.

'He got you in the backside with a dart,' he said. 'The kind used to tranquilise animals. The drug's gone into your body, but I dare say you'll live.'

Griggs didn't reply. A dizzy sickness was forcing sleep upon him.

Ryker climbed into the driving seat, pulled off his black mask, and started the engine. He breathed a sigh of relief as the vehicle left Oyster Gables. He decided to mock his partner. 'Has anyone ever told you that you have a disgusting taste in underpants, Griggsy?'

Spring and Jonathan had joined the gathering round the caravan. Both were walking about in bare feet and pyjamas.

'I've found some clues,' Jonathan announced after doing a search of the area, 'A holdall with stuff in it, and a leather belt.'

'Give them to Daniel.' Sky's voice sharpened. 'And both of you put some slippers on at once!'

'Scooter's hurt.' Spring appeared from underneath the caravan. 'He's licking his ribs.'

'I'll see to him in a moment.' Sky was holding a tissue to Shack's mouth, trying to stop the blood which trickled onto his rugby shirt.

'What were those men after?' she asked Daniel.

He rummaged through the holdall and pulled out a bootee. 'By the look of this gear . . . Horses.'

'Rustlers?'

He nodded.

'Grief.' She shuddered slightly.

There was a rattle as the caravan's porch doors opened and Seamus appeared holding an oil lamp, his bowed shoulders draped in a quilt. He blinked, looking confused as the lamplight flickered across his craggy features.

'Blood and blunderbushes!' he exclaimed, looking at the mixture of emotions on the various faces. 'Somethin' amiss? Me brain be fair twizzled wi' all the noise.'

Just his confused presence helped lighten the atmosphere. In the excitement of what had happened, everyone had forgotten about Seamus.

Grins were exchanged, followed by a few giggles, and pretty soon the whole forecourt rang with laughter.

CHAPTER SIX

_____

Very little sleep had been had since Ryker's and Griggs's unsuccessful visit. Only a confused Seamus had considered it worth going back to bed. Sky had busied herself between tending to Shack's bruises and the wounded Scooter, Daniel had sat up keeping a close eye on the fallow buck, and Spring and Jonathan were far too excited by the morning's happenings to consider doing anything apart from bombarding everyone with questions.

'I think you should lend a hand getting breakfast,' Daniel suggested, entering the kitchen from the yard and washing his hands at the large butler sink. He was talking to Spring and Jonathan who were tagging his every move.

'It's Sky's turn to cook breakfast,' Jonathan said breezily.

'Sky's busy with the vet. She's worried about Scooter.'

'I couldn't cook bacon,' Spring set her jaw stubbornly, 'the smell would make me sick.'

Daniel dried his hands and reached into a cupboard for a box of cornflakes. 'This morning we'll all have juice and cereal,' he announced. He set each of them various kitchen duties. 'And don't forget Seamus,' he added. 'Top of the milk on his cornflakes, and tea without sugar.'

There was a slight roughness in Daniel's throat and redness round his eyes to remind him of the troubles of the previous 24 hours. He stretched and joined Shack at the table. Normally, he and Sky would take turns to cook breakfast, but this morning he was determined that Spring and Jonathan should do their fair share.

'Toast as well for me, please,' Daniel requested loudly, dropping a wink to Shack.

'Two sugars for me, kids,' Shack said, playing along.

'None for Sky.' Daniel turned his back and sat down, trying hard to stifle a smile. 'She has a sweetener from a little clicky container . . . if you can find it.'

'I know what she has.' Jonathan's blue eyes flashed with irritation as he lowered the kettle onto a hotplate. 'She is my sister.'

Shack was studying the leather belt left behind by Griggs. It was fairly ordinary and had Size 32 stamped near the buckle. He placed it to one side and emptied the contents from the recovered holdall onto the kitchen table. Bolt-cutters, head-collar and halter, two sets of hoof bootees and a half-empty packet of book-matches.

There was a sickly blueness about his mouth, and as he examined each of the objects in turn his face showed a hidden anger, with none of the cocky self-confidence that was usually so much part of him.

'We've got to stop this pair of thieves,' he said. 'If we don't do something, then no horse in the West Country is safe.'

'Owners should have their animals marked,' Spring replied.

'Micro-chipping, hoof-branding or freeze-marking of a serial number on the horse's coat,' Shack agreed. 'Trouble is, people just won't spend the extra money.'

Daniel began fiddling with the book-matches.

'Silver Seagull Restaurant at Ilfracombe.' He read the printed words from the book-match cover aloud. 'If they use this place on a regular basis then we might be able to track them down.'

'We didn't see their faces. They were wearing masks.'

'True, but we have descriptions of sorts.'

'Like one being big and one being skinny?'

'Did you notice anything else?'

'One was wearing pink knickers with yellow thingamies on them,' Jonathan chuckled. 'He looked a right dopey muppet.'

'He also had evil eyes,' Spring put in, distributing cornflakes into six bowls.

'I'm surprised you could see his eyes,' Shack said, folding his arms on the table and leaning forward. 'It was very dark.'

'She couldn't,' Jonathan stated. 'We were watching from an upstairs window.'

'Well . . . er . . .' Spring was struggling. She fidgeted before adding, 'Anybody who would deliberately kick Scooter must have evil eyes.'

'Darn snothead!' Jonathan said with feeling.

Daniel decided to swing the conversation back to where it mattered. 'Did you notice anything unusual about the man you were fighting?' he asked Shack. 'Anything at all?'

Shack fingered his swollen lip and shook his head despondently.

'Shacky was too busy punching him,' Jonathan put in, nearly overfilling the teapot as he shaped like a boxer. 'A left hook to the jaw . . . a right jab to the body . . .'

'Too busy *not* punching him,' Shack huffed, 'he was far too powerful. When he went for a head-hold I thought I was going to black-out—' he broke off, slapping the back of his neck with his palm. He stared a little oddly at Daniel as a piece of memory returned. 'Of course, the tattoo . . . how the hell could I forget that!'

'Tattoo?'

'Yes. He had gloves on but as he prised the torch from my fingers so the sleeves of his jacket slid up his arms. I saw it clearly. A birth-sign tattoo. On his right . . .' He paused, considered. 'Yes, definitely his right forearm.'

Daniel arched an eyebrow. 'Which birth-sign?'

'Scorpio. It was a large yellow and blue scorpion.'

'A mega clue, Shacky!' Jonathan exclaimed, dropping slices of bread into the toaster. 'If we can find the tattooed man then we should find Mister Rafferty, eh, Daniel?'

Daniel nodded, deep in thought. He was quietly pleased. The tattoo was major information and now at least they had something to follow up. A plan began to form in his mind as Spring placed mugs of tea and bowls brimming with milky cornflakes on the table.

'Odd behaviour,' Shack murmured to Daniel, picking up Griggs's belt. 'Why would anyone risk losing their jeans?'

'To steal a greyhound?' Daniel suggested.

'Degsey? You're joking.'

'It's the only thing that makes sense. They were both standing by Degsey when we spotted them.'

'And a fat lot of use she turned out to be.' He sniffed his disapproval. 'It was all she could do to barely manage a growl.'

Daniel dug into his cornflakes, and between spoonfuls told Shack the full story about the torch, the tooth and the rifle.

'She held my gaze, her tooth shimmering . . . almost blinding me,' he went on. 'I lost all sense of where I was. It sounds crazy, I know, but things happened that were beyond my control. Degsey's inner energy, or whatever you want to call it, released the gun's safety-catch and her mental powers forced me to pull the trigger. I fought against it . . . But if she hadn't influenced me to fire, then the tattooed man might have killed you.'

Shack let his breath trickle out slowly. He sat back in his chair looking totally confused. 'I had no idea,' he said quietly. 'Thank you, Degsey.'

'It was Fin's gold.' Spring had returned to the table holding Seamus's filled breakfast tray. She'd caught most of Daniel's words and was glowing with pleasure.

'It's the most enchantedest and powerfullest gold in the world,' Jonathan piped up, doing a bad copy of Seamus's Irish accent.

'Sure is, little dude . . . sure is,' Shack said, standing up and stretching before taking the tray from Spring's hands.

Sky entered from the back door, nearly stumbling into Shack as he made his way outside. She kicked off her rubber boots and hung her white coat on a peg. Her hair was ruffled against her forehead and her eyes were gritty through lack of sleep. She pulled up a chair and sank into it, giving a breathy sigh.

'The vet's just left,' she told Daniel. 'He's very pleased with the way you nursed the buck through the night. The animal's had an injection and seems settled. I'll be treating the wounds caused by the snare so we'll just have to keep our fingers crossed. Scooter's okay too—just bruising—no cracked ribs.'

'Where is he?' Jonathan asked, bringing hot, buttered toast to the table. Spring followed behind with Sky's cornflakes, juice and tea.

'Sitting on the caravan foot-board with Degsey. Seems the two of them have become great friends . . .' Sky paused, suddenly aware that she was being waited on. 'What have I done to deserve this VIP treatment?' she asked, sipping her orange juice. 'My little brother and sister getting breakfast? Are you both feeling unwell?'

'We thought we'd do our bit . . . All pull together and that kind of stuff.' Jonathan avoided Daniel's eyes and looked a bit sheepish as he jerked out the words. 'You've been up all night . . . working very hard and that . . .'

Sky shot Daniel a questioning look. He pushed fingers through his thick hair and shrugged innocently.

'Well thank you—both of you.' Although weary she managed an impish grin. 'As you're obviously in a caring mood, can I ask one more favour?'

'Not the washing up?' Jonathan gave a groan.

'No, something far more exciting.'

'Like what?'

'Three hedgehogs are due for release today.'

'Oh, yes please!' Spring's eyes flung open to their very limit.

Sky went on to explain that she intended to send Shack home early so that he could rest and recover from his injuries. Megan and Hannah would take over Shack's normal duties, while she and Daniel released two foxes at Scamperbuck Ring.

'When I released the vixen we captured at the garage,' Daniel murmured reflectively, draining his mug of tea, 'I got a fair bit of abuse from a passing farmer at Horseshoe Coppice.'

'There's always been that kind of trouble,' Sky explained. 'Farmers don't like foxes, sometimes with good reason—so we're caught in the middle. It's Oyster Gables' custom to treat all wild animals equally. In our eyes they're all God's creatures.'

Shack returned with Seamus's breakfast tray. Both the cereal and the tea were untouched.

'Isn't the old boy hungry?' Daniel queried.

'Nope.' Shack's eyes appeared troubled as he shook his head. 'It's a bit worrying really. He says his aches and pains are playing him up, but I think there's more to it than that. He looks sort of grey . . . washed out.'

'Shall I call a doctor?'

'Seamus see a *doctor*, are you kidding?' Shack smiled, stretching his bruised mouth with a painful wince. 'I left him mixing up some herbs. He seems sure he can cure himself.'

'There's only one real cure . . .' Spring began hesitantly.

'Mister Rafferty,' Jonathan said. 'He wants to get back on the road and he's worried for the old horse. Whenever I talk to him he asks if there's any news.'

Shack crunched toast and exchanged a knowing glance with Daniel.

'The vet told me that three horses were stolen in the early hours from Penhill,' Sky murmured. 'It must have been the same men. We were very lucky not to lose Excalibur and Sir Galahad.'

'This horse stealing is getting out of control!' Shack said forcefully.

'Can't we . . . Can't we do something . . . ?' Spring broke off with a shudder.

Daniel saw the exchange of looks pass between them, the eyes showing anger and helplessness. He nibbled on a slice of toast as a plan began to form in his mind. If a carrot was dangled in front of the rustlers' noses something they couldn't resist—then he reckoned they could be flushed out and caught.

His kept his expression calm as he said, 'Don't worry, Spring. We'll catch them—and soon.'

*   *   *

Griggs was far from happy.

He'd been drugged for around six hours and had woken suffering dizziness and a splitting headache.

Ryker had put him to bed and was now holding a plastic bucket propped against his partner's chin as once again his face reddened, his chest heaved and he coughed up a mouthful of sickness.

'Mind what you're doing!' Ryker flared, clicking his tongue as his shirt cuff was suddenly stained with a yellowish slime.

'I'm about to croak, Tony,' Griggs spluttered, gripping the bucket and wiping spittle from his mouth with the comer of the duvet. 'T-that dart must have contained enough poison to put down an elephant.'

'They don't contain poison, they contain a tranquilliser.'

'B-but I'm dying.'

'You're not dying. Your body's reacted badly to the drug, that's all.'

He heaved again, retched, and managed a noisy burp. He pushed the bucket away and sank back onto the pillow. His eyes were hazy and he was sweating slightly.

'Anyway, you deserve to be feeling lousy,' Ryker told him. 'Running away like a wimp—leaving the holdall behind.'

'Did I?' Griggs looked confused.

'Of all the stupid things . . . All because of that flamin' dog.'

'The greyhound at Swiftly . . .' He groaned as an image of Degsey filled his head. 'I remember now! You were gripped with capturing the dog, and I paid the price. With all the mad stuff that went on it's no wonder I forgot to pick up the bag.'

'I'll dock the price of the tools from your next pay-packet.'

'Ta, you're all heart.'

'Luckily nothing can be traced. It was all old gear, bought years ago.'

Griggs cringed slightly as he shifted position in the bed. 'My backside's throbbing like hell,' he complained.

'Good,' Ryker said. 'You wouldn't have been shot if you hadn't panicked. Now, because you're laid up, everything will have to be delayed for a couple of days. I'd scheduled three horses at Okehampton and the two at Tiverton for tonight's haul . . . Now all my plans are totally messed up.'

'*Oh, I am sorry!*' A thick vein bulged and jumped in Griggs's temple as he lifted his head from the pillow. 'I'm ill, don't you understand? I'm laying here distressed and in pain. All I need is one of my nosebleeds to crown the whole thing off.'

'Don't you dare bleed over the duvet. A bloodstain won't wash out.'

Griggs glared at him.

'What about the old nags?' Ryker continued. 'Our Belgium contact is expecting the shipment on Saturday. You're supposed to be driving them to Harwich.'

'No chance. You'll have to postpone it.'

'Until when?'

'Until I'm fully recovered! Now leave me alone to get some rest.'

Ryker made for the door. He turned as he reached it. 'I suppose you're expecting me to muck out the horses and feed them?'

'Well, someone's got to do it.'

Ryker cursed under his breath.

'The sooner you start,' Griggs added, 'the sooner you'll get finished.'

'And the cooking? What about that?'

'Don't worry on my account. I couldn't eat a thing.'

Ryker's mouth bunched in anger. 'I'm not asking if you'd like anything, I'm asking you if *you'll* be doing it!'

Griggs shook his head with a deliberate slowness and once again reached for the bucket. 'Food's in the fridge,' he said, burping twice and managing a small dribble of spittle. 'You never could get the hang of the microwave. All those timing gadgets and buttons. Well, now's your chance to learn.'

*   *   *

'A trap?' Sky said, glancing at Daniel. 'So who or what is the cheese?'

'Either of the livery horses,' Daniel replied. 'We'll let them steal one—but we'll be a step ahead of their every move.'

They had left Swiftly village and were driving towards Scamperbuck Ring in Daniel's estate car. Degsey and Scooter had come along for the ride and were lying in the rear behind the dog-guard. Spring and Jonathan occupied the back seats, holding three transporting cages. Two contained foxes, the other held three hedgehogs.

They would all be released where they had been found. The foxes at Scamperbuck Ring, which was non-hunting land, and the hedgehogs in the nearby grounds of a large country house.

The injuries suffered were fairly common and Sky had dealt with similar casualties in the past. One fox had lost an eye in a fight, whilst the other had damaged its pelvis when in collision with a car. All three hedgehogs had been found in a compost heap where they had received wounds caused by a garden fork. The creatures had been sleeping when the accident had happened, and a very concerned gardener had immediately brought them to Oyster Gables for treatment.

'Here are the keys, kids.' Sky turned in her seat and handed a leather pouch to Jonathan. 'Mr and Mrs Blake are away on holiday so use the large brass key to open the garden gate. Walk past the lawns to the summer-house and release the hedgehogs close to the rose arbour. They'll be fine.'

Daniel slowed the Volvo and indicated left as he turned the vehicle into a huge tree-lined driveway. The roof of an elegant Georgian house was just visible above neatly trimmed blocks of tall hedging. Daniel rolled to a halt on crunching gravel and parked just short of the garden gate where a wrought-iron sign had been scrolled to form the house name: 'Greenacres.'

'Half-an-hour,' Sky informed her brother and sister, glancing at her watch. 'We'll be back by then. Take Scooter and when you've finished walk back down the driveway and wait carefully by the road entrance for us to pick you up.'

Jonathan and Spring leapt from the estate car anxious to complete their mission. They lifted out the cage holding the hedgehogs and opened the hatchback door to collect an eagerly panting Scooter. Sky waved and Degsey pressed her wet nose against the rear window, watching keenly as Daniel reversed the Volvo into the turning circle and backtracked the vehicle down the drive to the main road.

'Are you sure we can catch the horse thieves?' Sky asked, picking up the earlier conversation as she leaned over her seat to check the cages protecting the two foxes were secure. 'I couldn't risk any danger to a livery horse—not unless the plan was completely foolproof.'

'It's perfect,' Daniel told her. 'We'll need a small Rice trailer to tow the horse. Can you borrow one?'

'That shouldn't be a problem.' She nibbled on her lower lip and eyed Daniel suspiciously.

'I hope you're a good actress,' he said.

'Actress?' Sky's eyes sparkled with curiosity.

'Shack's checking something out for me. I'll talk it over properly with you if all the pieces drop into place.'

'But Shack's supposed to be at home resting.'

'The checking will be done tonight. It's Friday so he'll be visiting Sophie at Ilfracombe as usual.'

Sky said nothing, just frowned.

'There's a restaurant in the town called the Silver Seagull,' Daniel told her.

Sky looked vague. 'I know. What about it?'

'I'm pretty sure it's used by the rustlers. What I need to know—and what Shack will try and find out—is whether they have a routine for calling there. For my scheme to work the timing has to be perfect.'

Daniel eased the Volvo clear of the driveway and into the queue of traffic threading its way towards Fremington. Immediately next to Greenacres was a huge expanse of Ministry of Defence training land whose advertising banner announced: FOR SALE. 130 ACRES. The location, spanned by a high wire-mesh fence, had once been used by the Royal Marines for military exercises but had long since been abandoned and left to the elements of the weather.

As Daniel adjusted his rear-view mirror he noticed that Degsey was taking an interest in the now empty site. She was standing stiffly behind the dog guard, her muscles quivering, and her eyes full of hidden secrets as she stared at a large, partly destroyed building. It had originally been built to look like an enemy fortress which could be invaded during military action. The windows had been blown out and the now crumbling brickwork had been studded with gunfire during mock battles. For some reason it fascinated Degsey. She began to growl . . . a deep growl which suddenly turned into persistent barking.

'Shhh, Degsey.' Sky turned, following the dog's gaze to the tumbledown building behind the wire. Her eyes flicked curiously to Daniel. 'What on earth's the matter with her?'

Daniel shrugged, confused by Degsey's actions. He knew that greyhounds rarely barked unless anxious for a racing or chasing event—and he'd never heard Degsey bark before—so her present behaviour seemed totally odd.

'Maybe she's seen a rabbit,' he said.

Degsey continued to bark until the Volvo had sped past the wire fence and the view of the abandoned building was replaced by thick leafy woodland. Daniel glanced in the mirror as she settled herself behind the dog guard, long legs stretched forward and chin resting on the lower securing bar. Her eyes were like huge droplets of cut glass and Daniel could see his own face reflected in them many times.

Scamperbuck Ring lay ahead.

Daniel glanced briefly at Sky. Her profile was shadowed against the strong sunshine streaming through the car window. He left the main road and steered the Volvo over some rough terrain and towards a clearing. All around there was birdsong and above them shafts of summer sunlight poked feathery holes in the branches causing patches of brightness and shadow across the rich green foliage. The Ring's atmosphere was stickily hot and Daniel felt his polo shirt tugging damply at his shoulder blades as he slowed and nosed the Volvo into a hollow of shade.

'I love this place.' Sky was relaxed and smiling as she swung her legs clear of the car's door. She could smell a mixture of humid earth and dry wood, of leaves and grasses, broken only by a faint scent of the wild creatures which had made Scamperbuck Ring their home. She stretched sleepily, letting fragments of sunlight play across her bare arms.

Daniel opened the hatchback and couldn't resist a grin as he spotted the blue Oyster Gables advertising sticker fixed by Jonathan to the Volvo's rear window. He attached a lead to Degsey's collar and watched Sky reach into the vehicle for the two transporting cages which contained the foxes. She smiled at him as she stretched forward; her hair was teased into its usual wildness—a kind of tawny warmth which added to the line of her cheekbones. He smiled back, knowing he'd earned her friendship, but now he hoped for an extra special kind of closeness. He knew only too well that just being near to her made him feel giddy and light-headed . . . He also knew that given the slightest advance from her it would only be too easy to fall head-over-heels in love with her.

'Here we are, boys.' Sky knelt and spoke to the foxes as she positioned the transporting cages on a carpet of grass well inside the Ring. 'I don't want to see either of you back at Oyster Gables,' she added positively, 'so stay out of trouble.'

Degsey lay by Daniel's feet, her ears twitching as she waited for the foxes moment of release. They sensed freedom—smelled it—spinning around in their cages. Daniel took a firmer grip on Degsey's lead in case she decided to give chase.

Sky nodded to Daniel then slipped both catches on the hinged doors.

The foxes flew out. They were just a reddish-brown blur as they separated and made the 50-metre dash across open ground for cover. Foxes were well-known for their hurdling abilities and Sky laughed, Daniel grinned, and Degsey gave a tug on the lead as they showed this off by jumping a high bank of gorse and bracken before disappearing into a dense thicket of hazel.

'They'll soon go to ground.' Sky's eyes sparkled as she cupped a hand to her forehead, shielding her face from the sun. 'There are several fox families in this part of the Ring.'

Daniel noticed a pause as she pressed her lips together and sighed. The foxes had gone and now she began to look a little distant. Various cheerless expressions darted across her face as she re-fastened the doors on the transporting cages and climbed to her feet.

'You okay?' he asked.

She allowed him to hold her fingers. Her nails were well-tended and smoothly manicured in a business-like, practical manner.

'Releasing casualties is supposed to be the best part of the job,' she murmured, making an attempt at a smile, 'but it still leaves me with a large lump in my throat. I suppose I shouldn't get so fond of them.'

'You care deeply for the animals,' he said softly, pressing her fingers. 'It's only natural to feel sad when they go.'

'The foxes have their freedom but I'm being selfish.' She tilted her head on one side so her tawny mass of hair swung free across her face. 'So you see Daniel, I'm not such a toughie after all.'

He began to play with her fingers. 'I'm glad I'm seeing the real Sky Patakin.'

'I was pretty nasty to you when you first arrived.'

'I know.'

'I'd requested another female for the assistant manager's job.'

'Sexist.'

'I'm sorry.'

'You're forgiven.'

They stood motionless, just looking at each other as they inhaled the pleasant scent of fir and cedar. Daniel's throat felt dry and he knew he desperately wanted to hold Sky close and kiss her. But would she accept such a move? Was his timing completely wrong as it had been in the past? The questions tumbled over in his mind and he could feel his neck muscles tighten as he searched unsuccessfully for answers.

Degsey was still lying at Daniel's feet, long white legs stretched in front of her as she panted in the heat. Daniel's gaze shifted from Sky to the greyhound as he remembered how Seamus had told Jonathan about Degsey's smile. Was it possible that he was seeing it now? Certainly her open mouth curled up at the corners, lifting long folds of flesh in a curious, quirky way that added to the mysterious twinkle in her eyes. They seemed to be reading his every expression, every gesture, and every move.

He watched the pinkness of her tongue slide between her two sharp lower canines, wetting the gold tooth which now winked at him as it was caught by a ray of sunlight. Instantly everything became beautifully simple—and he knew, in some way, his thoughts and actions were being influenced by Degsey's presence.

His arms had developed a movement of their own as he moved his hands to Sky's hips and then gently traced a finger over her neck, her lips, and her nose. She bent her forehead to his shoulder, her hands clutching at his waist. She wanted to stay there forever as he cradled her in the warmth of his arms.

Daniel kissed her closed eyes and the tiny pulse that beat at her temple.

Sky's heartbeat quickened. She gave a gasp of pleasure.

'I'm very glad I came to Swiftly,' Daniel murmured, his lips on her cheek.

'Me too.' She rested her hand on the nape of his neck where his damp hair had curled in the warmth of the sun.

Daniel kissed her lips and Sky responded by clinging tightly to him for slightly longer than she intended.

'Wow!' Daniel broke the kiss and laughed suddenly, his gaze dropping to Degsey. 'When you do things girl, you certainly do them properly.'

Sky's cool dark eyes lingered on him. 'Me?'

'No, Degsey.'

'You were talking to Degsey?'

'Mmm. When I first held you I was hesitating whether to—'

'Daniel Rusk, are you saying a dog made you kiss me?'

'Well, yes . . . I mean no . . . It wasn't like that. Oh, hell! I wanted to kiss you desperately. Her tooth helped things along, I suppose.'

'*Her tooth!*' she exclaimed. 'You don't still believe in Seamus's magical hocus-pocus, do you?'

'I'd be a liar if I told you I didn't,' he said with mild humour.

'So it wasn't a *natural* kiss?'

'Of course it was. I think I'm falling in love with you.'

'But you needed a nudge.' Her face flushed hot at the thought as she folded her arms and looked down at Degsey. She stared at the greyhound, her eyebrows raised. 'Apparently Daniel needs

131

your approval before he can be guided by his heart. I don't believe you have special powers, but if you're trying to be clever, then stop it!'

Degsey moved closer to Daniel then looked up at Sky with her huge brown eyes.

Sky picked up the transporting cages and turned smartly away. 'We'd better collect Jonathan and Spring,' she said abruptly.

* * *

There was no sign of the children waiting at the bottom of the slip-road that led from 'Greenacres'. Sky tut-tutted and checked her wristwatch as Daniel swung the Volvo clear of the main road and cruised gently to a halt alongside a grass verge.

Degsey had her nose pressed firmly against the rear window and was making nervy little movements with her head. She could see the Ministry of Defence training area and once again the mass of energy which normally hummed quietly inside her body had started to race wildly. She began to bark loudly and with urgency.

'Oh no, not again . . . !' Sky began, then blinked and swallowed hard. She'd turned her head to subdue the greyhound but stopped short on seeing an empty transporting cage propped against the high wire fence.

'Spring and Jonathan were definitely here,' she said, touching dry lips with a dry tongue. She pointed. 'That's the cage that held the hedgehogs.'

Daniel immediately flung open the car door, jumped out of the driving seat and sprinted across to the fence. He could see that a section of wire mesh had been cut and bent back, leaving just enough room for a body to squeeze through. A quickly suppressed flash of panic came and went from his eyes as he took in the warning words of a notice pinned to a metal post. It read: PRIVATE PROPERTY. KEEP OUT. UNSAFE & DANGEROUS.

Degsey's muffled barking was still beating at Daniel's ears and he knew he desperately wanted the dog with him. The greyhound had a sixth sense—of that he was sure and now he intended to put her talent to its full use.

Sky had exited the Volvo and was shielding the sun from her eyes as she frantically scanned the length of the wire fence. Daniel shouted to her, indicating the gap in the mesh. 'I reckon they've gone through here,' he said, his breathing suddenly jerky. 'Bring Degsey!'

The greyhound responded to Daniel's voice and dived clear of the hatchback the moment it was opened. She ducked past the leather lead held in Sky's outstretched hand and made an immediate dart for the fence. Daniel felt her body streak past his legs as she powered herself through the gap, setting a blistering pace towards the partly wrecked hangar-sized building that resembled an enemy fort.

'This fence has been deliberately cut,' Sky said, easing through the gap. 'Spring and Jonathan would never do that.'

'Vandals would,' Daniel responded, following her. 'The clipped ends of the wire fence have gone rusty. It's been like this for ages.'

Degsey had settled on all fours beside a tumbledown wall which at one time had served as a barrier during military action. She could hear noises that were soundless to the human ear and the thought of what she must do made her muscles quiver. She now had a clear view of the rickety, bullet-scarred building which had prompted her earlier unease. She'd felt odd sensations prickle the hairs along her backbone when Daniel had first driven past it in the car. Now a warning was prodding at her razor-sharp senses and it indicated terrible danger. She padded her way forward, avoiding obstacles and sharp pieces of metal. She knew Spring, Jonathan and Scooter were inside the building and she also knew they were in desperate trouble.

CHAPTER SEVEN

'**D**egsey's sensed something!' There was a note of desperation in Daniel's voice as he dodged across a concrete compound pitted with bullet holes. He'd taken Sky's hand and they were weaving their way past old tyres, rusty oil drums, huge wooden spools which had once held cables, and the chewed-up remains of a training area now hindering their progress.

'Perhaps Degsey's found—' Sky began, then stopped in her tracks as the letters of a large worn and battered notice-board came into view. It was nailed to what was left of the hangar-sized building's front door and the message made her gasp. Written boldly in red paint it stated: KEEP CLEAR. THIS STRUCTURE IS IN DANGER COLLAPSE.

Sky uttered a faint moan. 'Oh, no, please tell me they haven't . . .'

'Take it easy,' Daniel said, steadying Sky's arm. 'We can't be sure that Jonathan and Spring are inside,'

A couple of throaty barks—unmistakably Scooter—ended all further questions. Sky and Daniel exchanged worried glances.

'Stay behind me, stay close, and watch your footing,' Daniel said, cursing as he knocked his ankle against a boulder. He kicked some loose rubble clear in order to reach the door. It was already half-open and hanging at a wonky angle by one hinge . . . easy enough for small bodies and dogs to get through but not wide enough for him or Sky.

He pushed it stiffly, hearing a groan before it opened fully under the pressure from his shoulder. A shower of powdery brick-dust whirled downwards, covering Sky's hair and clinging to her eyelashes. Daniel heaved a cough as the dust caught in his throat and stuck grittily to his forehead. A few seconds passed as both waited for the air to become breathable before they made their way inside.

At eye-level there wasn't much to see—just a huge expanse of empty space and Scooter panting fretfully and running round in circles. The air smelled of damp concrete and rotting wood. Daniel blinked to clear his vision and focussed on Degsey.

Through a haze of dust he saw the greyhound had used her springy power to leap onto an old metal-framed canteen table still sitting in the centre of the room. The building's roof had caved inwards leaving a gaping hole where a few slates still hung dangerously suspended.

Degsey lay perfectly still under the broken roof, her head and body bathed in a pattern of sunlight. Her eyes were gleaming and alert as they recorded the dangers around her.

'Up there!' Sky's voice rose shrilly as the creaky movement of an old metal staircase flickered at the corner of her eye. 'Something's moving. Is it . . . ?'

Daniel squinted towards the roof to where a balcony was linked to the staircase and ran the length of one wall. There, huddled in a corner were Spring and Jonathan.

'It's them.' Daniel swallowed.

Sky just stared, a flush reddening her face.

'W . . . we can't get down!' Jonathan shouted the words, shifting his position slightly on the balcony. He'd taken off his shirt and was holding it in a tight little bundle on his lap. There was a bruise on his forearm and his fingernails were thick with dirt. 'We came up here to rescue a barn owl. It was hit by a lorry at the roadside. We watched it while we were waiting for you to pick us up . . . and it flew into this old building.' He pointed to his torn shirt, adding, 'I've got it here . . . wrapped up. I think it's busted a wing.'

Daniel was becoming aware that every time Jonathan drew a breath his shoulders would flex against the wall and cause the whole balcony structure to move. Little puffs of red brick-dust rained downwards as the fixing points for the metal staircase moved alarmingly.

'Don't talk and don't move,' Daniel instructed, edging forward, his feet crunching over broken glass. 'I'll come up and get you.'

'But it's not safe,' Sky whispered the words. 'If you put your weight on those stair treads then the balcony could collapse.'

'I've no choice, cross your fingers.'

'I'll go . . . I'm just as capable,' Sky said.

'Not a chance. There's no way I'm risking you getting injured.'

'Then we have to get help.'

'No time.'

'There must be some other—'

Sky paused with her mouth open on hearing the ugly squeal of metal rasping against metal, followed by a loud crack. One end of the balcony dropped ten centimetres nearer the ground. Scooter let out a distressed bark as brick chippings rained down on him. Spring screamed in terror as both she and Jonathan were now tilted at an angle which threatened to take them on a roller-coaster ride to certain injury.

'Grab hold of the rails!' Daniel reacted immediately. 'Don't slip! Hang on tightly!'

Daniel's palms were sweating as he wrapped his fingers around the iron banister. His knuckles showed chalky white as, in one bound, he spanned the staircase to the third step, praying inwardly that the balcony would hold his bodyweight.

No such luck. The metal treads rasped a noisy warning and shuddered violently against the balcony.

Spring and Jonathan bounced slightly as the whole structure tilted perilously lower. There was a noise like gunfire as bolts pinged out of their sockets. Dust billowed and loose roof tiles clattered to the floor as a huge gash opened up in the wall behind Daniel just as he jumped clear of the staircase. He watched the large crack rip through the plaster as it continued upwards. It was like a can-opener splitting a tin and it ran from floor to ceiling, its progress shifting one of the roof rafters.

Sky felt herself being pulled to one side by Daniel as the rafter crashed with ear-stunning force to the ground. Sharp wooden splinters scattered in all directions narrowly missing her face but she was barely aware of the danger. Her thoughts were with her brother and sister as she stood, her hands twisting her hair, damp with fright, as her eyes focussed upwards in an unblinking stare.

'We're slipping! Please, please help us!' Jonathan's breath came in harsh gasps. He was clinging to an upright rail with one hand, while the other hand stopped Spring from falling as it clutched at the belt of her jeans.

It wasn't fear that whitened Daniel's face; it was the brutal fact that in his own hands lay the decision of how to perform a rescue.

His mind zigzagged wildly as he looked up at the two helpless figures hanging high above him. How long would they be able to hang on? Would the whole building collapse? Would he and Sky be smothered and crushed?

There was a deep rumbling noise which shook the very foundations of the building. Sky clung to Daniel as the sound of shifting walls and crumbling bricks crashed around her ears. She knew she was trapped in the middle of a nightmare that was only seconds from reaching its climax . . .

'Degsey! Degsey!' Spring's shrill voice cut through the destructive noise. Tears smarted under her eyelids as swept by sudden giddiness her head lolled sideways and she glimpsed the unmoving greyhound. 'Use your special powers, Degsey . . . Oh, smile for us, please!'

Degsey's soft eyes lifted towards Spring and blinked sleepily against the shafts of sunlight which poured in through the gash in the roof. Slowly, very slowly, her lower jaw dropped and her muzzle quivered, forming deep little crinkles in the supple skin. The outside edge of her bottom lip was black and shiny, clashing with her pink tongue as she displayed her sharp, gold canine tooth.

Suddenly, unbelievingly, there was a tomb-like silence.

No more rumbles, crashes or tremors. No more falling bricks. Nothing. The only sounds were the ticking of Daniel's wristwatch and Jonathan's heavy breathing.

'W . . . what's happening?' Sky swallowed rapidly, her throat pulsing.

She turned to look at Degsey, lifting a hand to shield her eyes from the laser-bright glint of the tooth. A blinding gold halo seemed to expand and brush against the walls of the building.

'No time to waste.' Daniel knew exactly what was happening and immediately launched himself up the staircase.

He powered over the steps—each one now easily accepting his weight and holding firm.

The balcony loomed ahead of him. It was hanging at a lopsided angle where the metal had buckled, distorted, and tilted downwards like some horrific fairground slide.

'She . . . she's slipping . . .' Jonathan's mouth was twisted in a grimace as he strained to keep hold of Spring's belt. His arm and fingers had gone numb under the pressure and he could feel his sister begin to slide from his grasp.

'Daniel . . . !' Spring shrieked the name as Jonathan had no option but to release his grip.

'Stay on your back!' Daniel yelled hoarsely, dropping to his knees and spreading out his arms. 'Don't be frightened. I'll catch you!'

She lost a shoe as she spun towards him.

Twenty metres . . . ten . . .

The balcony uprights flashed madly past her eyes but there was no time for fear. She held her breath as she bounced a couple of times, then felt a gush of relief as Daniel's strong hands halted her progress, sweeping her upwards and cushioning her against his chest. He held her there for a comforting moment, marvelling at the fact that although weary she could still manage a bright, dancing smile.

'Make your way carefully down the staircase,' he instructed, lowering her feet to the treads. 'Sky's waiting for you.'

Degsey watched Spring's progress with her all-seeing gaze. Nothing escaped her attention. Neither her smile nor the halo of light faltered as she watched Spring's journey to the safety of Sky's arms. Scooter darted around gleefully and there were lots of hugs as sister was reunited with sister.

Jonathan was now standing upright and gingerly testing the balcony for strength. The laser-bright halo from Degsey's tooth danced across his legs as he shifted his bodyweight this way and that. Nothing moved. The structure was as steady as a rock.

He edged his way down the balcony towards the staircase. He was still clutching the barn owl in his torn shirt and despite barely managing to remain upright he refused Daniel's offer of help and remained stubbornly independent of making it on his own.

Sky, Spring and Scooter watched anxiously from floor level.

Degsey remained on the table, bathed in sunlight.

'There . . . did it!' Jonathan almost collapsed with exhaustion as he finally reached the staircase. He grabbed Daniel gratefully, shaking and giddy with effort.

'Let's join Sky and get away from here,' Daniel said. 'Degsey can't keep smiling for ever.'

Jonathan accepted a steadying hand as he carefully made his way down the treads. He had his eyes fixed on Sky and Spring, showing them both a shaky but relieved grin, whereas Daniel kept snatching sideways glances at the greyhound.

Degsey had come unexpectedly into his life.

And now she had saved his life . . . All of their lives.

Not forgetting Seamus and Fin and a gold tooth.

The series of events tumbled over one another in Daniel's mind. He knew that had it not been for Degsey's help the staircase and balcony would now be just a tangled mass on the floor. He reflected grimly that the wall behind him was ignoring gravity by remaining upright. By rights it should have collapsed and brought the building crashing down around them.

The whole episode couldn't be explained sensibly and would only be believed if witnessed first hand. Any interested party, listening when the story was later repeated, would find it about as real as a hologram.

'Sweetheart!' Sky gathered Jonathan in her arms, planting tiny kisses on his forehead. 'Are you sure you're alright? No broken bones—just bruises?'

'I'm fine.' Jonathan exhaled a short sigh of relief to keep his nerves in check. His bare body was gleaming like moist putty and he displayed the purplish knock on his forearm with pride. 'I got the bruise rescuing the bam owl,' he said, handing the little body still wrapped in his shirt to Sky. 'It *will* be okay, won't it?'

Sky's lips were pressed together regretfully as she looked down at the owl's beautiful, heart-shaped face. The eyes were closed and as she felt inside the shirt, stroking the soft mottled brown wings, the lack of warmth confirmed the worst.

'Is he dead?' asked Spring in a half-whisper.

Sky nodded uncomfortably.

Jonathan looked away, distressed. 'H . . . He was alright when I picked him up from the balcony. He was dazed, but he was moving. That's why I wrapped him up in the shirt.'

'My guess is he broke his neck when the lorry hit him,' Sky said, applying gentle pressure at the base of the bird's head. She nodded to herself, confirming her thoughts. 'What you witnessed was probably just a series of nervous twitches. It happens. I'm very sorry.'

Jonathan nodded and let out a long, slow breath. 'I'll take him back to Oyster Gables and bury him.'

Degsey was getting restless. Daniel threw an anxious glance at her, watching as she shifted into a more comfortable position on the table. He was overwhelmed by the strength of her spirit but he could see that she was suddenly looking exhausted, panting now as she tried to gather more energy.

'We really ought to be moving,' he said, throwing a note of urgency into his voice. 'I know Degsey can work miracles, but we're pushing her special powers to the limits.'

Spring, Jonathan and Sky turned to look at the greyhound. In the heat of all the dramatic happenings they had failed to notice that Degsey was rapidly tiring as she constantly took stock of everything around her. The reassuring gold light which had seared at their eyes had lost its bright edge and was now gradually beginning to soften.

Scooter let out a yelp and jumped backwards as a piece of crumbling concrete plunged down from the roof. It narrowly missed his front paws, shattering into fragments.

'Something's happening to Degsey!' Spring exclaimed with nervous loudness. 'Her tooth . . . It's losing—'

'Its strength,' Jonathan put in, swallowing hard.

Daniel immediately saw the danger. He could feel a rumble beneath his feet as the crack in the wall began to widen. Little puffs of plaster indicated another tremor. 'Everyone outside!' he urged, grasping Scooter's collar. 'Degsey's powers are weakening so go now . . . Hurry!'

Feet trampled over floor debris in the rush for the door. Sky wrapped protective arms around Jonathan and Spring as she shepherded them outside. Daniel followed, grabbing Scooter's collar in order to get him clear of any danger. The boxer didn't want to leave Degsey and he was making his feelings firmly felt by sitting on his rump and stubbornly resisting. Daniel heaved and strained on the thick leather collar before physically dragging Scooter away.

Outside, everyone stood looking at everyone else. All faces were exhausted by the ordeal. Matted hair, faces smeared with brick dust, torn clothing and tiny cuts and scraped knuckles became apparent when examined in the bright sunshine.

The building shuddered once more. Daniel looked up as tiles shook loose and began to slide into the roof's gaping hole. They seemed to fall in slow motion—as if some mad magician was performing a trick with a gigantic pack of playing cards.

'Wait over there.' Daniel indicated a safe area about ten metres away. 'We're all standing too close. This building could collapse at any moment.'

They all felt weary and their eyes reflected their exhaustion as they began to walk to the point of safety—everyone that is, except Spring. She stood her ground, her lower lip jutting out stubbornly as she grabbed Daniel's arm to voice an urgent question.

'Why isn't Degsey with us? Why hasn't she followed us?'

'She's probably waiting for us to get clear,' Daniel said. 'She's still using her powers to prop up the structure . . . giving us time to find safety.'

'But you said her powers were weakening. She'll be killed if she doesn't come out.'

Daniel shifted uneasily. There was a tight pause.

The taste of salt fell on Spring's lip as she glared at him. 'We can't leave her . . . we just *can't!*'

'She'll be alright. She's a very clever dog who can take care of herself.'

Spring opened her mouth to argue but no words came. She was staring at the red warning sign attached to the building's door. Only it wasn't—not any more. Pressure from the loose bricks above had forced out the nails, splitting the wood and sending it crashing to the ground. A main supporting girder followed, dropping with such force that Daniel had only a split second to react. He threw both arms around Spring's waist and using almost a judo throw, lifted her, spun his body, and dived to safety. He landed heavily on his side with Spring cushioned protectively against his ribs.

'Are you alright, Daniel? Are you hurt?' Jonathan was behind him, trying desperately to pull him well clear of the building.

'I'm okay.' He mumbled the answer and winced from the pain in his side as he tried to sit upright.

Sky helped Spring to her feet and they all managed to stagger the few extra metres to complete safety.

Then the unthinkable happened.

The fallen girder released a reaction of ruthless demolition. In a tidal wave of force each of the four walls folded like cardboard and tumbled inwards. It sent bricks thundering earthwards to be reduced to rubble.

Spring's head was bent, her fair fall of hair obscuring her features as she clasped her hands to her ears. Sky and Jonathan had both covered their eyes and turned away, leaving only Daniel to witness the scene of destruction. In less than ten seconds the entire structure was reduced to nothing more than a flattened pile of debris shrouded by a dust cloud rising slowly into the atmosphere.

As the noise gradually ceased, Sky turned to take in the scene. She looked calm and controlled. 'Did Degsey manage to get out?' she asked Daniel. 'Have you seen her?'

He gave his head a vigorous shake.

Jonathan bit into his lip, adding numbly, 'Is she dead?'

'Don't speak like that!' Spring's eyes grew bright with unshed tears. 'That's a cruel and wicked thing to say. She's probably lying injured . . . waiting for us to help her . . . like she helped us.'

'Don't worry, Spring.' Daniel smiled to put her at ease, all the while keeping a sharp eye on the surroundings as little pockets of dust began to thin. 'If she's alive, we'll find her.'

Sky and Daniel moved forward with Scooter at their heels. It was like walking into a dense fog and they blinked repeatedly as floating grime stung their eyes. They picked their way carefully over the fallen rubble, holding hands to keep themselves steady as they used their limited vision to seek out any sign of the greyhound.

Scooter appeared hopeful. He'd got wind of a scent and had bounded away, barking as if to be followed. Sky tried to call him back but he just disappeared into a dense swirl of dust, his stump of a tail wagging furiously.

'I'm not holding out much hope of finding Degsey', Sky said, keeping her voice low so that Spring couldn't catch the words. 'I hate to say it, but maybe Jonathan's right.'

Daniel nodded reluctantly and squeezed Sky's hand, pointing out danger in the shape of a broken window frame surrounded by spikes of glass. They skirted round it, both now aware that a constant, freshening breeze had sprung up. It ruffled their hair and helped blow away the dust. Suddenly, fractured slabs of concrete previously just a hazy blur, were now taking on a more definite shape.

Seconds passed—then amidst all the rubble they saw Scooter.

A pocket of dust had swirled away at ground level revealing the boxer encircling the legs of the metal-framed canteen table. Sky and Daniel exchanged glances and blinked at each other as if they had just woken up. They both held their breath as the upper cloud of murky dust lifted and was wafted away on the breeze.

'*Degsey!*' Daniel's bruised side caused him to wince as he shouted out the name. How the table had survived the destruction was a total mystery to him. And how the greyhound still came to be lying on it was nothing less than a miracle.

Spring and Jonathan both gave a yell of delight and sprinted over the rubble to join the group. Sky was already at the table, running experienced eyes and hands over the dog's head and body, checking for injuries. She had spotted a bright sheen of blood as it trailed in a lacy pattern along the back edge of the table and she was now trying to trace the cause.

She said, gently and with great relief, 'All I can find is a cut just above the base of the tail—not deep enough for stitches—just a bit messy. It was probably caused by the edge of a falling roof tile.'

'Can you fix it?' Daniel asked.

'Not here. I didn't bring my first-aid case.'

'Better leave it to Seamus,' Jonathan said sensibly. 'He'll have some leaves or bits of old twig to help heal a cut. He won't want you fiddling with it.'

Tears glittered in Spring's eyes as she leaned against the table. She pressed her face against the greyhound's muscular neck and brushed her lips across the brindle ear markings. 'Seamus said you were a special dog. I know you've hurt yourself, but thank you so much for smiling.'

Degsey rested her head in the crook of Spring's arm and looked up at her with peaceful, contented eyes. Spring squeezed her tightly, flushing with pleasure as the greyhound nuzzled closer.

'How come Degsey didn't get crushed?' Jonathan threw Daniel an inquiring glance. 'By rights the table should have been flattened . . . I don't get it?'

'I don't understand either,' Daniel admitted, fingering his jaw for inspiration. 'My guess is—and it's only a guess that she surrounded herself with some sort of protective force-field.'

'Force-field? You mean electricity?'

'Maybe.'

'Or magnetism might work,' Jonathan speculated.

'Who cares how she did it,' Sky put in. 'Let's all be grateful that she's safe and that because of her, we're safe too.'

'Oh, so it *isn't* hocus-pocus?' Daniel put his hand on her shoulder, a mischievous query in his dark eyes. 'You believe in Degsey's special powers?'

'I didn't,' she confessed quietly, 'especially after what happened at Scamperbuck Ring. But now I believe Degsey is a greyhound with an incredible gift.'

She heaved a sigh and looked almost relaxed as she spoke. Daniel's arm lifted and she slid under it to be drawn close to his side, her head coming to rest quite naturally on his shoulder.

Daniel ran his fingertips through her messed up hair and glanced at the smudges of brick dust on her face. 'Ms Patakin you look terrible,' he said.

'Ditto, Mr Rusk,' she responded with amusement.

Jonathan was puzzled by his sister's earlier words. 'Scamperbuck Ring?' he queried, blinking blue eyes. 'I don't understand. How could releasing some foxes change your mind about Degsey?'

Daniel and Sky exchanged confidential little glances but said nothing.

'Is it a secret?' Jonathan pressed.

'Could be,' Daniel hedged.

Degsey appeared to have recovered her spent energy. She looked knowingly at Spring as her left eyelid drooped in what could have been a final shaking off of fatigue, or maybe a subtle wink.

'And Degsey's keeping the secret,' she said.

*　　*　　*

Tony Ryker's patience was wearing thin. He wasn't used to carrying out menial tasks—to fetch and carry—but that's exactly what circumstances had forced him to do. He was dressed in overall-type trousers, tucked into rubber boots, and an old shirt buttoned tightly across his flabby stomach. The sleeves were rolled up and sweat patches stained the neck, back and armpits.

'Damn you Griggsy!' he said loudly and with feeling, letting his words echo around the walls of the warehouse.

Nobody heard him but the sudden outburst caused one of the stolen Penhill horses to turn it's head and give a loud snort. Ryker responded by yelling abuse at the animal and only just resisted hurling a broom in its direction.

The old fertiliser warehouse had been converted to hold up to twenty horses in separate stalls—and many times in the past it had been bursting to overflowing. Now, as Ryker swept the last pile of soiled bedding and manure into a muck sack and heaved the load onto his shoulder, he pondered on the unsatisfactory fact that at present it housed only three.

Thursday night's haul would have meant plenty of profit if things had gone to plan and they'd returned to Hele with the full ten-animal haul. But, as Ryker lugged the waste manure to the outside dung heap, he reflected bitterly that through his partner's stupidity to avoid a knock-out dart, the evening's work had been barely worthwhile.

'Glad you're coping alright.' Griggs suddenly appeared from nowhere. He was wearing a clean white shirt, with the sleeves rolled up over his bony elbows, and neatly pressed jeans complimented by a new pair of trainers. A smirk settled on his face as he decided to turn the tables and take pleasure in Ryker's present discomfort. 'Try and distribute the weight more evenly on your shoulder, Tony, otherwise you might drop the dung.'

Ryker swung his body as if to let the load fly in Griggs's direction. The sudden movement caused his partner to duck, but Ryker stopped short, cursed under his breath, and let the steaming contents of the sack shuffle out to add another layer to the huge manure heap.

'Tut-tut.' Griggs wagged a mocking finger at the big man. 'I thought for a moment you were going to unload that on me. Temper, temper, Tony, think of your blood pressure.'

'I was thinking more about my wallet,' Ryker replied sourly. 'This pile of dung has reached the point where it's worth eighty pounds to the local garden centre—so I'm not wasting any of it on you!'

Griggs gave a humourless chuckle. He was looking and feeling much perkier than yesterday—a fact that hadn't gone unnoticed by Ryker.

'How come you're looking so healthy, Griggsy? You could have driven the old horses to Harwich—no problem.'

'Did you manage to postpone it?'

'After a lot of phone calls and excuses, yes. I've put the trip back a week.'

'Good. I still feel a bit fragile. I'm in no fit state to drive the travelling box.'

Ryker gave him a sharp look. 'So how come you're out of bed and bothering me?'

'Thought I'd show willing. Maybe do a bit of housework.' Amusement edged his words as he added, 'Nothing too taxing . . . some light dusting around the home perhaps.'

'How about feeding the old horses and cleaning out the water troughs?'

'Too hard, Tony. You're forgetting I was shot at.'

'I wish I *could* forget it,' Ryker said, barely curbing his impatience as he strode towards the paddock. 'If you're not going to make yourself useful then stop annoying me. Go back to the mobile home and rest.'

'I'll stick around for a bit . . . You know, put my personal pain to the back of my mind. Partners like us should always have a caring and sharing attitude.'

Griggs was enjoying the role reversal game too much to back off now. Ryker had propped a bale of hay against the paddock's five-barred gate and Griggs watched, arms folded, as the big man gave him a glowering look and cut the string with a pocket knife. As half the bale was removed, Griggs made a generous flourish of lifting the latch on the gate and beckoning Ryker through.

'Don't over burden your strength, Griggsy,' Ryker breathed in a loud exaggerated way. 'I would hate you to add a slipped disc to the rest of your troubles.'

The six elderly horses were at the far end of the paddock when they heard the gate creak open. They all turned to look, and depending on their physical state, either managed a shambling trot or a reasonable canter in their efforts to be first to the hay. It was almost a mini cavalry charge and Mister Rafferty headed the group. Clumps of earth flew as the chestnut cob braked, pivoted, and very nearly bulled into Ryker's shoulder. Having unbalanced the big man, he tore out a lump of fodder with his teeth, before skittering away.

'Get back!' Ryker brandished the broom handle at the remainder of the snorting horses and regained his footing. As they scattered away he turned quickly to Griggs. 'I had problems yesterday with that caravan horse,' he grated. 'The animal's a definite trouble-maker.'

Griggs's mouth quirked at one comer as he gazed at Ryker with a gleam of amusement. 'Face facts, Tony. You just can't handle 'em—you never could.'

'Don't talk rubbish.'

'You're too soft . . . I'm telling you.'

'They're a bad-tempered bunch of nags because you starve them,' he said stiffly, thrusting the half bale of hay into Griggs's hands. 'I'm aware of your secretive games, my little ferret. I warned you about cutting back on their food and pocketing the extra money. Now shake that hay out—and make sure they each get a fair share!'

Griggs curled his lip in a gesture of defiance but the steely glare in Ryker's eyes told him the balance of power had once again shifted back in the big man's favour.

'I keep 'em hungry for a reason,' Griggs said, watching Ryker stroll back to the gate. 'With me around they know who's boss. They respect me. One word from Griggsy and they do as they're told.' He faced away from Ryker and pursed his lips in a shrill whistle. The sound brought five of the six horses obediently back at a very slow, wary trot.

'I think I've just proved my point,' he called out smugly, doing a cocky little walk as he distributed the hay at various feed stations around the paddock.

The point was proven—almost. The only fact he hadn't bargained for was Mister Rafferty's Irish antics. The old chestnut cob had cantered a full circuit of the paddock and was fast approaching Griggs from the rear. Ryker glimpsed the horse but said nothing to his partner. It was like an accident waiting to happen the big man thought, fighting down a grin as he leaned casually against the five-barred gate.

'I can't handle them, eh?' he murmured to himself. 'So let's see if you can.'

'You say something?' Griggs muttered sullenly.

Ryker shrugged and shook his head.

Griggs turned to make his way back to the gate in a slow fashion and began absently picking stray bits of hay from his white shirt. He wasn't really looking anywhere—certainly not to his rear—and he appeared totally unaware that Mister Rafferty was heading straight for him.

The old cob horse had dragged out some hay from a feeding station and this was now streaming from his mouth as he munched, ran, and homed in on his target. Old and stiff he very definitely was, but he could still show a swift turn of foot when a devilish mood was upon him.

Griggs saw the horse—just a Chestnut flash at the corner of his vision—but it was much too late to avoid any action. Mister Rafferty arrowed in, ears flattened, eyes determinedly set. He blundered into Griggs shoulder-blades, hammering all breath from his body and tipping him forward into a mound of steaming, freshly dropped manure. Griggs gurgled, coughed, and thrashed about on the ground.

'Respect? Boss-man?' Ryker threw Griggs's earlier words back at him and laughed loudly—a rich oily chuckle that seemed to come from far down below his sagging belt. 'I suggest you remind this old horse that you're in charge!'

Mister Rafferty eyed the broom in Ryker's hands and decided not to take any chances. He turned quickly on his haunches and wheeled away to join the rest of the group.

Griggs bit teeth which needed brushing into his thin bottom lip and lifted himself up on his elbows. He cursed the dark wet stain which was spreading across the front of his neat white shirt and frantically mopped up the streaky beginnings of a nosebleed with the back of his hand.

'Blood and horse pee everywhere!' he yelled at Ryker. 'These clothes were fresh on. Now look at the state I'm in!'

'I'm looking, my little ferret.' Ryker's stomach threatened to burst from his belt as he laughed. 'It couldn't have happened to a nicer person. Tut, tut, what a terrible, terrible accident.'

'It wasn't an accident! You said that the old horse was a trouble-maker.'

'But then I could have been wrong,' he mocked softly. 'Unlike you, I'm not an expert. According to the Martin Griggs Book of Horse Knowledge—a rather slim little pamphlet—I know very little about horses.'

Griggs ignored Ryker's sarcasm and exhaled bitterly as he climbed to his feet. His eyes focussed on the group of old horses and narrowed with evil intent as they settled on Mister Rafferty.

'The sooner that old cob ends up as dog meat,' he spat, 'the happier I'll be!'

CHAPTER EIGHT

Saturday morning found Jonathan and Spring standing by the caravan watching attentively as Seamus began snipping a bandage dressing from the base of Degsey's tail.

'Hold her . . .' Seamus's voice was a little croaky so he began again. 'Hold her head nice and steady now. Good, good, that be fine.'

Degsey didn't flinch at the scissors—just stood erect and still, switching between the trusting, affectionate gaze she kept for her master and the loving, watchful glances she reserved for her offspring.

The three pups played on the grass verge nearby, getting up to mischief by taking little nips at Scooter's ears and then using the speed in their whippy light-framed bodies to avoid the boxer's playful revenge.

Little Degsey appeared to be growing up fast. She was far more agile than her two brothers and had the most energetic nature. In common with her mother she seemed to fear nothing, and also possessed the uncanny ability to sense things that were about to happen—especially when Spring was close at hand. This telepathic instinct was still very new but Spring had experienced it in a few simple ways that couldn't be explained.

She knew that she only had to concentrate very hard on the puppy's name and Little Degsey would be there to find her—to protect her from harm.

Even this morning's dip in the sea with Jonathan at Delight Cove had resulted in a type of rescue. At the water's edge Little Degsey had made a nuisance of herself by running in front of them, tripping them up, encircling their legs and making it impossible for them to swim. They had managed no more than a brief paddle before the puppy's persistent barking and frustrating blocking tactics had forced them to abandon any sort of beach enjoyment. On the walk back to Oyster Gables Jonathan had called the greyhound an 'irritating pest' and given Spring firm instructions never to bring Little Degsey to Delight Cove again.

Only later, by listening to the local radio news, had they discovered that the hot weather had brought thousands of poisonous Orange Compass jellyfish to the Swiftly coastline. Thirty bathers had needed treatment in hospital, and only by not swimming had Spring and Jonathan avoided the possibility of a very nasty sting.

'Can you use your wee fingers to lift off the herb from me darlin' girl's tail,' Seamus was saying to Jonathan without much response. He looked up from Degsey, pushed his glasses further up the bridge of his nose and raised a wispy eyebrow. 'Are we disturbin' your thoughts, me boy? You look t'be miles away 'n all.'

Jonathan *was* miles away. He was still feeling a bit sheepish about his earlier remarks to Spring, especially as his sister had given a blow-by-blow account of what happened on the beach to all at lunchtime. When asked for his comments he had brushed off the jellyfish episode as nothing more than 'over excitement' on Little Degsey's part. But in private he had to admit he was probably wrong.

Now, as Little Degsey gave up the game with Scooter and turned to hold Jonathan's gaze, he could see something in the puppy's eyes; an all-seeing, all-knowing twinkle which only she and her mother possessed. It was strange; a sort of bottomless depth around each coal-black pupil where every shade of brown merged into brilliance.

'S . . . sorry.' Jonathan blinked rapidly to shake himself free of Little Degsey's gaze and focussed on Seamus. 'W . . . what did you ask me to do?'

'The sphagnum moss.' Seamus's watery blue eyes narrowed slightly. 'Can you be liftin' it off so old Seamus can look at the wound there.'

Jonathan carefully removed the herbal package that resembled an old tea bag from the base of Degsey's tail. The cut had knitted together nicely, leaving only a thin trail of scar tissue.

'It's mended t'be sure.' A smile wafted briefly over Seamus's face. 'Me wee girl be as good as new.'

'What is sphagnum moss?' Spring queried.

'Looks like green gunge.' Jonathan pulled a face as he examined the piece in his hand.

Seamus explained that it was a forest herb containing natural iodine and other healing properties. He went on to reveal how he'd first cleansed the wound with a strong extract of rosemary leaves and added some meadowsweet herb to Degsey's drinking water to help the repairing powers of her body.

'It's healed remarkably quickly,' Spring observed, runnning a hand over the greyhound's neck. 'I think even Sky would be surprised.'

'There be many sorts of doctorin,' Seamus pointed out, 'but y'both know that me wee girl be used to the ways of this old tinker. I be admittin' that y'sister be specially fine at curin' the woodland creatures of their ills—far, far better than old Seamus. It's true . . .'tis tings I've seen her do wi' me own eyes. Marvellest tings. Sewin' and stitchin', mendin' broken wings, splintin' fractured bones . . .'He moved his head in a series of slow thoughtful nods, adding, 'Ah sure, by Jaminee, she be a saviour—a wonderful girl.'

'Who's a wonderful girl?' Shack loomed over Jonathan's shoulder. It was another hot day and his unfastened check shirt hung loosely over his jeans. 'You can only be talking about Degsey. I heard she'd been hurt again—what a heroine! When Daniel told me how she saved your lives in the collapsing building, I thought . . .'He didn't finish the sentence, just looked at the dog and gave a long whistle of admiration.

Degsey's tail flailed at the air as she gazed up at him fondly.

'Is the fallow deer alright?' Spring asked, concerned, 'I went to look for him this morning but he must have been moved.'

'He's doing well. He's in his own outside pen now and the damaged hind leg is improving daily. With luck he'll be released next week.'

She nodded, pleasure showing in her pale-lashed eyes.

'Your busted lip's looking better,' Jonathan told him.

'It's fine.' Shack fingered the slight blemish on his mouth.

'You must have used the famous sphagnum moss cure.'

'The what?'

'Seamus used it on Degsey. It's slimy green stuff, Shacky, but it healed her cut.'

Shack caught the lilt of humour in Jonathan's voice and fell in with the joke. He grinned, said he'd used cold compresses on his lip, and then glanced at Seamus. 'Degsey looks no worse for yesterday's ordeal. You seem to have fixed her up a treat.'

'Tis true, she be well fit. Back to her old self and no mistake.'

Shack regarded him steadily. 'And how about you, Seamus? Are you back to *your* old self?'

'I—I be fine,' he mumbled, making a determined effort to look as healthy as possible.

Seamus had always taken a pride in his personal appearance—always looking neat and well-groomed, whatever the occasion. But now, to Shack's observant eyes, there was a loss of vitality. His waistcoat had been wrongly buttoned so that one side was higher than the other; there was two day's growth of stubble shading his jaw; and the brightly coloured strip of cloth that usually fastened his pony-tail had been substituted for the convenience of an elastic band.

Shack was also aware that he seemed to have dramatically aged just in the last few days. His skin had a waxy look, his eyes lacked their usual sparkle, and his entire appearance had clouded over with either distress or pain or a combination of both.

'How's your chest?' quizzed Shack.

'Er . . . chest?'

'You had a moan about a burning sensation when I brought you breakfast this morning.'

He gave a little shivering movement of his head and shoulders. 'It was nothing, young 'un, I be fussin' too much. It was a wee twinge—a touch of indigestion maybe.' He flexed his jaws, working hard to show a smile and added, 'Sky's cookin' be very rich. It be so luverly that I reckon old Seamus be eatin' too much.'

His voice hinted of weariness and he wasn't fooling anybody about 'indigestion', especially Shack.

'You can't be eating too much,' Spring announced, blinking puzzlement. 'Daniel said that you hardly touched your food this lunchtime.'

'Are you ill?' Jonathan asked bluntly.

'A few aches and pains, me boy. Old age be creepin' up fast.'

Shack's eyes were troubled. 'Megan prepared a lamb casserole yesterday,' he said, 'but she told me you refused to even taste it.'

'I be more inclined towards veggie food now,' he replied quickly.

'Then I expect you ate the cauliflower cheese,' Spring said.

'Ay, it was grand. I fair scoffed the lot.'

Shack knew he wasn't telling the whole truth—which for Seamus was totally out of character. He didn't want to pester the old man, but he was seriously worried that he might need a doctor.

'You may have picked at a bit of the cauliflower,' Shack pressed his point home, 'but the majority of it ended up being fed to the puppies.'

Seamus looked baffled. Creases ran up his forehead and his mouth opened and closed several times.

'H . . . How you be knowin' that? You be away yesterday . . . At home, restin'.'

'Yep, I was.'

Jonathan and Spring exchanged puzzled glances.

'You had visitors just after Hannah brought your lunch.' Shack looked at Seamus coolly. 'They came to inspect Oyster Gables and asked if they could have a guided tour of your wagon.'

'Oh ay.' He nodded and moistened his lips. 'It was a Mr and Mrs Wilson.'

'And Mrs Wilson was very worried when she saw you giving your grub to the puppies. She thought you looked breathless and unwell and she blamed herself for disturbing you.'

'Never heard of people called Wilson,' Jonathan piped up. 'Do you know them, Shacky? Are they friends of yours?'

'They're my mother and stepfather,' he said simply. 'They've come down from Yorkshire, touring Devon in their camper van. After Megan told them I was off sick they popped in to see me and dad at Yelland.'

'And you talked about Seamus.'

'Amongst other things.'

Seamus's face lengthened expressively as he looked at Shack. 'You havin' lots of names be confusin', he grumbled, fingering his earring. 'I don't know where I be with all this choppin' and changin'.'

Spring looked at Jonathan. He shrugged.

'Not lots,' Spring pointed out to Seamus. 'Only his surname is different because his mother remarried.'

'And his first name be diff'rent too.'

Shack cleared his throat with an embarrassed little cough. 'I have to move off,' he said quickly. 'There's a staff meeting ... in the office. They'll be expecting me. See you ... er ... later.' He finished weakly and began backing away.

Jonathan could sense Shack's discomfort and guessed that Seamus had touched a raw nerve. He reckoned there was some fun to be had at Shack's expense so he wasn't going to let the matter drop.

'His first name's Shack, his surname's Skinner,' he told Seamus, deliberately raising his voice just enough to halt Shack in his tracks. 'Nobody ever calls him anything else.'

Shack turned, waiting for a word he didn't want to hear.

Seamus puffed his cheeks and continued, 'Mrs Wilson, she be askin' where she could find Cedric. It's me son, she be tellin' me and he be workin' on some trainin' thingumy at Oyster Gables.'

'Cedric!' Jonathan exclaimed. His eyes lit up, then rolled comically. 'Ha! So Shacky's first name is really Cedric! No wonder you were messed up.'

'Fair twizzled t'be sure me boy. I be tinkin' Mrs Wilson be at the wrong animal shelter. No Cedric here I tells her, only Danny boy and Shack the donkey man.'

Jonathan laughed out loud.

'Is Cedric really your name?' Spring looked from Jonathan to Shack and stifled a giggle.

Shack scowled and made a grunting sound as he nodded.

'Can . . . can we call you Ceddie for short?' Jonathan was barely able to squeeze out the words.

'No you can't!' Shack ran an agitated hand through his hair. 'Haven't you any work to do, little dude? Like cleaning Mister Rafferty's harness? I thought that was a weekly chore?'

'Not much point, young 'un.' Seamus drew a small breath of hopelessness as Spring's elbow prompted Jonathan to stop laughing. 'It's time this old tinker be knowin' that his poor old cob horse be gone for good.'

Shack walked the few steps back to the group, tucked his thumbs into his belt and faced Seamus. Jonathan was still grinning, but for the moment at least he was silent.

'I can't promise anything,' Shack began, 'but there's a possibility—a small one—that we may have a lead as to where Mister Rafferty's being kept. I don't want to raise your hopes because we might be too late. The horse may have been sold on to someone else. I think we'll know tomorrow. Trust me.'

Seamus stared at Shack. There were tiny flutters in his throat but he said nothing, just nodded, letting unspoken words pass between them.

'No time to waste,' Spring announced. She crossed to the rear of the caravan and opened the pan-box. She began lifting out various pieces of Mister Rafferty's harness, threading an arm through the huge coil of reins and heaving them onto her shoulder.

'I'll get the buckets, saddle-soap, silver polish and cloths from the tack-room,' Jonathan said, bobbing his head approvingly at Spring's actions. He walked quickly past Shack, avoiding any eye contact as he struggled to hold back a grin.

Seamus realised the significance of Shack's words and was grateful for his honesty. A warm wave of excitement washed over him and his eyes now reflected a flinty brightness that spelled hope.

'Look . . .'Shack began, 'you do realise this harness cleaning could all be a waste of time?'

'But you did say there was a chance,' Spring said.

'Yes I know,' Shack agreed. 'But I also said it was only a small one.'

Jonathan made sure he was well out of Shack's reach before risking one final comment. 'It was your idea that we do some work,' he quipped, calling out over his shoulder before making a dash for it. 'Well now we're ready . . . *Ceddie!'*

*   *   *

Sky gathered up the animal record cards she had just updated, stretched her arms and switched off the shelter's computer. She turned in the work-station chair to face Daniel who was making coffee. The three were in the Oyster Gables office and the staff meeting was about to begin.

'So tell us everything about last night's excursion,' Daniel prompted Shack. 'Every little detail—I'll be making notes.'

Shack swivelled back and forth in the squeaky chair behind the roll-top desk and began by giving a blow-by-blow account of his visit to the Silver Seagull at Ilfracombe. He'd travelled there with his stepfather, he told them, leaving his mum and dad at home in Yelland to catch up on each other's news.

They'd taken a mini-cab, and during the drive Shack had given precise details to his stepfather of all the recent happenings. He'd spoken about Mister Rafferty's disappearance, the outbreak of horse rustling in the area, and the early morning visit they'd had from the tattooed man and his partner. He had explained about the book matches and the reason for the evening's outing. Everything, including the possible outcome, had been discussed and mulled over. By the time they'd picked up Sophie, Shack had decided to let his stepfather do the talking at the restaurant. The landlord of the Silver Seagull, he reasoned, might respond more willingly to an older person's questioning.

'So you and your step-dad are finally getting on,' Sky remarked, taking her mug of coffee from Daniel's outstretched hand.

'Yes . . . everything's cool between us. I suppose I couldn't be bothered to get to know him before—but last night we became good mates. He seems nice enough and I'm pleased for mum . . . His name's Ken by the way.'

Daniel handed Shack a coffee, sat on the chair by the workbench and began making notes on a clipboard that was stuffed with paper.

'So what did Ken manage to find out?'

'He did really well. They talked about golf for a bit—that's the landlord's game. There are loads of trophies and shields around the bar, so as Ken plays too he soon latched onto the small talk.'

'Were you at the bar with them?'

He shook his head. 'I got a couple of Cokes and sat with Sophie at a table nearby. I didn't want to cramp Ken's style.'

Sky asked how the topic of stolen horses had entered the conversation.

'Ken made up some story about wanting to buy a pony for his daughter. He'd just bought a house with a few spare acres at West Down, he told the landlord, and he mentioned very matter-of-factly that a neighbour had spoken of a horse-trader who could sometimes be found at the Silver Seagull.'

Daniel leaned forward with his elbows on his knees. 'Did Ken get a name?'

Shack nodded and went on to explain that several names were suggested. About four horse-traders used the Silver Seagull on a regular basis and his stepfather had listened to the comments on each, patiently playing along, and nodding in all the right places. Anyone of the horse-traders, Shack explained, could have fitted the description of the big man in the mask—but everything changed when Ken dropped the scorpion tattoo into the conversation.

'The landlord knew immediately,' Shack went on. 'He named him as Tony Ryker and told Ken he had a partner named Martin Griggs. He wasn't sure where they lived—fairly local he thought—but here's the good bit . . .'Shack sipped his coffee and paused for effect. 'They visit the Silver Seagull every Sunday for lunch. One-thirty, on the dot. They never miss. Apparently Griggs does the cooking for six days of the week, and he insists on having a Sunday break.'

'Griggs being the skinny one?' Sky queried.

'Yep, pink panties—the one Daniel darted.'

Daniel scribbled more notes on the clipboard. 'Ken did great,' he said. 'Now we can pin Ryker and Griggs to a definite time and location.'

'It's Sunday tomorrow.' Sky flicked a concerned fingernail against her bottom teeth.

'No problem.' Daniel sounded confident as he drained his coffee. 'My plan can be put into action at any time—besides, we can't afford to wait another week.'

'Which brings us to Seamus,' Shack put in. 'I'm very worried about him. He's been complaining of chest pains. He should see a doctor.'

'He's a stubborn old boy,' Daniel said. 'I've suggested it many times but he won't listen.'

'How bad is he, Shack?' Sky asked after a short silence.

'I think he looks terrible. He's a shadow of how he looked when I first met him. I just know that something is very, very wrong.'

'Mister Rafferty's the cure,' Daniel stated, drawing a long concerned breath. 'Just let's hope the old cob horse is still alive.'

Sky pressed an index finger to her lips thoughtfully. 'I agree he's pining for Mister Rafferty, but we better not take any chances.

After we've finished this meeting I'll ring the surgery and arrange for a doctor to call Monday morning.'

Daniel swung the conversation back to the rescue plan. He turned to Sky. 'Did you make arrangements to borrow a small Rice trailer?'

She nodded. One of our livery clients is bringing it over tonight.'

'Perfect.'

'Are we going to steal Mister Rafferty back?' Shack queried.

'No, the stealing will be done by Ryker and Griggs. They're the experts.'

'I'm not really following this?' Sky looked bewildered.

'I'll explain everything in a moment. Just remember *you're* the main person in this plan.'

'I've another piece of gen . . .' Shack said, remembering. 'The landlord mentioned Ryker's make of car. He was doing his best to persuade Ken to use another horse-trader—calling Ryker "dodgy" and suchlike—but Ken kept trying to suck out more info and insisted that Ryker came highly recommended.'

'So the car . . . ?' Daniel prompted.

'A red BMW—almost new. The landlord spoke of it in case Ken wanted to meet up on a weekday. If Ryker's in the Silver Seagull, he said, then you'll always see his car parked on the forecourt.'

'Drinking and driving never mix.' Sky tut-tutted.

Daniel agreed but he was impressed with this latest piece of knowledge. 'Pity we can't get a look at the car. I'd like to know if it's fitted with a tow-bar.'

'It is.' Shack was definite. 'Ken told me that Ryker uses a large travelling horse-box to go to the auctions, but for private deals he hitches a solo job to the BMW.'

'This couldn't be better.' Daniel placed some more ticks in the paper margin on his clipboard. His pencil hovered against one item and his eyes flicked to Sky. 'We'll need a couple of nets something big and strong. Does the shelter have any?'

'There are some nets in one of the tack-room hampers. We used them once to rescue a muntjac deer.'

Sky's words were rewarded with a grateful nod from Daniel as another tick found its way onto the clipboard.

'What exactly are you doing, dude?' Shack fingered his chin.

'Double-checking that we have all the equipment.' He flicked over some pages, checking each tick. 'We do. Everything has come together just great. We're ready.'

Shack winked at Sky and leaned towards Daniel. He deliberately lowered his voice to a whisper. 'Is it a secret or are you going to give us the details of this plan?'

Daniel hunched forward in concentration. 'Right,' he began, 'what we do is this . . .'

CHAPTER NINE

Martin Griggs crammed a final forkful of roast chicken into his mouth and blotted gravy from his lips with a paper napkin. His cheeks inflated as he burped a couple of times—loudly. It was just after two p.m. and they were finishing their regular Sunday meal at the Silver Seagull.

Ryker looked up from his roast beef lunch and glared. 'Didn't your mother ever teach you any manners?' he rasped. 'Belching like that is damned rude.'

Griggs reached for the free book of matches clipped to the menu and tore a couple out as he shifted moodily in his chair, His face held a bored expression as he struck them, letting them splutter and flare before blowing them out.

Ryker leaned forward, forearms on the table; knife and fork held upright as if to stamp his authority, 'Okay, so what's the matter? Why the old woman act? I can always tell when you're crabby.'

'Sunday should be a day of rest,' he muttered, probing about inside his mouth with a dead match until he'd fished out a shred of chicken from a back tooth, 'I thought, just for this afternoon, we could give work a miss. I'm fed up with tearing round the countryside looking for horses to steal. I'm still not fully recovered. My body is telling me that I should be enjoying a lazy afternoon . . . watching a DVD or something.'

'Your body can be bone idle when you're moody.'

'Untrue. I'm still in the recovery. It's always rush, rush, rush with you.'

Ryker exhaled silently. 'Time is a luxury, Griggsy, which I can't afford to waste. I'd like to be back in Berkshire, playing golf, having a drink with my friends at the Country Club—but I'm prepared to stick it out because I've a wife who spends money like it's going out of fashion and two kids at a private school. Lazing around in your mobile home doesn't increase the wad of money in my back pocket. Horses do!'

'Well I'm getting pretty sick of horses. I smell of 'em and my clothes stink of 'em. Even the chicken I've just eaten tasted of 'em.'

'So next time have a shower before you come out. Your hygiene habits are non-existent.'

'Ha-ha, very damn funny,' he replied, almost to himself. 'Have a dig at Griggsy . . . he's always good for a cheap laugh.'

'So what do you want to do?' Ryker responded. 'Break up the partnership?'

'Maybe.' He paused, his mouth surly, brooding on it. 'It's a possibility.'

Ryker was unimpressed. It was a familiar pattern and he'd heard the same old record being played many times. There was only a month left before they went their separate ways, and his partner was getting bored—maybe even a little frightened. But Griggs wasn't going to quit now, Ryker told himself. He'd moan and groan, but he'd finish the season as he always did and be back for more of the same next year.

'So what will you do?' Ryker asked, still mocking him slightly. 'Go back to stealing wallets and signing on at the Social Security Agency?'

'I told you—I'm thinking about it!' He glared and rose from his chair. 'I'm going to the loo,' he added, pulling a handkerchief from his pocket. 'I can feel a nosebleed coming on. It always does when you get me stressed. Sometimes I think you do it deliberately.'

'If you have any more nosebleeds, my little ferret, your brains will fall out.'

Griggs ignored the sarcasm. 'Do you want me to order coffee?'

'Whose turn is it to pick up the bill?'

'Mine.'

Ryker smirked. 'Then make it two coffees and two brandies.'

Griggs bristled aggressively at that. 'But I bought the drinks when we arrived!'

Ryker just looked at him with a long, unblinking stare.

Griggs mouthed a swear word, turned and threaded his way towards the men's room.

* * *

Sky, dressed in jodhpurs, lightweight polo-neck jumper and leather riding boots was perfectly positioned on the Silver Seagull's forecourt. She'd arrived in Daniel's Volvo with the Rice trailer hitched to the tow-bar and had managed to park alongside Ryker's BMW. Following the plan to the letter she'd then opened the Volvo's bonnet and was now peering worriedly into the rather dirty engine.

All of this was being watched by Griggs from a small frosted top window that was slightly ajar in the toilet. The men's room overlooked the forecourt, and he was perfectly positioned to spy on her every move.

He studied the chestnut horse in the trailer, experience telling him that he was looking at a classy show animal and not a run of the mill hack.

Spring had spent several hours plaiting Sir Galahad's mane and forelock and then weaved in eye-catching strips of coloured ribbon along the dock of his tail. Sky, Daniel and Jonathan had all pitched in and performed various grooming tasks. Body brushes, curry combs and wisps had all been used to great effect and the end result of highlighting the neck, shoulder and quarter muscles was spectacular. The final polishing had been left to Shack who had become quite an expert at 'strapping' a horse with a stable rubber. He had worked like a demon, not stopping until Sir Galahad's coat shone like the finest spun silk.

Griggs nodded his approval, gently blew his nose, and switched his gaze back to Sky. She had moved from the engine to the cab and was playing her part convincingly as she tried the ignition several times, letting the engine turn over noisily but unsuccessfully. She knew the Volvo wouldn't start because she'd switched on the immobiliser under the dashboard, but the impression to anyone watching—and she hoped they were—was one of typical frustration shown by a motorist having problems.

Certainly, the act had fooled Griggs. He was watching her every move, a faint smile playing around his lips as he heard Sky utter several loud curses and kick at a tyre with her boot. She then moved to the Rice trailer, stood on the rear ledge, and appeared to be saying a few calming words to the horse.

Unbeknown to Griggs she was having a whispered conversation with Daniel and Shack who were crouched uncomfortably under the belly of Sir Galahad.

They'd rehearsed the hiding routine with expert precision last night. Nothing had been left to chance. Spring and Jonathan had guided them this way and that and told them the best position to adopt to be tucked away . . . then chalk marks had been etched on the floor as an aid for their feet. Luckily, Sir Galahad was big enough and the trailer compact enough for them to be neatly hidden and screened from prying eyes. Even Degsey had been hidden from view. She was curled up in a straw-filled corner and covered with an empty bran sack.

'We're parked next to Ryker's BMW car,' Sky told them through half-closed lips. 'I've angled the trailer so it's level with his tow-bar.'

Daniel shifted position. He lifted his head level with Sir Galahad's hind leg and grinned up at her reassuringly. 'Thumping the tyre with your foot was a neat touch . . . we could hear your loud swearing from inside.'

'I didn't think you knew such filthy words.' Shack grinned and rubbed life into a knee that was suffering pins and needles.

A smile showed in her eyes. 'Only acting,' she said.

'And remember,' Daniel offered some quick advice, 'don't use Sir Galahad's real name. It could be known to Ryker and Griggs and they mustn't suspect that you're connected with Oyster Gables.'

'Understood. From now on he'll be known as Buckingham. I thought of it last night . . . It sounds royal and it suits him.' She patted the horse's rump and jumped down from the trailer's ledge.

Martin Griggs was still at the window. He watched all Sky's actions—saw her reach into the Volvo for a black velvet riding jacket and toss it casually over her arm. She was talking to herself, saying things which he presumed were angry grumbles about the breakdown, but which in reality were words of personal encouragement. She was trying to play down her fears and convince herself that she could carry off her part in front of strangers. She took a long prayerful breath and strode purposefully towards the Silver Seagull's entrance.

Griggs wiped his nose and left the men's room. The restaurant's bar was abuzz with laughter and chatter as he shouldered his way past customers and hurried back to Ryker.

The big man didn't look up as Griggs almost fell into his chair. He swirled a brandy round in his glass and said irritably, 'I suppose you've had another nosebleed? You've been gone long enough. The drinks arrived and I had to pay—'

'Shut up and listen.' Griggs cut him off.

Ryker immediately looked up. He was startled by Griggs's directness.

'There's a girl—late teens—with a horse and trailer in the car park.' Griggs tried to keep his voice level, but it was edged with excitement. 'Her car's broken down, so she's stuck. It looks like an expensive show-horse to me. Probably worth four or five times more than the stuff we usually steal.'

'Are you saying . . . ?'

Griggs nodded and took a swig at his brandy. He swallowed too much, coughed, and hiccoughed as the raw spirit burned his throat.

'Are you saying,' Ryker began again, 'that we should relieve this young lady of her four-legged friend?'

'If you mean steal the horse yes!'

Ryker showed a lopsided smile. 'That's not the way we operate, my little ferret. We always do our business under the cover of darkness. That's part of the reason we've never been caught. Going against a tried and trusted method could mean complications.'

'But this horse is being handed to us on a plate, Tony. We simply unhitch it from her car and re-hitch the trailer to the BMW.'

'I thought you were sick of horses? The smell, the—'

'I'm sick of driving all over the county to find 'em!' His words tumbled out angrily. 'This would only take us a couple of minutes and we could relax for the rest of the day . . .' His eyes flashed as he sucked in a noisy breath. 'Oh, why do I bother . . . ?'

Ryker's fingers drummed on the table. He was thinking.

'I'm surprised you're using your brains, Griggsy. Does this mean you're back on the firm? No more talk of ending the partnership?'

Griggs went to answer but pulled himself up. He could see Sky at the far end of the bar. She'd stopped to order an orange juice and was now picking her way towards the restaurant.

'Keep your voice down. Here comes the girl.' His words were clipped with tension. He gnawed at a thumb knuckle and lowered his eyes to the tablecloth.

Sky did a very good impression of ignoring them as she strode past, her gaze fixed on a landscape picture which hung on the far wall. Five tables were being used by diners, mainly those offering a view of the harbour. There were three unoccupied and one was perfectly positioned just to the rear of Ryker and Griggs.

She sat at it, placed her velvet riding jacket on a spare chair and began casually flicking through the menu. Her eyes scanned the various dishes of the day but her thoughts were very definitely elsewhere.

Ryker was wearing a short sleeved shirt and she'd instantly spotted the scorpion tattoo on his forearm.

Everything in Daniel's plan seemed to be coming together perfectly. She was sitting at the right table, watching the right men. Of that she had to be certain, and now she was. And yes, she thought fleetingly, letting her gaze stray to Ryker's partner—Spring had guessed right. Martin Griggs did have evil eyes.

'So?' Griggs asked in hushed tones. 'What do you reckon? Shall we have the horse away?'

'Maybe,' Ryker said, 'I'm thinking about it. I want to be convinced she's genuine. No need to be hasty. The girl's the one with the problem. Let's see how she intends to sort it out.'

Sky took a sip of her orange juice and pulled her mobile phone from the pocket of her velvet riding jacket. She could feel Ryker's eyes on her face, studying the various changes in her expression as she pressed several digits on the key-pad.

The number burred in her ear and then, as expected, Oyster Gables answering machine clicked in. She thought briefly of Megan and Hannah attending to the shelter's animals and then listened to her own recording on the machine's opening message. She kept up the pretence of appearing worried by flicking a concerned fingernail against her bottom teeth and then started a one-way conversation that she'd spent most of last night rehearsing. She spoke with a classy accent, deliberately rounding her vowels in order to portray an expensive upbringing.

'Hello, daddy darling . . . yes it's me . . .' She paused briefly, snatching a quick glance to Ryker and Griggs. They were both sitting silently, heads tilted, listening to her every word. She continued, 'I've got some beastly news . . . I'm not going to make it to the Somerset County Show. The car's been an absolute pig—you know misfiring and things—and now it's given up the ghost altogether. I've had a wretched time of it, daddy, and it's left me feeling totally drained.'

'Poor sad thing,' Ryker whispered to Griggs, lifting his eyes mockingly as he sipped at his brandy. 'She sounds a right stuck up little madam.'

Sky pretended she was listening on the phone, and then went on, 'No, it's simply impossible. The dressage competition starts at three and I have to check in with the course secretary at least an hour before.' She sighed heavily as she glanced at her wristwatch. 'I know it's a ghastly state of affairs but what choice do I have? It's doubly disappointing because Buckingham would have been brilliant in the classical dressage.' Another fretful pause as she tucked a strand of hair behind her ear, then, 'Yes, of course he's alright, and no I won't let anything happen to him . . .' She raised her voice just a touch and delivered the line which she hoped would be irresistible to a pair of horse thieves. 'You don't have to remind me of that, daddy! I'm well aware that Buckingham cost you over twelve thousand pounds!'

Griggs's eyes grew large as he stared at Ryker. 'She said twelve, Tony . . . *Twelve* thousand quid! Hellfire, you can't turn your back on this one.'

Ryker was beginning to look as if he couldn't. His lips were pursed and almost watering with greed as he listened intently to Sky as she began to pacify 'daddy' by naming competition venues for which Buckingham had already qualified. These included the International Show in West Germany and the Horse of the Year Show at Wembley in London.

'I bet there's someone on your "private" list who will pay top money for a show-horse like that.' Griggs's lips hardly moved as the words slipped out silently.

'Maybe,' Ryker admitted. 'I dare say, with fake paperwork, I might just be able to sell it on for three thousand.'

Griggs nodded, pleased with the price . . . and so was Ryker. He had a worldwide register of dishonest buyers waiting for class horses. He knew that he could easily place the animal for five thousand pounds, maybe six, but if his partner was happy to accept a percentage of a lower figure then that was fine by him.

Sky shifted her position as a waitress arrived to take her order. She held the phone in place with a raised shoulder, pointed to something on the menu, and then continued her make-believe conversation.

'I've just ordered a smoked salmon salad, daddy . . . not that I'm hungry . . . just a morsel to pick at while I'm waiting.' She paused, listening to nothing but a hum on the line, and added, 'Yes, I'm at the Silver Seagull in Ilfracombe. Could mummy use the Range Rover to pick me and the trailer up? I'll phone for a breakdown service to deal with the car—but you know how these silly garage people can take absolute ages.'

'Oh, forever and ever,' Griggs murmured softly, his smile confident. He looked at his partner. 'Are we on?'

Ryker's nostrils arched. He nodded.

'Bless you, daddy dear. Both me and Buckers think you're an absolute poppet.' Sky wrapped up the call. 'Half-an-hour, then . . . byeee.'

Griggs was up and away, barging through patrons as he headed for the door. Ryker took his time in draining his brandy glass, and finally rising from his chair. As he turned he collided briefly with a waitress and realised that Griggs's speedy exit had meant that the bill for the meal had been left unpaid.

'Here's fifty pounds,' he said, grunting with annoyance as he fished a note from his wallet. 'It's the smallest I have and I'm in a hurry. I'll call back tomorrow for the change!'

He pushed the note reluctantly into the hands of the waitress, cursed inwardly and made his way out of the restaurant.

So far so good.

Things were running exactly to plan.

Sky couldn't resist a small secretive smile as she watched him go.

* * *

Degsey was the first one to hear Griggs. The bran sack slid from her neck as she lifted her head, muzzle quivering, ears eagerly pricked.

Daniel reacted quickly by nudging life into Shack who was dozing as he rested his back against the inside of one of Sir Galahad's forelegs. He woke with a start but Daniel clamped a hand over his mouth and indicated that something was happening outside the trailer.

'This could be it,' Daniel whispered, putting the sack back over Degsey. 'No noise . . . all perfectly still.'

The mood of teasing excitement which had existed between Daniel and Shack during the drive from Swiftly had changed to one of quiet anticipation. They waited, listening only to the sound of advancing footsteps and their own breathing.

Griggs was whistling softly as he approached the trailer and Daniel tried to judge his movements from the outside sounds. He'd be checking the Volvo first, he imagined, possibly looking at the engine before moving round to peer in the windows . . .

'Oh, hell . . .' Daniel's face suddenly changed colour as a thought hit him. He stared at Shack, his cheeks bleaching to an anxious whiteness. 'Jonathan's blue advertising sticker,' he murmured. 'I forgot to remove it from the Volvo's rear window.'

'Too late to worry,' Shack observed bleakly. 'If he's fairly clued-up then he's noticed it by now.'

Griggs had noticed it. His eyes had drifted over the words: OYSTER GABLES ANIMAL SHELTER—SWIFTLY . . . but the real meaning of the sticker hadn't registered. It should have rung huge alarm bells in his head but fortunately he was far too occupied with eyeing the contents of the Volvo's interior.

He had walked casually past the bonnet, which was still up, and was now peering into the passenger window. On the seat was a folder marked 'Show Documents' and a road atlas. Next to these, and all packed in polythene bags, were three pairs of riding gloves, two velvet hard hats and several white shirts with black ties. Two pairs of jodhpurs and a spare black velvet jacket sat neatly on a wooden hanger which dangled from the passenger's interior hook. A wicker tack hamper labelled 'Somerset County Show' had been positioned invitingly on the rear seat.

Griggs was unaware that every article had been borrowed from the saddlers shop in Swiftly and placed in the car with the sole intention of creating the illusion that Sky was a keen competition rider. Certainly it had him fooled and he gave a nod of approval and carried on whistling an as he edged his way round to the trailer. Commonsense told him that the clothes must have cost a fortune and were all necessary show wear. Ryker's fears were groundless, he convinced himself. Both the girl and the horse were genuine.

Daniel and Shack exchanged relieved glances as they heard the rattle of the safety chain and the rasp of the locking pin being slid from the trailer's coupling.

'Panic over, stay cool,' Shack whispered, managing a tight grin.

The tension in Daniel relaxed a little but inwardly he was cursing his own stupidity. He'd been so thorough in his planning, not leaving anything to chance—and then he'd very nearly tripped himself up by forgetting to remove something as obvious as a window advertising sticker.

Griggs continued to whistle as Shack and Daniel squeezed closer to Sir Galahad's underbelly, positioning themselves level with the chalk marks, expecting to hear someone's foot mount the rear ledge at any moment.

They weren't to be disappointed.

Ryker was suddenly at Griggs's shoulder. 'Does the girl's story ring true?' he asked, stepping onto the ledge and leaning over the top edge of the trailer.

'The car checks out,' Griggs told him. 'It's full of her show gear. Loads of designer stuff. She's a spoilt little rich girl alright.'

'And the horse?'

'He's no gymkhana hack. His condition is ace. I bet "daddy" employs an army of stable staff to keep him tip-top.'

Ryker grunted, leaned further in, and ran a hand over the groomed check quarter-marks on the horse's rump. Every slight shifting or scrape of feet echoed spookily in the trailer. Daniel was well tucked in and had mentally braced himself not to flinch if he caught a glimpse of Ryker's hand.

'Can't see much while Buckingham's boxed up,' the big man was saying, 'but he's short-coupled with good rounded quarters . . . and very well turned out, I'll give you that.'

'Stinks of money, eh, Tony?'

'Mmm, possibly.'

Daniel's stomach lurched as Ryker leaned as far over the top edge of the ramp as his body bulk would allow. Daniel glimpsed the big man's fingers dangling in front of him and took a gulp of air, holding it as he tried to ignore the diamond-studded ring shimmering in front of his eyes.

'Is the tow-bar fitted with a locking device?' he heard Ryker ask Griggs.

'A simple pin and chain,' he replied. 'No problem. It was easy to disconnect.'

Ryker's fingers ceased their stroking and probing and stretched as far as they could to a point just short of Sir Galahad's stifle. The arm was now at full stretch and the scorpion tattoo was being displayed to Shack in all its unforgettable glory.

He shivered as the memory of Thursday night came flooding back. His tongue crept out to wet the blemish on his lip as a small voice, deep inside, held him in check. Keep calm, it repeated over and over . . . remember Mister Rafferty . . . remember the plan.

'This seems too easy.' Ryker sucked on a tooth, pondering. 'It's all fallen into place so well that I'm beginning to get suspicious.'

'You think it's a set-up?' Griggs scratched the nape of his neck.

'I don't know. I've got a feeling . . . just a twinge in my stomach.'

'That's indigestion. You stuffed your gob full of beef.'

'No, it's something else. Maybe I'm being over cautious but . . .'

Daniel and Shack listened nervously as Ryker began voicing the events that had supposedly brought Sky to the Silver Seagull. He was questioning every detail of Daniel's carefully laid plan, looking for weak spots.

Daniel stared at the floor, his fingers crossed tightly.

Minutes dripped by like the slow drops of sweat trickling between his shoulder blades.

'Okay, it's all feasible . . . even though the damsel in distress bit sounds like something from a fairy tale.' Ryker wound up his probing of events and posed a question to Griggs. 'Are you sure the stuff in the Volvo looks authentic?'

'I'm sure.'

'Perhaps I should double-check.'

Daniel traded swift glances with Shack. Martin Griggs had failed to make the connection with the sticker, but they both knew that the mistake would not go unnoticed by Ryker's eyes.

'No need.' Griggs huffed. 'I've done it and I'm satisfied. You'd simply be wasting your energy.'

Ryker looked at his watch. 'Alright, time's short so let's get on with it.' He snapped out the order, his voice echoing around the inside of the trailer.

'Phew! That was close.' Shack shuddered with relief as the big man lifted his arm from view. There was a small metallic groan as the trailer's springs relaxed from the extra weight and Ryker stepped from the ledge.

With the danger gone, Degsey's eyes appeared from under the bran sack. Her whole presence radiated wisdom as she looked from Shack to Daniel and up to Sir Galahad. She understood everything, Daniel thought, and nothing ever escaped her attention. He guessed that she'd recognised Ryker's and Griggs's voices from their early masked visit the other morning—and possibly even before that. It now seemed highly possible they had also caused her shoulder injury, and if this was the case then the incident was far from forgotten.

'He's shifting the BMW into position,' Shack whispered the words as the smooth purr of an engine drifted through the trailer's walls.

Daniel nodded, feeling a shudder of movement ripple through the floor as the towing arm was uncoupled. The switching of vehicles would be easy, he reasoned; just a case of Griggs heaving the trailer clear of the Volvo and re-hitching it to the ball-socket on Ryker's tow-bar.

Daniel could now feel a movement in the trailer's tiny wheels. He listened carefully to every sound, going through the various manoeuvres in his mind until finally the trailer stilled and there was a hollow clunk.

'We're coupled up,' he said to Shack, knowing it was now safe to ease his cramped body into a more vertical position. He unhooked two large nets that had last seen action rescuing a muntjac deer and handed one to Shack. 'Did you remember the rope?'

Shack nodded and tapped the back pocket of his jeans.

'Okay. Then it's time to get ourselves organised.'

CHAPTER TEN

Sky had positioned herself by an outside staff door and was observing the forecourt activity from beneath a leafy overhang of branches that provided shadowy cover. She waited until the trailer was well on the move, watching the red BMW exit the car park before crossing quickly to the Volvo.

She shut the bonnet, flicked off the ignition immobiliser, and spun the front tyres as she swung past a few straggly parked cars. The Volvo bounced over a traffic hump as she swung left out of the Silver Seagull's forecourt before joining a one-way system that would take her along part of the High Street.

The pavements were bustling with Sunday sightseers and vehicle movement was heavy. There was a bus, a van, and four cars in front, all slowing her progress—and to make matters worse she was heading due south with the sun blazing into her eyes. She pulled down the driver's visor and snatched a look down every side-turning she passed, just in case Ryker had slipped free of the main stream of traffic.

No sign.

She was clear of the High Street now and three cars and the bus peeled off at the next road junction. That left one car and what she now identified as a baker's box van in front of her. She gave a shaky sigh as she realised she was fast approaching a set of traffic lights with a right-hand filter. Now she had the BMW and trailer in her sights. They were stationary, caught on the red filter light. Suddenly she didn't want to be this close. The main lights were already green and she knew that if she took that route she would have to double-back, which could mean losing them. If she decided to turn right and use the filter she would be sitting directly behind them, just begging to be spotted.

Luckily, the baker's van solved the problem. As the car in front flashed through on the green, the van indicated right, giving her the cover she so desperately needed.

'Thank you, thank you,' she heard herself saying, braking and waiting, glimpsing the logo on the van's rear doors. 'I promise I'll always buy Bosworth's Bread from now on.'

Seconds passed and then the filter light changed to green. Ilfracombe was behind her but she was looping back to the sea on a narrow country road signposted: HELE BAY. Farmers fields flashed past for the next two miles as she hugged the van's rear end, catching the odd glimpse of the trailer as the tight bends forced it to swing wide.

Habitation now; a dozen or so houses and a variety of small stores. Sky eased off on the accelerator as the baker's van indicated its intention to pull into a slip road by the shops. She drifted the Volvo to the kerb and came to a halt behind the partial cover of a bottle bank and a parked motorbike.

She had a clear view of the red BMW car and trailer. They were some two hundred metres ahead of her and climbing a fairly steep hill. She'd wait until they reached the top, she told herself, and then follow at a safe distance.

The waiting was unnecessary. Without giving a signal the BMW and trailer veered off to the right and disappeared from view. Sky immediately engaged a gear, swung clear of the parked motorbike and revved the Volvo's engine.

The turning was barely visible from the road. Sky cruised up the hill and only spotted it because she knew it had to be there. It stood well back from any passing traffic; an unmade track where brambles were left to the haze of roadside exhaust fumes.

The steering wheel vibrated in Sky's hands as the Volvo bounced through a cluster of potholes. The width of the track had increased over the years by the constant journeying of Ryker's travelling horse-box. There was a single raised strip of grass running up the middle of the track and deep earthy tyre marks either side.

Sky struggled to control the steering as the Volvo pitched in and out of the ruts. Suddenly the track divided and she decided to fork left for no better reason than it looked less bumpy. Now she found herself heading up an incline and a blind bend lay ahead. She slowed to a crawl, not knowing whether to get out and walk or press on and maybe risk being seen. The safety of the estate car appealed more, so she eased the Volvo gently round a curve and breathed a sigh of relief as the track gradually widened to reveal a large ramshackle building.

Suddenly, carried on the wind, she heard somebody shouting instructions.

'A bit more . . . Easy, easy! Hold it . . . that should do you!'

She immediately jerked on the Volvo's handbrake and switched off the ignition. The estate car's front windows were open and although the voice was faint—a very long way off she instantly recognised it as belonging to Griggs. There was a fair bit of revving, which she guessed was coming from Ryker's BMW, and she hoped this had masked any noise of her arrival.

Her mouth was prune-dry as she calmed herself to take stock of her surroundings.

She had halted close to some barbed-wire fencing at the rear of what appeared to be an old warehouse. It was a tall building and the fierce afternoon sun was bouncing off the roof and casting long shadows across the Volvo.

She couldn't be seen, she decided, grateful that she'd taken the correct fork in the track. Whatever action was now taking place was happening at quite a distance on the other side of the warehouse. She opened Sir Galahad's hamper of tack and pulled out a bridle, keeping her fingers wrapped tightly round the snaffle-bit to stop it from rattling.

She trampled through dried bracken as she made her way awkwardly along the rear of the warehouse. Nettles and brambles clawed at her jodhpurs as, still concealed by the cloak of shade, she ran the length of the building's wooden cladding to the corner.

She pulled her phone from her jacket pocket, letting her eyes roam over the property's six acres. The paddock for old horses, the mobile home, and the rusty iron structure which housed the travelling horse-box were all now visible.

And so were Ryker and Griggs.

The trailer had been backed under a leafy mass of some huge oak trees but both men became visible as they stepped out of the shadows and into the sunshine.

'Do you want Buckingham put in a stall?' Griggs was saying. 'Or shall we let him stretch his legs in the paddock?'

'I want the horse in the warehouse and out of sight,' Ryker replied, climbing out of the BMW. 'The girl's probably reported him stolen by now.'

'What about the trailer?'

'We dump it. The cops could come sniffing around and I don't want it found on the property.'

Daniel and Shack could hear the conversation clearly as they crouched motionless against the inside of the trailer's ramp. They held their nets loosely, ready to spring into action, their eyes fixed on the inside keepers that located the outside bolts.

'Okay, drop the ramp and get him out,' Ryker was saying. 'I'll put down some fresh bedding in one of the stalls.'

Daniel cursed. He turned to Shack, adding softly but firmly, 'We need them together. If Ryker and Griggs separate we've had it.'

Shack pointed to the metal chains that ran either side of the trailer's interior. They were there to give added strength and support to the ramp when it was lowered—but they could also have another use. Shack gripped the chain at his corner tightly and by using sign language prompted Daniel to do likewise.

He nodded, following Shack's actions.

Breaths were held as Griggs started whistling yet another unrecognisable tune and the bolts were slid free of their keepers.

Two stringy hands with badly bitten nails wrestled to release the ramp. Shack and Daniel took the strain on the chains. They rattled but the ramp didn't budge.

'What's up with this?' Griggs grumbled. He turned and called out to Ryker. 'You'll have to give me a hand, Tony. The flamin' thing's stuck!'

Shack lifted a thumb to Daniel and grinned. The action of gripping the chains wasn't part of the original plan, but it was working.

'Can't you handle anything on your own?' Ryker was saying irritably, striding back. 'Are you sure the bolts are off?'

'Of course I'm sure. I'm not stupid.'

'That's open to question, Griggsy.'

Daniel swallowed hard and Shack nibbled on his lower lip as Ryker checked the bolts before his big sturdy hands joined forces with Griggs's. They pulled at the ramp together and the strain on the chains was enormous.

'On the count of three . . .' Daniel said on a raw whisper. 'One . . . Two . . .'

'*Three!*' Shack added his voice to the count, and both chains were immediately released.

The ramp flew open, rocking on its hinges and leaving everybody's ears ringing as it crashed to the ground with the noise of a small explosion.

Suddenly there was chaos. Everything happened at once.

In an ultra-fast movement Daniel and Shack jumped from the trailer, their nets billowing in their hands . . . Ryker and Griggs stepped backwards, unnerved, confused, blanketed in dust thrown up by the ramp. Sky broke cover, running at full tilt . . . Degsey leapt out . . . and Sir Galahad, frightened by all the din swayed sideways, muscles rippling violently in his quarters as his head went up and he snapped his halter.

'What the . . . !' Ryker's lips moved back on his teeth. The net had covered him but he was still lashing out at Daniel with a crazy strength.

Griggs was snared too. His eyebrows flew up in terror as Shack dived at him, bringing the net down over his head and bony shoulders and forcing him to his knees. The netting clung to his face, making his eyes bulge hugely as he wriggled against Shack's strength.

'Lie on the ground!' Shack pulled the net free and twisted the collar of Griggs's shirt. 'Don't even *think* of escaping!'

'W-who . . . ?' Griggs gave a strangled little cough as a bubble of spittle puffed from his lips and popped. 'A-are you cops or something?'

'Or something,' Shack said, nudging Griggs's thighs further apart and forcing him face down in the dust. He pulled some rope from his pocket and began tying Griggs's wrists and ankles, looping the two ends together so he would be trussed up like a chicken.

Daniel was having far more of a problem.

He'd managed to get a grip around Ryker's thick waist and was holding his own—until fate and Sir Galahad intervened. Sky was reaching to grab the loose horse's head-collar when its hindquarters struck heavily into Daniel.

The impact knocked all breath from his body. Suddenly he had no air, no voice, and his lungs were burning. He staggered sideways, somehow managing to remain upright as he tried to regain his senses.

Ryker had freed himself from the net and intended to take advantage of Daniel's dizziness to the full. Grunting heavily he body-charged Daniel, knocking him to the ground and sending stars pin-wheeling before his eyes. Ryker paused briefly for the dust to clear before balling his fists and moving forward as if to finish the job.

'Leave him!' Shack confronted the big man. He stood with arms folded, legs set aggressively apart.

Ryker's eyes suddenly flashed as he remembered every detail of Shack's face. 'Well, well, if it isn't the cocky kid who tangled with me at that Oyster place at Swiftly. You've done well, sonny boy—you set me up and I fell for it . . . the trailer breakdown, the show-horse, the girl with the plummy accent . . .'

'I've made a call on my mobile phone,' Sky chipped in, hot-eyed and flushed. She was still holding Sir Galahad by the broken halter. 'The police and RSPCA will be here at any minute.'

Ryker's gaze was on her. 'So what would you like me to do, Miss Plummy Voice—*stay?*'

Sky said, 'You can't get away. Your horse rustling days are over. Both you and your sickening trade are finished.'

'Nobody tells Tony Ryker what he can and cannot do!' His face darkened dangerously. 'You animal welfare people are all the same. You're an irritating bunch of do-gooders with empty lives. I can set up again . . . anytime, anywhere. And believe me—I'll be long gone before the cops arrive.'

'We've got your partner,' Shack reminded him, tilting his head towards a wriggling Griggs. 'He won't be going anywhere.'

'So keep him. He suffers from nosebleeds and he's more trouble than he's worth.'

Ryker took a couple of sideways steps towards the BMW.

'Don't make for the car,' Shack warned, 'or I'll—'

'You'll what?' Ryker focussed on him sharply. 'Set the dog on me?'

Degsey was lying by the paddock gate, motionless. She seemed very cool and focussed and she was watching Ryker's movements. Mister Rafferty stood on the other side of the gate, sniffing briskly at the air. He had been reunited with his old friend and he capered and pranced excitedly behind the woodwork.

'I wouldn't pin your hopes on the dog,' Ryker went on, laughing without humour. 'That greyhound could barely manage a growl when we last met.'

Daniel leaned against Sky as she helped him to his feet. He let out a wheezy groan as he clung to Sir Galahad's neck for support. Shack's eyes flicked briefly towards the group. It was a foolish lapse of concentration and time enough to allow Ryker to seize his escape opportunity. He lunged suddenly for the BMW's driving door and had his fingers curled around the handle and was yanking it open before Shack noticed the movement.

He reacted but it was too late. Much too late.

He hurled himself at Ryker in a cannonball dive—but the big man had expected the move and swung the half-open car door into his path. It crashed painfully into Shack's side, lifting his legs from under him and sending breath hissing through his teeth. He righted himself, clutching his ribs, hearing the BMW's engine throb into life and a noisy grating of gears as Ryker floored the accelerator.

'He's getting away!' Sky turned her gaze to Daniel.

Daniel could only watch helplessly, waiting for his strength to return as he clung to Sir Galahad's mane.

There was a smell of rubber in the air as a wave of dust surged from the car's powerful wheel spin. Shack managed to stagger clumsily away as he felt a wisp of air from the trailer whoosh past his face. The tiny wheels rumbled away from him; the still-lowered ramp bouncing and rattling over the uneven surface.

Degsey was now standing by the paddock gate. She stretched and shook life into her taut muscles, knowing exactly what she must do . . .

'Can I have some help with this?' Sky released Sir Galahad's head-collar and was struggling both to hold the horse and attach the bridle.

'I'll do it,' Shack said. He was still rubbing his side but looked in far better shape than Daniel.

Degsey sprang forward like a cork leaving a bottle, adopting her powerful racing stride as she flew past the group's legs. Shack, who had never seen her at full stretch before, let out a soft whistle of amazement.

'Jeez,' he murmured, the whistle causing his bruised ribs to grate painfully under his denim shirt, 'that's one hell of a fast greyhound.'

'The best.' Daniel straightened his back, working life into his shoulders.

'Flamin' devil dog . . .' Griggs jerked out the words as he wriggled against the ropes twisting into his side. A nosebleed had begun, the redness caking his nostrils and streaking to his lips as he corkscrewed his neck to glimpse Degsey.

'She's going after your boss,' Sky told him, accepting a leg-up from Shack and vaulting onto Sir Galahad's bare back. 'She'll have something planned—you can bet on it.'

'And you?' Daniel asked, the colour returning to his face. 'What are you planning to do?'

Sir Galahad was gusting breath, one hoof pawing impatiently at the ground. 'Catch Mr Ryker,' Sky said simply.

Daniel exchanged a worried glance with Shack, but neither spoke. They could both see that Sky looked determined, her eyes direct and steady—and they both knew there wasn't a word they could say that would stop her.

She gathered the reins and tapped her heels firmly against the horse's flanks. Sir Galahad sprang forward, knowing she meant business as he changed his gait from canter to full gallop in one graceful movement.

Ryker was weaving a dangerous course around the property's perimeter track. He was hindered by the trailer; the ramp rumbling and jolting, creating resistance whenever the BMW approached a sharp bend. He'd rattled past the rusty iron structure which housed the travelling horse-box and was now on the other side of the paddock surging away from the mobile home and heading towards the warehouse. If he reached the fork in the track, then he was away and clear.

Sky spanned the paddock fence on Sir Galahad, cutting a path through the startled old horses as she thundered across the patchy turf. She used the shortest route possible before bracing the muscles of her back and cresting the fence on the far side. Riding without a saddle wasn't easy but she kept her seat secure, forking her body tautly, tightening her legs around the horse's ribs.

She continued to cut every corner, using her show jumping skills to coax the chestnut horse this way and that, spanning ditches and jumping barbed-wire fences in an attempt to head off the BMW.

The task was too great. Ryker was watching her in the rear-view mirror and he had no intention of being outsmarted.

'No chance, Buckers,' he murmured through clenched teeth, stamping hard on the accelerator. 'Compared to the car you're badly lacking in vital horsepower.'

The warehouse loomed ahead. Ryker gave a grunt of satisfaction, dropping down a gear as he approached the fork in the dirt track.

Suddenly his vision blurred over . . .

His fingers immediately tightened on the steering wheel.

A penetrating light was searing at his eyes, boring into them with such fury that he fumbled frantically to flip down the car's sun visor. It jammed—he pulled—it broke off in his hand.

'What . . . ?' Through screwed-up eyes Ryker could just make out the shape of a greyhound. It was standing stock still where the track forked, muzzle drawn back, head tilted upwards towards the sun. A pinpoint of dazzling light radiated from one of its teeth, growing, expanding, and enfolding him. Its strength smothered the car, shimmering through the windshield and blinding him with a circle of brilliance.

'No! No! I can't see!' He yelled the words at Degsey, cupping a hand to his forehead.

A mixture of emotions twisted his features as Griggs's warnings about the dog flashed into his thoughts. A gold tooth? Was it possible? Is that what he'd seen in the headlights on the journey back from Marshwood? Is that why he'd swerved? Griggs had always claimed that it was a devil dog. Now, as Ryker's uneasiness tightened, he was beginning to wish he'd listened to his partner's warnings.

He spun the steering wheel this way and that, hoping to break free of the energy-sapping beam.

No reaction—his efforts didn't alter his course and the wheel ran free in his hands. The car had suddenly developed a mind of its own . . . taking a very definite route, accelerating under its own steam and putting him on a collision course with the warehouse.

He felt dizzy. His heart was pumping fast.

Degsey was unmoving. She held her position and blinked . . .

There was a click as the BMW's central-locking system snapped on, sealing the doors. Ryker heard the noise and knew what was happening. His unsteady fingers fiddled with the electric window switches as he wrenched frantically at the driver's door-handle.

No response.

He was panicking now, real white-faced panic, stamping on the foot-brake in an attempt to stop the car. He pumped at the pedal, but there was just a soft hissing sound and the hollow slap of his foot making contact with the floor.

Try the handbrake, try the handbrake . . . The words echoed hotly in his head, running through the veins bulging between his forehead and ears. In a last-gasp effort he fumbled for the brake lever, almost wrenching it from its metal housing. Once again there was no pressure, no tension. Only slackness. It slopped about in his fingers, as if the cable had been cut.

He cursed loudly. In the past he had always been in charge of whatever situation presented itself . . . prided himself on always being in control. But now he had never felt so helpless in his life. Helpless and frighteningly weak. The wooden framework of the warehouse was closing by the second . . . and he knew he was going to crash.

Blind that dog's eyes! Send that greyhound to hell!

Ryker wrapped his arms around his face as the red BMW slammed powerfully into the warehouse doors. Wood splintered as the building's heavy metal locking bar buckled under the thrust of the car's radiator grille. It lifted and spun, punching a spidery hole through the BMW's windshield as it lanced past Ryker's shoulder and jammed itself into the leather upholstery. Tiny arrowheads of glass rained onto Ryker's lap as the car ploughed on.

Ahead were the stalls—empty apart from the three stolen Penhill horses. They were tethered to securing rings and these twisted jarringly as the animals whinnied and snorted as they tried to skitter away from the impending danger.

Ryker's knuckles whitened on the steering wheel as he braced himself. His eyes were squeezed tight shut as he waited for the impact of the car striking horseflesh—waiting for the obvious bloodshed which would surely follow.

Only it didn't.

The brakes came on.

The tyres screamed for grip, lurching Ryker forward and causing his ribs to bounce against the steering wheel. Four black strips of rubber showed across the warehouse floor as the red BMW skidded sideways and came to a shuddering halt.

The engine stuttered and died. Only the noise of Ryker's loud, breathing could be heard above the hiss of steam escaping from the car's cracked radiator.

Sky, on Sir Galahad, trotted through the gaping hole and into the warehouse. The horse was lathered, foaming, and shining with sweat. It quivered and trembled still as Sky gentled it before swinging a leg over the withers and sliding to the floor.

The sound of a police two-tone siren began to gain in strength. Ryker now knew he was only minutes away from arrest.

He yanked at the door handles but they were still firmly locked. Glaring at Sky he thumped a fist against the dashboard. 'Caught by three snotty teenagers and a flamin' dog!' He coughed out the words, wiping spittle from his mouth and giving her a look that was evil and brutal.

'*We* didn't catch you, Mr Ryker,' Sky said, quietening the Penhill horses as she gazed at him through the ragged hole in the windshield. 'Your *greed* did that.'

*   *   *

Seamus Horrigan's whole body was shaking with delight. His proud, sensitive mouth had curled into a huge smile and this had caused his crease lines to treble.

'Praise be to God and Mary, Peter, Paul and Patrick,' he said, tears of relief pricking his eyes. He fondled Mister Rafferty's ears and blew gently against the chestnut cob's muzzle. 'I be full of gratitude to you all. Me heart be fair burstin' with the joyestest of feelings . . . I never thought I'd be seein' the old rascal again.'

Mister Rafferty lifted his head and whinnied jubilantly. He rolled back his top lip and exposed well-worn, slightly brownish teeth.

Jonathan, dressed only in surfer's shorts, ran a hand over the old cob's coarse, uneven mane and exchanged a delighted grin with Spring.

It was early evening and Daniel, Shack and Sky had arrived back at Oyster Gables. Their faces held a look of triumph, but their bodies were suffering muscle fatigue brought on by the afternoon's events. They had each given statements about Ryker's and Griggs's horse-napping activities to the police and then assisted the RSPCA inspectors in sorting out the stolen horses. The three from Penhill were easily identified, but the six old animals from the paddock proved more difficult to identify. Eventually five were matched against the Society's computerised records of thefts—and of course Degsey had no trouble in establishing

Mister Rafferty as the sixth. Both the old cob and the greyhound were devoted friends.

'Where's Sir Galahad?' Jonathan asked, standing by the trailer and running a finger over the dents and jagged scratches that scarred the ramp's leading edge.

'We only had room for Mister Rafferty,' Daniel explained. 'The RSPCA will drop him off later when they return the Penhill horses.'

'You've hurt your face.' Spring indicated a plaster that covered a small graze on Daniel's temple. Both he and Shack had received first aid treatment at the local police station.

'Was there lots of fighting, Shacky?' Jonathan's eyes lit up as the questions tumbled out. 'How many were in the gang? Did they use weapons? Was there lots of blood and spit and stuff?'

'There wasn't any gang,' Shack said, fingering his bruised ribs. 'Although sometimes it felt like it.'

Degsey was showing everyone her pleasure at being reunited with Mister Rafferty. She stood under the cob, looking up at him as she weaved in and out of his legs. It was a game they had played many times in the past and the old horse hadn't forgotten the routine. Whenever Degsey's wagging tail presented itself he would turn and dip his head, trying to knock her off balance.

'I expect Mister Rafferty has lost a bit of weight,' Sky remarked to Seamus, smiling at the animal antics as she leaned into the Volvo and folded the borrowed riding clothes neatly over her arm. 'We'd better put him on a special diet for a week to build him up.'

Seamus said nothing, just looked slightly embarrassed as he toyed with the strip of brightly coloured cloth that secured his pony-tail.

'You will be staying for a bit?' Spring asked.

He shook his head. 'I be doin' a lot of tinkin' and it be best if old Seamus be makin' a move.'

He spoke the words so calmly that Jonathan could only open his mouth and stare. 'You're leaving . . . What now?'

'T'morrow mornin', boy—after breakfast. Ireland be callin' old Seamus. It's time me and me family be on our way.'

Daniel, Shack and Sky exchanged glances. They knew only too well that once Mister Rafferty had been found there would be nothing to keep Seamus at Swiftly; but hearing talk of his sudden departure still came as a blow. They had all become part of his life, his problems, his mysterious ways—and all of them had gained from the experience. Life at Oyster Gables would go on—the way it had in the past—but with Seamus gone, a little chink of colour would always be lacking from their lives.

'You'll be sadly missed,' Daniel said, 'by all of us.'

'And I shall be missin' all of you.' Seamus's watery eyes crinkled as he looked at each face in turn. 'You all be me special family—and Mister Rafferty and me darlin' Degsey will be tinkin' of you with every roll of the wagon's wheels.'

Spring was looking at Degsey, trying to blot out thoughts of never seeing the greyhound again.

Seamus caught her look and glanced at Sky. 'Can I be askin' a special favour?' he said. 'Me babbles be growed so big that there barely be room in me wagon to keep the wee rascals. So I be wonderin' . . .'

He paused, rubbing his jaw.

'You were wondering . . . ?' Sky prompted.

Spring stared at him hard, her pale lashes rolling back. She waited desperately for the words she wanted to hear.

'Ay, Seamus be wonderin' whether Jonathan and Spring would do him the favour of keeping Little Degsey.'

In a breathy voice, Spring asked, 'For always?'

'Ay, for always.'

'Epic!' Jonathan gave him a jaunty salute.

Spring had already climbed the caravan's steps to the footboard and was peering over the top of the porch doors. Little Degsey jumped up to greet her. Spring's smile was huge as she turned to blow Seamus a kiss.

Shack moved forward to take the halter from Seamus's hands. Tonight, at least, Mister Rafferty would be spending a safe night in Oyster Gables' stables.

Daniel followed behind the old horse with Sir Galahad's hamper of tack. Seamus smiled at both of them, thanking them quietly for their help and their courage and telling them he'd say his 'goodbyes' in the morning.

Daniel thought the old Irishman seemed to be at peace with himself. His face had lightened and for the first time he looked relaxed—free from the stress of the past week.

Even Daniel's weariness had lessened. Mister Rafferty was safe and that's all that mattered—that's all that had ever mattered. Every bruise, graze, ache and pain had been worth the effort.

Shack turned, glancing over his shoulder. 'Good to see the old boy looking so happy. All's well that ends well, eh, Daniel?'

Daniel smiled. 'Amen to that,' he said.

CHAPTER ELEVEN

Staff and helpers usually arrived in stages for breakfast at Oyster Gables but this morning was no ordinary morning and Sky had her work cut out to cope. Due to Seamus's departure everyone was appearing at seven on the dot.

Shack and Daniel had finished their mucking out and cage cleaning duties and were at the large butler sink sharing a joke and washing their hands. Megan and Hannah had made a point of coming in early to help with the animal feeding and were now slicing bread ready for the toaster. Spring was clicking on a timer as she prepared to boil herself two fresh eggs . . . and even Jonathan, who was always an hour behind everyone else, was generally getting under Sky's feet as he played with Scooter.

'So the police phoned here last night and asked if we could offer an explanation . . .' Daniel chuckled to Shack as he dried his hands. 'They couldn't shift Ryker because all the BMW's doors were *welded* shut. They said they'd never seen anything like it. In the end they had to use cutting gear to get him out.'

'What about the smashed windshield?' Jonathan posed the question.

'What about it?'

'Couldn't they pull him out that way?'

'He was too fat. They tried but he got jammed.'

Shack caught his breath in a giggle. 'Did you tell them that the doors were Degsey's fault?'

'Would you have told them?'

'And let them think I'm crazy?'

'Exactly. The true story would have got me an appointment for brain treatment!'

Sky had resorted to using two large frying pans. One sizzled away with sausages, bacon, frying bread and tomatoes, whilst the other was ready with heated cooking oil to accept seven free-range eggs sitting in a nearby rack.

'Nice smell, Miss Plummy Voice,' Daniel mocked softly, enjoying her closeness.

'Thank you Mr Rusk.' Sky grinned mischievously and put on her Silver Seagull accent and joined in the game. 'Cooking breakfast is a frightfully tiresome business, but one appreciates being appreciated.'

His warm breath touched her earlobe. 'I wasn't talking about breakfast. It's you that smells delicious.'

Sky laughed, tilting her head.

'Who's Miss Plummy Voice?' Jonathan broke in, the question interrupting Daniel's thoughts.

'Er . . . It's a sort of nickname,' he explained. 'Invented by one of the horse thieves.'

'There seems to be a lot of this nickname stuff going on,' Jonathan said, flicking a glance to Shack. 'I mean who would have thought that Shacky—'

He stopped abruptly as Shack glared at him and made a throat-slitting gesture.

'Thought what?' quizzed Sky.

'Oh,' he swallowed, having to think quickly. 'That . . . that the horse thieves would be jokers.'

'Takes all sorts, little dude.' Shack's features relaxed.

Sky asked Daniel if he would try to persuade Seamus to join them for breakfast. 'As it's his last morning,' she added, 'it would be nice if we could all eat together.'

'He always has his meals in his wagon.' Jonathan stated the obvious.

'Make yourself useful, Jonathan.' Sky said the words firmly, her eyes dark and direct. 'Please set the table for eight.'

'Seamus won't come. He's far too stubborn.'

Sky gave him a no-nonsense stare. She opened the cutlery drawer and just pointed.

'I'll see if I can manage a bit of arm twisting.' Daniel made his way to the door. 'But you know Seamus—it won't be easy.'

'Tell him I've prepared a packed lunch to eat on the road,' Sky added, remembering.

'And ask him if he'd like some cans of dog food for Degsey and the pups,' Spring said brightly, helping herself to a yoghurt from the fridge.

'Will do.'

'And Daniel . . .' Sky stopped him in his tracks.

'Yes?'

'Don't be long. Breakfast is nearly ready.'

Sky's mouth had softened, the corners turning gently upwards into a warm, open smile.

Daniel knew things had finally come right between them. He closed the door softly at his back, stretched, and stepped out into the misty early morning sunshine.

Crossing the forecourt he almost half expected to see Mister Rafferty in the caravan's shafts. He knew Seamus was an early riser so it wouldn't have surprised him if the old cob had been collected from the stables and tacked up, ready for the long journey ahead.

No horse, but the caravan's pan-box was open and some pieces of harness lay in a messy tangle on the ground.

Not only harness, but a man's shoe. An old-fashioned leather brogue shoe that Daniel recognised as belonging to Seamus.

Suddenly his spine felt chilly.

Something was very, very, wrong.

'Seamus!' he shouted the name, ducking under one of the shafts and scooting up the steps to the porch.

The porch doors were wide open, revealing the three pups huddled together on the skin rug. They looked up at him, shivering—not with cold—but with a fear of the unknown. His eyes travelled past them to the bunk bed beneath the rear window where hazy sunlight filtered in through the shutters.

He saw Degsey first, standing on the patchwork quilt which lay crumpled on the floor . . . and then he saw Seamus.

The old Irishman was sitting loose-limbed on the bunk, his face like wax, and his head lolling sideways. He was fully dressed apart from one missing shoe and his blue eyes were staring unseeingly at Degsey.

Daniel crossed quickly to the bunk, hearing the greyhound give several throaty whimpers as she stretched her long neck, nudging persistently at Seamus's arm, trying to wake him.

Daniel knelt, checking the old man's pulse and breathing; knowing inwardly it was hopeless. Seamus's leathery skin still felt slightly warm to the touch as Daniel closed the old man's eyes with a sweep of his hand.

Degsey nuzzled closer to Seamus, sniffing and gently licking at his fingers, her eyes wide and midnight black, willing her master to waken.

Daniel wished it could all be imagination, a memory of a night's bad dreaming. He looked at the greyhound and took a shuddery breath.

'Seamus has gone, Degsey,' he said softly. 'Your master is dead.'

The words had a stunning effect.

She immediately lifted her head to the window, catching the slatted rays of the sun across her face . . . and then she howled. At least, Daniel assumed it was a howl. He'd never heard anything like it before, and never wanted to hear it again. It was a quivering wail which when it broke free, shot through his senses like an explosion and causing him to reel backwards. It grated painfully against his ears and jangled the raw edges of his nerves.

Every muscle in Degsey's body was bunched and strained as she stretched her neck higher. The gathering of black skin around her muzzle lifted and rumpled back to reveal her gold canine tooth. Set against the glistening pinkness of her gums, it was pulsing with an overwhelming brilliance.

Daniel shielded his eyes, squinting through fingers that were trembling. For the first time he was feeling real fear.

The wailing continued, raw and intense. It bubbled in the greyhound's throat and forced Daniel to cover his ears.

Something was happening to the tooth, which in turn was causing the weather outside the window to change. Clouds were suddenly massing darkly overhead.

It was as if both were linked. The gold was slowly disappearing and the sunshine was noticeably fading. Daniel watched open-mouthed as a single shaft of the now-weakening sun's rays enfolded the tooth, sapping the gold away; spinning round as it licked at the precious metal and replaced it with a hard milky whiteness.

Degsey's special powers were ebbing away . . .

A flash of lightning briefly lit up the caravan's interior followed by a loud clap of thunder. Large droplets of rain began to bounce on the leaded roof, hitting the outside chimney stack and echoing down to the old Colchester stove.

Degsey was quiet now. She looked weak and she was panting softly as the final fragments of sunlight vanished from inside the caravan. She placed her chin on Daniel's thigh, focussing on him, the deep grief of losing Seamus reflecting in her eyes.

Inside, Daniel guessed that the rain on the window was Degsey's tears. The water pattered behind the velvet curtains and trickled down the rear window glass.

Tears of sadness, he convinced himself, stroking her long, beautiful face.

Tears for Seamus.

He put a finger to Degsey's muzzle and lifted the soft flesh to glimpse the tooth. No bright sparkle of gold, no mystical powers—they had all died along with the old Irishman. Now there was just a healthy white canine in the lower jaw. Degsey was back to being a normal greyhound. How it should be, Daniel supposed. How, without Seamus to protect, it was always meant to be. Suddenly the thought of what had happened no longer frightened him.

'Mr Rusk?'

Daniel turned towards the porch steps not recognising the voice. The rain had stopped as quickly as it had started and the early morning sunshine had returned. 'Yes . . . Who . . . ?' He squinted towards the outline of a tall, male figure standing on the footboard.

'My name's Doctor Becker. I've been to the house and Ms Patakin sent me here. She phoned the surgery on Saturday asking for an early Monday morning call.'

Daniel's brain whirred. With all the happenings of late, Shack's request for a doctor to see Seamus had completely slipped his mind. 'I'm sorry . . . Yes . . . Come in . . . He's here.'

'The patient is a Mr Horrigan I believe?'

Daniel nodded, sadness showing in his face. He stood up and coaxed Degsey to one side, leaving a clear view of the bunk. As the doctor removed his rain-soaked jacket he glimpsed Seamus and the situation became only too clear.

'I found him like this,' Daniel said in hushed tones. 'I'm afraid he's dead.'

Doctor Becker rolled up his sleeves and sat on the bunk. He had iron grey hair and iron grey eyes to match. He opened his medical bag and took out some pieces of equipment.

Daniel heard the sound of feet on the caravan's wooden steps. He crossed quickly to close the bottom half of the porch doors just as Jonathan reached the footboard.

'Sky sent me,' he said, his blue eyes scanning Daniel's face. 'She's going ballistic. You were expected back ages ago. Your breakfast will be all dried up.'

'Tell Sky I'll have some toast later. I have to stay with Doctor Becker.'

'Is Seamus alright?' He shook rain from his anorak, pulling the hood back and trying to crane his neck past Daniel's deliberately blocking shoulders.

'Can you take the pups back to the house?' Daniel asked.

'I suppose I can.' He looked suspicious. 'What's up? Why are bits of Mister Rafferty's harness dumped by the pan-box? And what's that shoe doing there?'

'Don't ask so many questions, Jonathan.'

'I bet he's poisoned himself with all that herbal stuff he keeps in the cabinet.'

'No he hasn't.'

'Well let me see him.' He pushed at the porch doors.

Daniel had his foot jammed firmly against them. 'He's with the doctor. Just take the pups—alright?'

'Let me in and I will.'

Daniel turned and called the pups to him. There was a scramble as he opened the porch doors just enough to let them squeeze through.

Jonathan stifled a sigh. 'At times you can be really freaky, Daniel. Are you sure Seamus is alright?'

Daniel ignored the question. 'Tell Sky I'll join her as soon as the doctor leaves.'

The sun was coming through quite strongly now and pale patches of hazy blue were showing overhead.

'You're as weird as the weather,' Jonathan went on. 'Was that some sort of freak storm or what? It only lasted a minute. We don't get crazy stuff like that back home in Sussex.'

'Thank you for the weather information, Jonathan. I'll see you later.'

He walked backwards down the steps and gathered the pups around him. 'Seriously freaky . . .' he said again.

Daniel closed the top half of the porch doors and pushed home the bolt.

Doctor Becker had finished his physical examination and was now going through the contents of the veneered table-top cabinet. He opened tiny containers stuffed with twigs, barks and leaves, and sniffed curiously at the bottles of oil.

'You don't think any of those are to blame?' Daniel spoke with more ease than he felt. 'I thought they were harmless.'

'All perfectly innocent. They're just the normal assortment of herbs used in folklore. I thought I'd better just check—having overheard the boy's observations.'

'Yes, of course, so . . . ?'

'A heart attack killed him, Mr Rusk. He's been dead about an hour. I saw the harness and shoe when I arrived—so putting all the pieces together I'd say it's very probable that he struggled too hard getting the harness from the box. He more than likely collapsed, losing his shoe in the process. He's a very old man—middle to late eighties, I'd say . . . but he was wiry and being the outdoor type probably as tough as old boots.' He paused, and then added in a controlled voice, 'It's my guess that after Mr Horrigan collapsed he dragged himself back into the caravan to die.'

'To be near his darlin' Degsey.' Daniel deliberately used Seamus's words as he patted the greyhound.

Doctor Becker began replacing the containers of herbs in the table-top cabinet. 'Ms Patakin explained that he was an Irish tinker spending some time in Swiftly. Did he have any relatives?'

'He never spoke of anyone.'

'Mmm.' He paused to close his medical bag and glanced at Seamus. 'Well, things have to be done. Would you like me to take care of the initial arrangements?'

'Moving him you mean?'

'Yes, until his affairs get sorted out.'

'Thank you.'

Doctor Becker had replaced all the containers and bottles but the drawer was jamming as he tried to close it. He fiddled for a while without success and then decided to pull it out from the cabinet to find the obstruction.

'There's something catching at the back . . .' he began, placing delicate fingers around a large rolled up envelope which kept uncoiling itself. 'Here we are . . . got what was causing the jam.'

He flattened it, placed it on top of the cabinet, and closed the drawer.

Daniel's face was intense as he recognised his own name. He was baffled as to why the foolscap envelope should be addressed to him. But there, in black ink were the words: *MR DANIEL RUSK.*

Doctor Becker was watching Daniel's eyes. He tapped the bridge of his nose with a knuckle and said, 'I think you should open it. It could be important.'

Daniel nodded and looked at Degsey as he swallowed uneasily. He tore open the flap and pulled out the contents. It contained one large double sheet of thick paper, folded lengthways, and a brass key with a label attached.

'Locker seat opposite the policemen.' Daniel read the words on the key tag aloud.

'Policemen?' Doctor Becker gave him a searching look. 'Does that mean anything to you?'

He indicated with his eyebrows. 'The old Colchester stove,' he responded, as the breath caught in his throat. He glimpsed the main heading on the document. It read: *This is the Last Will and Testament of me Seamus Horrigan.*

Daniel looked uneasy as he handed the document to Doctor Becker. 'I've never had to read one of these before,' he said. 'Why the heck is it addressed to me?'

The doctor's eyes scanned the first page. 'Mr Horrigan must have trusted and admired you a great deal. He's named you as sole executor of his will.'

Daniel had heard the term before — he remembered that his father and uncle had both been executors of his grandmother's will, but he still wasn't exactly sure what it meant.

'You're the trustee of Mr Horrigan's estate,' Doctor Becker explained. 'It will be your job to make sure that his last wishes are carried out to the best of your ability.' He turned the document over and glanced at the date and signatures. 'This was signed and witnessed only a few days ago. It's a perfectly legal and valid document.'

'But Seamus didn't have any money . . . Well, I mean, he never *spoke* of having anything.'

'Perhaps he'd found the pot of gold at the end of the rainbow.'

'Perhaps he had.' Daniel thought briefly about the tooth and stretched out his fingers to stroke Degsey, knowing that the doctor's words weren't a million miles from the truth.

'Anyway, this isn't for my eyes—it's for yours.' Doctor Becker placed the will back in the envelope and gathered up his jacket and medical bag. 'When you've read it go and see a solicitor.' He extended a firm hand for Daniel to shake. 'Good luck, Mr Rusk.'

Daniel thanked him and opened the porch doors, watching as he strode briskly across the forecourt to his car. Daniel waved a goodbye, then turned back to face Degsey.

'So what's this all about?' He showed the greyhound the tagged key. 'What mystery is this going to unlock?'

Degsey padded behind him as he crossed to the Colchester stove. He knelt by the locker seat and turned the key easily, sliding open the polished doors.

It seemed to be full of neatly stacked blankets and towels but when Daniel shifted these to one side he found a cardboard box containing two brown paper packets tied securely with thick string. On the smaller packet was written a number two, on the larger packet a number ten.

He blinked, mystified. 'Your master has given me a few surprises this morning,' he murmured to Degsey. 'We'd better go back to the house and sort some of them out.'

During the examination Doctor Becker had placed Seamus into a more pleasing position. He was now lying fully back on the bunk, his head on a pillow and the patchwork quilt covering his legs. The lines of his face seemed less noticeable and he looked to all the world as if he was sleeping.

'Time to leave, girl.' Daniel spoke coaxingly to Degsey as he gathered up the will and the brown paper packets. He edged towards the door.

The greyhound was unmoving. She had returned to the bunk and was resting her head on Seamus's chest. Her eyes flicked from Daniel to the splendid brass lamp fixed to the window ledge.

Daniel followed her gaze and knew what she wanted.

The Angel lamp.

Seamus would have wanted it lit and Degsey was prompting him to do just this.

Seamus's pipe and matches were on the chest of drawers. Degsey's eyes tracked Daniel's every move as he collected the matches and crossed to the Angel lamp. She watched him check that the ruby red oil container was full before he removed the globe and the chimney and put a match to the wick.

He closed the wooden window shutters and adjusted the burner so that the lamplight rippled over the lower bunk. Seamus was bathed in the glow. He looked perfectly at peace.

'Is that what you wanted?' Daniel turned to Degsey. The greyhound blinked contentedly as she looked into the light. She left Seamus's side and followed Daniel to the door.

*　　*　　*

'Fifteen thousand pounds?' Shack stared at Daniel, slack jawed, his eyes reflecting his puzzlement. 'How could old Seamus save that amount of money?'

It was long past breakfast and Daniel, Sky, Shack, Jonathan and Spring were now seated in the Oyster Gables office. Earlier, when Daniel had broken the news of Seamus's death there had been lots of silent tears but now—gradually—the sadness had lessened to quiet disbelief and everyone, in their own way, had come to terms with the situation.

'I expect the money represents a lifetime's savings,' Daniel said in answer to Shack's question. 'Seamus told us he used to do odd jobs during his travels . . . well this was probably collected over sixty or more years.'

Everyone was looking at the various banknotes that were spread on the desk in front of Daniel. They were the contents of packet 'ten' and comprised English, Irish and Scottish paper money.

Daniel ran his finger along the handwriting in the will, telling all that it was Seamus's last wish that the cash should be spent on rebuilding the stables.

'I wasn't aware that he'd ever seen the stables.' Sky's eyebrows drew together. 'I probably put the idea into his head.'

Shack looked a little guilty as jigsaw images floated out of the past to prompt him. 'It was the night we were all sitting round the fire listening to the story of Degsey and her gold tooth. Seamus mentioned that he did weaving to gain a few pennies, and I joked that he should teach us the craft. That way, I said, we could earn some extra cash to repair the stables.'

'They are very grotty,' Daniel stated. 'It's great news.'

'Thank you, Seamus,' Sky said softly to herself. 'Thank you for thinking of us.'

Daniel struggled with some of the misspelled words and the phrasing. 'Me old cob, Mister Rafferty,' he read aloud, 'will be allowed to live out the rest of his natural life at Oyster Gables. He will be used to pull me wagon whenever it's agreeable.'

'Is the caravan a gift?' Sky asked.

Daniel's eyes dropped back to the will. He nodded. 'The wagon and all belongin' to it have been gifted to the shelter.'

'We could rent it out for short breaks,' Shack said, liking the idea. 'Caravan holidays are pretty cool in Devon. Families would love it and we could use the extra cash to buy new stuff for Oyster Gables. Everyone would benefit.'

'Especially Mister Rafferty,' Jonathan observed.

Spring had been sitting tight-lipped and pale. Only now, was she managing a smile.

'He would be back between the shafts—travelling again. Seamus would have wanted that. I think it's a brilliant idea.'

'It will need careful planning,' Sky said. 'We'd have to run a proper advertising campaign.' She paused to give Shack a nod of approval. 'But yes, Spring's right. It is a brilliant idea.'

'And it's a proper wagon,' Jonathan put in, 'not a modern piece of cruddy junk you see in most holiday adverts.' He cleared his throat and did his usual bad impression of Seamus. 'Ay, she be a genuine Reading, built in the early nineteen-hundreds and weighin' thirty hundredweight.'

'It is a classic,' Daniel agreed, relaxing a little. 'A piece of history. Oyster Gables is very lucky to have it.'

Shack nodded. 'Whenever it's rolling we'll be reminded of Seamus. The old boy's memory will always be with us.'

Daniel returned to the will and tapped the packet numbered 'two' with a pencil. 'Seamus has also left four thousand pounds to cover funeral expenses. He's requested that he be buried in Ireland at the village church in Knockgrafton.'

'At the foot of the Galtee Mountains . . .' Sadness entered Spring's tense little face as she remembered the story of Degsey's birth. 'He wants to be near Deggoran Odyssey. He wants to go home.'

'Yep, you're right, little Spring.' Shack gave her a comforting smile. 'Seamus will be resting in one of his favourite places.'

Sky turned to Daniel, her face showing a mixture of emotions. 'May I see the will?'

'Sure.' He handed it over. 'Is something bothering you?'

'Just curious about who witnessed it. As Seamus rarely left his caravan I was wondering—'

'A Mrs Helen Wilson and a Mr Kenneth Wilson,' Daniel said from memory, expecting the question. 'They've given a Yorkshire address—tourists I suppose.'

She turned to the back page and shrugged. 'I've never heard of Mr and Mrs Wilson.'

Jonathan's eyes were fixed on Shack. He moved his head to avoid their point of focus.

'They're my mother and my stepfather,' he said eventually. 'They called in at Oyster Gables last week unaware that I was off sick. They told me later that they had looked over Seamus's wagon, but I didn't know they'd signed his will.'

'Well, that solves the mystery.' Sky looked reassured.

'Names can be confusing,' Jonathan said pointedly, pursing his lips as he strolled casually to the computer and back. 'I know they had old Seamus confused.'

'Not now, little dude,' Shack cut quickly.

Jonathan returned to his chair and folded his arms as Spring changed the subject.

'Any mention of Degsey and the pups?' she asked.

'A request that Degsey should live at Oyster Gables,' Daniel told her, 'and the pups be found good homes.'

'They'd probably make excellent racers . . .' Shack began, and then caught a breath as he pulled himself up. He shook his head as if to rattle some sense into it. 'What on earth am I saying? That's the last thing Seamus would have wanted. What was it he told us round the camp fire? Degsey and the pups should . . . ?'

'Run free to chase the wind,' Daniel said.

'And so they shall,' Sky promised. 'Mum and dad have agreed that Spring and Jonathan can keep Little Degsey and I know I can place the other two in caring homes.'

'And big Degsey?' quizzed Shack, deliberately throwing amusement in his voice. 'Surely we don't want that old dog hanging around . . . flashing her gold tooth and getting in the way.'

'I'm afraid we do.' Sky's lips actually curved at Shack's comment. Her first smile. 'She'll live here just as Seamus requested.'

'She'll be company for Scooter,' Jonathan said.

'And she'll bring us all good fortune,' Spring put in, visibly brightening.

Daniel swivelled uncomfortably in his chair. So far he had made no mention of the gold vanishing from the tooth and he wasn't too happy at having to recall the event to all the faces now looking at him. He sat forward, gathered his thoughts, and explained what had happened.

As the details of this body-blow sank in, everybody was silent and Daniel continued, 'So Degsey's back to being a normal dog again. She can't influence things any more. From now on she's just an ordinary pet greyhound.'

'She'll never be ordinary,' Spring said. 'She'll always be special.'

'I suppose the gold couldn't last forever,' Sky remarked.

'We were very lucky she had her powers when we needed them,' Shack added.

Jonathan, showing his wisdom, said, 'She's going need a lot of extra affection now Seamus has gone. She mustn't be allowed to feel lonely or she'll pine. We'll all have to put in some extra effort . . . do our bit . . . show her that she's loved and wanted and that Oyster Gables is now her new home.'

His words caused a surprised look to drift across Sky's face. She looked at Daniel.

He finished placing the packets of money in a cash-box and turned the key. 'Sometimes, Jonathan,' he said, with a hint of dry humour, 'you never fail to surprise us.'

'Why, what's up?' He scowled. 'What have I said now?'

Daniel let the tension of the morning unwind a little before answering. Everyone was exchanging small, swift smiles.

'Probably what all of us wanted to hear . . . a lot of good commonsense.'

Sky grinned at the rather pleased look on her brother's face as the desk telephone rang for attention. She leaned across and lifted it from its rest.

The grin rapidly disappeared as a small tinny voice vibrated from the phone's earpiece. 'Oh, no,' she said with a groan, 'that means the whole of the north coastline will be at risk.' A long listening pause, then, 'Yes, Oyster Gables has the basic washing facilities. We've coped before; we'll cope again. Yes, we'll be ready. Thank you for the warning. Goodbye.'

All eyes were on Sky.

'That was the Coastguard,' she said. 'There's been an oil spillage—an Atlantic collision—and a tanker has ripped one of its tanks.'

'That means lots of gummed-up sea-birds,' Shack observed bleakly.

Sky nodded and shifted in her seat. 'We'd better get prepared. They reckon the wind's on the turn and the oil slick will hit Swiftly by morning.'

CHAPTER TWELVE

L ife at the animal shelter became increasingly busy which helped ease the drama of Seamus's death by directing everyone's minds back to the business of wild animal welfare.

The oil slick had invaded parts of the North Devon coastline and the long stretch of Swiftly beach had been one of the worst hit areas. Oyster Gables, along with other wildlife and bird rescue organisations, had joined forces in order to cope with the huge clean-up operation.

Jonathan and Spring had spent the remaining four days of their holiday helping to wash and groom the vast quantity of sea-birds which had been collected by volunteer helpers and delivered to the shelter. They comprised gannets, cormorants, razorbills, kittiwakes, terns, guillemots, storm petrels as well as the more common black-headed and herring gulls. It had been tiring, round-the-clock work, with everyone toiling through long shifts in order to keep casualties to a minimum. By the time the weekend arrived the number of new admissions was down to a tiny trickle and many hundreds of oil-free sea-birds had been boxed-up and collected by national welfare agencies. They would all be transported and released along the non-polluted waters of the South Devon coast.

Gradually things slipped back to normal and Saturday morning found Daniel and Sky at the stables. In about an hour Sky would be driving Spring and Jonathan back to the family home in Sussex so she was enjoying a brief break and combining the leisure time to check on the cleanliness of Delight Cove. Five miles of local coastline had been given the all-clear by the Department of the Environment, and the oil dispersal teams had moved on to tackle more stubborn pollution elsewhere.

'Race you to the beach.' Daniel swung into Sir Galahad's saddle and the horse sniffed the air briskly as he gathered the reins.

'I'm exhausted.' Sky yawned as she sat astride Excalibur. Her muscles felt stiff and aching. 'I couldn't manage more than a slow trot. My body's telling me it could sleep for a week. If you want to race then pit your riding skills against Degsey.' She gave him a teasing smile, adding softly, 'I bet you can't beat the greyhound.'

Degsey had now established herself at the shelter better than anyone had hoped. Not that it had been easy at the beginning. The first couple of days had been worrying, with the greyhound refusing food and steering clear of the house, preferring to spend her days and nights huddled on the caravan's footboard. Everyone had taken it in turns to sit with her, to talk to her, but no amount of patience and affection would coax her away. Daniel had reluctantly padlocked the porch doors but she didn't attempt to enter the wagon's interior by the flap. She knew Seamus was no longer inside—she'd watched the old Irishman being taken away by three men in a large black vehicle—but she wouldn't give up her territory until the oil in the Angel lamp had run dry. Only then, when the flame had finally flickered and died would she leave the caravan.

She was now circling the two horses as they made their way to the paddock. She didn't weave in and out of their legs—that trick was reserved solely for Mister Rafferty but she was enjoying the friendship, and never strayed very far from Daniel's side.

'I'm so pleased Degsey's settled.' Sky yawned again as she stood up in the stirrup irons pretending to lift the metal-keeper on the five-barred gate. 'I'm sure she's accepted us as her new family.'

Daniel was about to agree when Sky unexpectedly tightened her reins, restricting Excalibur's head movement and wheeling the mare around.

'Hold up . . . !' Daniel's breath came in a jerk as Excalibur's haunches flexed and quivered, dipping Sir Galahad's quarters and nearly unseating him.

Sky whooped a laugh as she veered away, applying pressure with her legs and pushing Excalibur into a canter. 'You caught me like this soon after you arrived,' she yelled back, her voice thin against the wind. 'Now I'm turning the tables!'

As Daniel's fingers fumbled to free the keeper on the five-barred gate he could only watch in astonishment as Excalibur, without fear or hesitation, breasted the fence. Sky performed the jump with such perfect harmony of balance that she was barely conscious of the slight jolt on landing.

'Exhausted, are you?' Daniel mouthed the words soundlessly, his heels immediately urging Sir Galahad into a canter. 'Couldn't manage more than a slow trot . . . *Ha!*'

Degsey streaked ahead of him as soon as the gate swung inwards. Spirited in pace and manner she flashed across the open turf, easily outrunning the horses.

Excalibur was now at full gallop, the mare extending her neck and flattening her ears. She was a good four lengths clear of Sir Galahad who was responding boldly to the surge of pressure from Daniel's legs.

There was no chance of Daniel closing the gap. The paddock was too short and the beach gate was already in view. Both riders saw Degsey crest the obstacle, tucking in her forelegs and raising her hind legs just sufficiently to cruise over the woodwork without faltering. Such was the power of the jump that she somersaulted on landing; tumbling over twice before her paws scrambled for grip in the damp sand.

Sky was only a few seconds behind, her concentration steady, her eyes fixed on the wooden obstacle as she drove hard and straight at it. Excalibur took the jump smoothly, the hooves of the mare's forelegs tucked into her chest, her hind legs using every muscle in her thighs; effortlessly lifting her bulk in a perfect take-off as she spanned the gate. Sky reined in and glided to a halt beside a heavily panting Degsey.

Sir Galahad followed in the mare's slipstream. Daniel kept the reins taut, holding them only millimetres from the animal's neck, but as they crested the woodwork he mistimed the jump and the gelding jarred slightly on landing. Clumps of moist sand flew at the impact of juddering hooves as Daniel stiffened his spine, bracing himself back into the saddle and braking to a dead stop alongside Excalibur.

Sky was flushed with the pride of her performance. The salty air whipped her hair into her eyes as she pranced the mare in front of him and smiled, teasing. 'A pretty convincing win, wouldn't you say?'

'For Degsey, yes,' he replied, keeping up an air of playful annoyance. 'You cheated. There's no way you would have beaten me in a fair gallop.'

She threw her head back and laughed.

The two horses trotted side by side, weaving in and out of the rock pools with Degsey scampering behind. She would pause to sniff at the tiny crabs stranded in pebbled hollows, flicking an inquisitive paw and sending them crawling for cover. It was a harmless game which had her spinning madly round in circles and left Sky and Daniel laughing aloud at her antics.

The sheltered bay of Delight Cove was surprisingly clean. A few remnants of black sludge still glistened as it clung stubbornly to the wooden uprights of the breakwater, but the beach was almost back to its silvery colour. The foamy waves at the water's edge were crystal clear and tinged with blue as they sloshed against the horses' fetlocks and nudged at a line of seaweed on the wet sand.

A cormorant spiralled in soundless circles above them. They rested the horses for a moment, squinting through the heat-haze and watching the bird's energetic antics.

'That's what makes all the hard work worthwhile,' Sky said, after a moment's reflection. 'We've given life back to over five hundred sea-birds.'

'Jonathan and Spring were a great help,' Daniel responded. 'I'd reckoned on a lot of moans and groans, but they really got stuck in with the dirty jobs.'

'I shall miss them.'

'Me too.'

'They've both grown up a lot'

'We all have.'

Sky let her feet dangle from the stirrup irons and swung one leg across Excalibur's withers. She leaned nearer to Daniel, swaying against his chest. He kissed her lightly, then more firmly, and hugged her.

Degsey lay close to the horses, missing nothing. She stretched contentedly in the sand.

Sky caught the dog's gaze and glanced at Daniel with mock suspicion.

'Nothing to do with the greyhound this time,' he pointed out defensively. 'That kiss was the genuine article. No prompting whatsoever. Go check her tooth if you don't believe me.'

'I have and I do.'

They both laughed.

Sky reached up and kissed his temple, her lips finding the pulse that beat there. She closed her eyes for a long moment as he held her.

'I love this place.' Daniel sighed, breathing out the taste of oil which seemed to have clung to his lungs for the last four days. He drew in a deep breath of the salt-fresh air. 'Swiftly, Oyster Gables, Delight Cove, Scamperbuck Ring . . . all of it.'

'I love it too. I couldn't live anywhere else.'

Daniel was deep in thought. He tented his fingers and pressed them against his lips.

'Penny for them?' Sky said.

'The past couple of weeks have flown by. They seem more like a couple of minutes.'

'The months will fly even quicker and then you'll be at university.' Sky traced the outline of his chin with a finger.

'Exeter's only an hour's drive away. Promise me you'll visit us every weekend.'

'You just try and keep me away,' he said.

* * *

'Well, goodbye, Ceddie!' Jonathan thrust his right hand towards Shack. 'I expect we shall see you in October. It's half-term so we're down for a week.'

'I shall mark it on my calendar, little dude. I shall be counting the days till you arrive.' Shack was having problems holding back a smile. His grip was firm as they shook hands.

Daniel carried the cases to the Volvo, stacked them safely, and then erected the dog-guard. He had offered the use of the estate car as it was more comfortable on long journeys than the van, and it would also keep Little Degsey secure.

'Goodbye, Daniel . . . Goodbye, Shack.' Spring reached up to give both of them a hug as her blue eyes misted a little.

Degsey and Scooter didn't need any prompting when it came to farewells. They had boundless energy and were using it to dash around the forecourt, skimming as close to the youngsters as possible in a display of showmanship.

Both Jonathan and Spring crouched, letting the dogs fly into their arms. Each were fondled individually, and then swapped to be given endless hugs.

'Goodbye, Degsey.' Spring knelt and pressed a moist cheek against the hollow of the greyhound's neck. Her eyes were closed as she whispered, 'I promise to take care of Little Degsey and bring her to visit whenever I can.'

The sun was hot as Daniel leaned against the Volvo, tanned arms folded, watching the show of affection. He could see the trusting look in Degsey's eyes as she listened to the softly spoken words.

'Are we all ready?' Sky appeared at the side door.

She looked freshly showered and her hair was worn loose, swaying across her face as it was caught by the breeze. She clutched a small overnight bag in one hand, and held Little Degsey on a lead with the other.

'Luggage is in,' Daniel told her, 'and you have a full tank of petrol.'

'Right, kids, let's go.' She ushered Spring and Jonathan into the Volvo. 'Wind your windows down or else the heat might upset Little Degsey.'

Shack got to grips with the greyhound puppy and lifted her into the hatchback, setting her down on a car rug. She gave a small throaty greeting as she spotted her mother padding briskly towards her.

'See you tomorrow morning.' Sky beamed a smile to Daniel and Shack as she slipped on a pair of huge sunglasses and settled herself in the driving seat. 'The RSPB should be here in an hour to collect the remaining seabirds. You'll find a fresh supply of cardboard carrying-boxes in—'

'The storage shed,' Shack cut in.

'Sorry.' Sky briefly pressed her lips together. 'Am I behaving like a mother hen?'

'Yes, you are. Now enjoy your night away. Oyster Gables won't fall to pieces in twenty-four hours.'

Daniel was standing to the rear of the Volvo watching Little Degsey respond to her mother's affections. He'd always been fascinated by the amazing resemblance of the pair. Apart from the duplicate body markings their facial expressions were alike. It was like looking at a mirror-image, he thought. The pair were as one; so close it seemed they shared heartbeats.

'Bye all!' Sky adjusted the rear-view mirror and turned the ignition.

Daniel closed the hatchback and Degsey briefly placed front paws on the bumper so, for a moment, both mother and daughter had their noses pressed each side of the rear window.

'See you tomorrow,' Shack shouted out. 'Drive carefully!'

Daniel called Degsey to heel.

Spring and Jonathan were both waving madly as Sky eased the Volvo out of its turning circle, past Seamus's caravan, crunching over dusty gravel as it headed towards the two huge conifer trees which flanked the driveway.

Shack and Daniel raised their hands in farewell as they watched the Volvo depart.

Little Degsey was standing up, looking back at the dwindling view of her mother, panting in the heat and swaying with the movement of the vehicle.

Daniel suddenly blinked. He felt his mouth drop open. The car's rear window seemed to glow as it was caught by the slanted rays of the sun. It glowed, then shaded over and for a baffling millisecond Daniel was certain that he'd witnessed the glint of gold in Little Degsey's lower jaw.

The Volvo swept past the trees and disappeared from view.

'Did you see . . . ?' Daniel gulped at the craziness of his own thoughts.

'See what?' Shack frowned.

'Little Degsey . . . The tooth . . . It was shimmering.'

He gave a strangled laugh. 'Very funny, Daniel. I expect she's inherited it from her mother.'

'I'm not kidding around. I saw it.'

'But Little Degsey hasn't got a gold tooth.'

'I know. Am I sounding like a complete idiot?'

'You're not making much sense.'

Daniel held his breath, unsure whether to be glad or frustrated.

'You saw a trick of the light, maybe,' Shack added sensibly.

'It could have been that, I guess . . .' He paused, as the doubts crept in. 'You really didn't see a thing?'

'Nope.' Shack was definite.

'But I was sure . . .'

'I reckon you're suffering from lack of sleep, dude. We all are. It's been a hell of a week.'

Daniel nodded. He felt embarrassed. Of course Shack was right—it must have been a trick of the light. He cursed his stupidity in believing otherwise.

Degsey hung back but Scooter plodded ahead as Shack turned towards the house.

'Shall we make a start?'

'Sorry . . . ?' Daniel blinked, slightly at a loss.

'You're the boss until tomorrow, Mr Rusk,' Shack said. 'Assistant manager and all that. I await your instructions.'

Daniel's mind was still running in little swirls of confusion. He looked at Shack blankly.

'Sea-birds,' he prompted, placing a strong hand on Daniel's shoulder. 'Cardboard boxes. One hour. Remember?'

'Of course.' Daniel's voice was suddenly more positive. He drummed up a smile and fondled Degsey's velvety ears. She was still standing just behind him. 'Work to do, girl,' he said. 'Let's go.'

Daniel didn't look back as he and Shack strode purposefully towards the house. Had he done so he might have noticed the slight swagger in Degsey's step and the springy swing in her tail as her gaze shifted from the dust trail left by the Volvo and settled briefly on Seamus's caravan. A fanciful, very private twinkle lurked in the depths of her eyes.